The New House

The New House

A NOVEL

DAVID LEO RICE

Whisk(e)y Tit
NYC & VT

Published in the United States by Whisk(e)y Tit: www.whiskeytit.com. If you wish to use or reproduce all or part of this book for any means, please let the author and publisher know. You're pretty much required to, legally.

ISBN 978-1-952600-14-2

Cover design by Matt Lyne.

Praise for *The New House*

Filled with pious, mechanical rage and ecstasy, David Leo Rice has created a catastrophe, a religion of some sort. Fishy as it may seem, Jakob (his zealous protagonist) blows our minds and charges our electric socket with his hysterical, esoteric coming of age. Severely disciplined by martinet parents, Jakob becomes a Trader Joe's frenzied witness of some sort. Rice has created a world like none other. An ophidian world dressed and fashioned for more devastation than revelation, more mother than meadow, more irresistible than blasphemous.

– Vi Khi Nao

The childhood of Jakob, The New House's young hero, is one unlike that of your typical coming-of-age narrative. His is a youth surrounded by prophetic dreams, religious schisms, and secretive conversations — plus some shocking scenes of violence. Rice's prose creates a mood abounding with mystery and dread, and The New House would fit comfortably beside the likes of Michael McDowell's Toplin and Iain Banks's

The Wasp Factory in terms of disquieting portraits of sustained alienation.

– Tobias Carroll, author of *Reel* and *Political Sign*

David Leo Rice achieves a superb naturalism in recounting the experiences of young Jacob, contraposed to the world of the book, where natural laws do not interfere. There is a profound freedom in the depiction of how material objects with extension interact with material objects with extension—that space can be filled twice. A non-metaphorical depiction of contradiction (that inside things there might be other things) undergirds a portrayal of the artist informed by an ambient mysticism but not of it. Rice's stunning manipulation of identity over time allows the book to relate a coming-of-age story and an anticipatory retrospective of the life of the artist at once. The New House leaves the reader to reflect on whether there is anything holding an identity together, or whether whatever we are was burned in the woods long ago.

– Charlene Elsby

Twisted, disturbing, and completely bizarro to the point of hallucinogenic. Rice is the master of fantastical Lynchian body horror and the surreally wacky—and if you read this book, he'll also be the master of your nightmares. An absolute must for fans of the weird and unexpected.

– Leah Angstman, author of *Out Front the Following Sea*

The New House is magic. It's a book so infused with dreams that it seems to be dreaming us into being—you and me and the families that form us, the towns that try us, the shadows that want to wake us or take us away for good.

I don't remember a book that captured dreaming so perfectly, or at least captured my dreams: the streets I repeatedly step down, the edges of town that scare the shit out of me, the sweetness that always seems to dissipate while I'm savouring it.... Sweet dreams, sweetheart!

– Derek McCormack

Like a Jewish magical realist bildungsroman, The New House is a darkly compelling exploration of sacrifice, love, the will to create, and the will to destroy. David Leo Rice finds the beating heart at the center of many interlinked questions and he opens it like a surgeon

– Lindsay Lerman

PART I

The Town
Museum

"Who's alive? Who is alive? Who's alive anymore?"—Guy Maddin, *My Winnipeg*

The Desert

Dream

Jakob finishes the rice pudding that's been enchanted to put him to sleep, and, like a dutiful baby, toddles out of the kitchen, ready for bed. "Tonight's going to be one of your dream nights," his mother shouts as he leaves, and he looks back at her and his father, who's staring at the floor. Then he nods and makes his way up the carpeted stairs on his hands and knees, like he's been taught to when the weight of incipient dreaming has built up in his belly. "Like you're about to give birth to a baby of your own," as his mother used to joke when he was little.

He crawls along the upstairs hallway, dragging his hair on the unsanded floorboards, until he's wriggling along with his lips in the dust, slithering like the snake that lives in the walls. It hatched from an egg he rescued from the depths of a puddle, and, instead of letting it go in the garden like he'd been told to, he fed it through a small hole in the sheetrock behind his bed, where it thrived and thrived and thrived and is still talking to me today, he thinks, whispering... if only I could make out what it wants me to do! Here he starts to lose focus. Everything goes deep red, then brown, then black, until he can't tell if he's on a softening ground or a still-hard bedsheet just before it gets all wet and creamy with dreaming, but he knows he's not himself anymore. He knows his eyes are closed, and he's slipping down a long tunnel, like the one he was born through, into his father's head, and in there it's storming, raging, smashing against its own edges.

He pulls the sheets up to his neck, aware that he's in bed now, but it doesn't feel safe like it should. His head's losing its hair and skin, becoming a vessel whose pulsing and boiling contents are clearly visible from the outside. Once the vision resolves, it's of his father, roaming a frigid lunar desert, the lights of one town vanishing into the distance behind him while the lights of another appear on the horizon ahead. Everything about the last town is downfall and ruin, sleaze and corruption and runoff, he thinks, while everything about the new town, getting closer with every step that he takes along with his wife and infant son, grows in luminescence, brightening like the sunrise, then merging with the actual sunrise, so now the icy desert blue is a welcoming Florida orange and the new town, the one they've come all this way to try their luck in, is no mere dot but an array of concrete slabs punctuated with wood, brick, and tree. Now he's depositing his wife and infant son in the new house he's had built just for them, as clean and snug as can be, careful to make sure they don't wake—the game he plays is, if I wake them, I must crack them like unhatched eggs, so they need never live knowing what I know. The world between towns, the abjection of highway and rest stop, the vast uncertainty between one tiny populous dot and the next. And now Jakob, the boy, is stirring in his bed, his sheets damp and his mouth dry from the dream, which, though it comes quite often, is never familiar enough to leave his saliva in his mouth where it belongs.

Jakob sits up in bed and looks around the room, which reminds him of his bedroom but doesn't quite feel like it. In the dream, he's always an infant, but now, awake, he's closer to ten, or perhaps even eleven or twelve, nearly old enough to slime his sheets and thirst for murder. I just dreamt I was my father, he thinks, but now I know I'm me. This is what he hopes. I love him, he reassures himself, but I do not wish to be him.

He wants to cry for his mother, but tries to hold off. It's what little boys do, he thinks, and I'm not a little boy anymore. I'm something else, not quite a big boy, but not little anymore, either. A medium boy, one who dreams of crossing deserts only to arrive right back where he started... except, and this is the scary part, every time I wake from the dream, it's a little different.

He looks at the books on his shelf—Gershom Scholem's biography of Sabbatai Zevi, Walter Benjamin's *Illuminations*, Spinoza's *Ethics*, the full deep history of his family, his ur-ancestors from before the line was cut and the Great American Exile began—and tries to convince himself that these are the same books he fell asleep with last night. My books, he thinks, digging into his long hair with his too-sharp fingernails. How lovely to wake up surrounded by my dear, sweet books. Isn't it?

He belches. The thing that he wants to be true doesn't feel like it is, and this feeling gives him gas. So he gets out of bed, carefully placing his feet on the floor in case the rug's turned to lava, and drags himself down the hallway with his ear to the wallpaper, listening for the snake whose message he knows he mustn't miss, if and when it comes, but there's only silence today. He slides down the stairs and teeters into the breakfast room, unsteady as an injured foal. He feels his life starting over, the ten or twelve years since his actual birth running parallel to a great number of timelines marking subsequent births and perhaps deaths and rebirths thereafter, twins who were almost born or were born in places that are almost but never quite here, such that today is, once again, Day One. The time known as *in the beginning*—"festival-time," as Mircea Eliade, a wise man though no friend of the Jews, according to his father, once put it. A time for the world to be ritually renewed so that its oldness doesn't grow terminal. He takes in everything around him—the clean white walls, the slick wood floor, the windows with their manufacturers' stickers still on them, doing all he can to imprint these as the familiar signposts of home before he has to face his parents, or those who now stand in for them, whose influence, he knows, will warp whatever impression he's managed to come to on his own. But weren't there piles and piles of papers last night, interspersed with unopened envelopes and parking tickets and plastic bags, he wonders, and rows upon rows of mugs moldering with their teabags stuck to their sides, lined up on these same countertops and windowsills? He can't remember. He knows he could ask, but he also knows that his parents will insist this is their home, their only home, regardless of what and where it really is.

When it's finally time to enter the kitchen, he finds his mother and father sitting at the table with cereal and coffee, stock-still like toys that can only be activated by his arrival. Indeed, he confirms, now that I've come down, they're already talking to me, trying to convince me that they're real.

"How'd you sleep, honey?" his mother asks.

Sitting down at the place that's been set for him, he grunts and fills his bowl with Wheaties. Then he holds out his half-sized coffee cup, which is what he uses for training, as his mother calls the process of learning to drink coffee like a full-grown person with a busy day ahead of them. She fills it from the French press and Jakob takes his first bitter sip. It tastes different than before, though, of course, he can't remember how it used to taste. He doesn't want to say that he's had the nightmare again, but, before he can stop himself, he's blubbering, "I was terrified, mom! I saw the Desert again, and dad was carrying me like a little trinket, and you too, both of us by the scruffs of our neck, and it was also me in charge, carrying everybody, but…"

His father, who'd been sitting silently across the table, throws his Wheaties at the window above the kitchen sink, which is the universal sign for, "time to take a walk by yourself." Jakob used to argue against this rule; he used to complain that it wasn't fair and that he wanted to stay at the table where the real decisions were made, but one broken arm when he was eight was enough to see that this wasn't the right approach if you were someone who wanted to live to a ripe old age without being crushed up like a goddam spider and left to flail in dead silence on the basement floor where you belong.

So Jakob gets to his feet as the milk and flakes drip down the window, and he puts on his sneakers under his pajamas and walks over the sacred threshold, a line between inner and outer as significant as his own skin. Then he walks through the door, down the driveway, and into the hot sun of wherever this is.

The Bridge

Now he's walking up the strange street his house is apparently parked on, past the neighbors out watering their lawns and playing with their dogs, neighbors who look friendly but indistinct, like whatever names they might have could be swapped with no one noticing, and now he's rounding the corner, off the side street and onto the main one. It's easy to find the way to downtown because that's where almost all the cars are going: this is the secret Jakob learned long ago, the secret that almost all adults behave in exactly the same way, while thinking there's never been anyone like them, and never will be again.

Soon he's drifting into what looks like the heart of downtown, past the church and the drug store and the hardware store, and now it's all coming back to him. The fog of the Desert Dream's burning off, as, he now remembers, it always does, especially on hot, bright

9

days like this one. Now he's much more certain that this really is his town, the one he was born in, and the one where he's lived all along with his mother and his father, who, though he can be mean, loves his only son to death. Jakob stands on a corner and zooms out of himself, high enough to watch the nightmare-steam rise from his hair in sickly green streaks and congeal into a dome overhead, admiring the image as if it were a painting he'd done of some unknown street kid about to suffocate in a town-sized terrarium.

Then he snaps back into his body, head now full of more pedestrian thoughts. No sooner has he wished for a dollar to buy a soda with than he sees a quarter gleaming in the sun at the bottom of a hill, which leads away from the center of town toward a river. A quarter's not much, he knows, but it's a start, so he sets out following the gleam, hoping it isn't a mirage like the kind he's heard drives Bedouins insane in the deep Sahara. He runs faster as the gleam plays tricks on him, getting harder, then easier, then harder to see, gleaming bright and then dark and then bright again, the way the world sometimes likes to.

Next time he looks up, the quarter's long gone and he's leaning against the edge of a bridge, panting, while six fishermen cast lines from the middle, their hooks slicing the air into jagged papery shards before sinking into the river that seems to define the absolute edge of the town. Or at least the edge of the sane part, Jakob decides, recoiling from the thought of what must lie beyond.

One of the fishermen spits a long white glob that tangles in his line as another says, "Then I popped her like a can of Schlitz," and all the others laugh so hard the bridge shakes, and Jakob's terrified it's about to collapse. He sees it collapsing, and, though he knows that, for the time being, it's just a vision, he also knows that no vision can resist coming true for very long. On top of all this, he's so sure the bridge wasn't here yesterday that he closes his eyes, trying to make it go away, and then he starts to run, as fast as he can, and doesn't stop until he's back in the house, at the kitchen table, where his mother's doing some work—whatever it is that supports the family—on a legal pad beside the password-protected laptop. Before he can catch his breath, he blurts, "Mom, I was downtown and I found this bridge that... well, yesterday the river was too wide to cross, and today there's six men sitting on top of it, popping cans of Schlitz."

His mother summons him into her lap and runs her hands through his hair and says, "Listen, Jakob, we've been over this, haven't we? Bridges do that. All sorts of things—bridges, roads, schools—what do they do?"

Jakob knows the answer but doesn't want to say it. He knows what'll happen if he doesn't, but, still, he stalls, staring at the Wheaties stuck to the kitchen window, counting them. When he's counted all fifteen flakes, plus smidgeons, he knows his chance to evade punishment is about to pass him by. So, because he's tired and all he wants is to go to his room—or *the* room—and lie down, he says, "Bridges, roads, and schools change sometimes. They remain in flux. It's only natural."

"That's right," his mother says, clearly relieved that no punishment was necessary this time. "It's only natural, sweetie. The universe isn't done being created. Small things change, but the big things, the ones that really matter, like our family, what do they do?"

"Retain their essence at any cost," Jakob recites, squirming out of her lap before she can kiss him.

As he runs upstairs, tiptoeing past the room where his father's thinking, he puts his ear again to the wallpaper and this time the snake whispers something, but he can't tell what it is. As he gets in bed with his drawing paper and pencils, he decides to draw the bridge he got stranded on. Underneath, instead of the river, he draws the snake. Its dripping fangs and red tongue reach up to where he stands looking down, in the same posture as those old drunk fishermen, men who have—Jakob decides, as he lies there drawing—given up on searching and accepted that where and who they are is all there is. Pulling out a new sheet, he draws an array of six sketches in which he feeds them to the snake one by one, dangling them from their own hooks like bait, hoping this sacrifice will be enough to protect him until he comes up with more to offer.

The Father's

Sermon

When the late afternoon has bled away outside the windows, Jakob is called down to dinner. He stirs, shaking off the nap that was starting to grow in his lower head, just above his neck, and slides down the stairs like he did this morning. He tries to retrace his movements as close to exactly as possible. The closer the better, he thinks, knowing full well how much life can improve when you manage to be precise rather than sloppy.

At the dinner table, his mother has set out three whole fish, grilled, and three carrots beside them, on identical plates. It is a matter of necessity in the family that all meals be identical, all portions precise. Without this, there is chaos. The void from which life emerged and back into which it would be more than happy to return.

Once they've taken their seats, taken one another's hands, and then unfolded their napkins in their laps, Jakob's father, draped in a long white robe and skullcap, stands. He and his mother look up, awaiting the speech that always accompanies the first dinner after one of Jakob's Desert Dreams.

"My whole life," his father begins, "is nothing but the tireless, fearless attempt to find a place of refuge for the two of you, my beloved wife and son, who are, as you know, all that I have in this world. All that I am, in the sense that, without your love, I would be nothing. I would be less than this," he holds up his fork, then drops it loudly onto his plate. "And less, even, than this," he holds up his napkin, then lets it flutter down to where it crumples on top of the fork, in an origami-like array that Jakob can't help but admire. How many times have I heard this speech? he wonders.

"And yet, there is a deep, deep problem in this house. A curse upon it, brought down by my inability to recall in actionable detail the house of my own origin. The one in which I was reared, and the family, if any, that did the rearing. The father, the mother, the siblings, if any. If a man can't remember his own childhood, what chance does he stand of being the husband and father he wishes to be, and that he knows he, in some sense, is capable of being?"

"None," respond Jakob and his mother in unison.

His father nods. "Last night, while the two of you

were sleeping soundly, free of all care, sealed inside smooth eggs of innocence, I had a dream. A dark, heavy dream, of a journey through a desert, a treacherous voyage that the three of us were making in search of the town of my birth, the one town where we might stand some chance of extending our roots into the soil and finally beginning to thrive. In that town, we will feast on pork, at last shucking off the mandate of self-denial handed down to us by the great Maimonides himself, who compels us to resist throughout the long, long epoch of exile, waiting for that final fruition when, at last, we arrive in the one town where the two of you hatch out of your semi-inanimate states and begin the long, arduous process of attaining full personhood. Out of the lives of dolls and into the lives of human beings, which, let me tell you, are no picnic... but this is the state that all living things, be they sufficiently humanoid, are compelled at birth to strive to experience. Are there, at this point, any questions?"

Jakob's father looks down at his plate, half-closing his eyes. This is the one night that the family members are permitted to ask about the things they might be puzzled by. Jakob has long since stopped. The question of whether they are moving from town to town, house to house, is never answered. Why does no one but us look the same, month to month, day to day? This too is a question that Jakob has stopped asking, because he knows the answers he'll get: because people are untrustworthy. Because they are enemies of all that is visionary in this world, trying to snuff the gift of prophecy because they can't buy and sell it.

Mouth shut, Jakob stares into the eyes of his mother, which reflect his father and nothing else. They are so riveted onto him, so without life of their own, that they make him squirm in his seat and paw at his hair, desperate to massage some life into his skull and thereby ward off the thing that has bewitched her beyond reach.

When he can't take this any longer, he stares down at his fish.

The fish stares back, trembling in a state between one life and another. Already Jakob pictures taking it to his room after dinner and hooking it up to the wires and clamps he found in the desk, and beginning to make an assemblage, an imaginary machine brought into the realm of the real, which will pump new life into the scaly hulk, rescuing it from the torpor it has fallen into on his plate. To think that he will soon be made to eat it is almost cause for tears, though the knowledge that he will manage to salvage the bones from the kitchen trash, assuming his mother retires to bed and his father to the garage in a timely enough fashion, provides some relief.

"Jakob," his father says, his voice straining against anger, "I fear that I'm losing you. Please, son, for your own good, bear with me."

Jakob looks up. Whether his father's talking about the long or the short term is impossible to tell. Either way, he knows better than to break eye contact again.

He fixes his eyes on his father's chin, where his mother's eyes are, too. The image of a man with four eyes on his chin almost makes Jakob howl with laughter. He has to clamp his teeth shut to avoid it and press his hands over the fish's eyes so it can't see him struggle.

"The first dinner after such a dream is a trying time, a time of great instability in my soul, for I am reminded of how much further there still is to go, how long the journey remains between wherever I am—wherever we are—and the town of my birth, which will, if my life is to be a completed project, be the town of my death as well. There is no God, but there are visions, and I am both blessed and cursed to be their bearer. Let me say, simply, before we part for the evening, that everything I do, I do for you. There is nothing in this universe that I yearn for more than the end of wandering and the beginning of the stable existence wherein you, Jakob, will be able to establish yourself in the town of my ancestry—and thus of yours, as well—and raise your family there, and feel safe and secure in your residence, not forever on the edge of the abyss, as I feel now, and have always felt, I'm sorry to say. For how can a house be a home if it is not the home of the father? All things rot from the head down. For all my years on this earth so far, excepting the remote possibility that my unremembered childhood was a happy one, I have existed in a state of nearly unbearable contingency, like a spider dangling by one leg over the fires of hell. But, while the two of you sleep your sweet, dreamless sleep, know that I am roaming the continent in my mind, leaping from vision to vision like a man twenty years my junior, filled with the strength of absolute conviction, searching for the right town, the one I'm from, the one to which I must return, and when I find it—and I will—I will then, without delay, uproot this house from its purgatory and carry it, heroically, on my back, with the two of you nestled safely inside, all the way to wherever that Promised Land may be, and there we shall be received at last."

With this, Jakob's father falls silent, dabbing his eyes with his inner forearm. Then he picks up his fish and says, "Excuse me, I—" and tramps out to the garage to eat alone, as he always does after his sermon, even though tomorrow morning at breakfast he'll say, "I don't know what came over me, that's never happened before."

When he's gone, Jakob and his mother look at one another, their two fish between them. His mother's face fills with compassion for her son, then, just as quickly, drains to a pale, soapy blankness. She picks up her plate and napkin and says, "I think I'll eat this in my room. Do you need anything before bed?"

Thrilled at the prospect of preserving his fish, whole and not in bones, Jakob shakes his head, trying not to let on just how excited he is. His mother, for her part, is too preoccupied to notice. He can tell that tonight is going to be one of her sleepwalking nights. "Goodnight, mother," he says, as she leaves the kitchen.

Then, forgetting the snake in the walls, Jakob runs upstairs with the fish borne out in front of him, as if to present it to a kingly version of himself waiting for the fulfillment of his decree, and barrels into his bedroom, closing the door behind him. If only it locked, he thinks, tingling with the frisson of a Forbidden Thought, since *We Do Not Lock Doors in This House* is first among the *Ten Cardinal Rules for Avoiding Schisms in Family Life.*

Sitting at his desk, he lays the fish out and hastily unspools the wire he found at the back of the innermost drawer, running it through both of the fish's eyes, then leaning down to fit the other end into the electrical outlet just below his desk.

As he's down there, struggling to shove the wire in deep enough to get a current flowing, the door bursts open and his mother flies across the room, like she's the one who's been sparked to life. Soon he can't tell which hurts more, the shock in his fingers or the pinching on his clavicles as she pulls him away from the outlet.

He blacks out.

When he comes to, he's on the floor with the fish in his lap and his mother seemingly all around him, above, below, and above at the same time, ripping out thick, wet handfuls of fish flesh and shoving them in his mouth, demanding that he eat, eat it all, eat it now, which he does, licking it from her fingers, sucking down the pasty white flakes which he imagines come from her body, the meat of a healthy living animal rather than a scaly dead one.

After all, he thinks, swallowing the last of it, I'm no damn scavenger!

When it's gone, his mother gets up, dropping him on the rug, where he lies slumped, pretending to be more distressed than he really is. She, on the other hand, storms out with real anger, muttering, "I was just about to nod off when I saw you burned to a crisp. I shudder to imagine what would've happened if I hadn't burst in here when I did."

Then she slams the door in such a way that, Jakob knows, means she'll only pretend to go to bed. Soon, she'll be in her slippers and nightgown, wandering the streets in search of something whose nature Jakob can't imagine, no more than he can imagine the town his father hopes to end up in at the end of the journey they're still clearly in the middle of.

The Mother's
Journey

Jakob lies in the fishy reek of his room, wondering how late it is and how long until it starts to be early again. That's the only thing that saves us, he thinks. Otherwise, life would soon get so late there'd be nowhere to go but down. He smiles at the thought, aware that it doesn't quite make sense, but more than happy to surrender to nonsense as a means of easing into sleep. There's no harm in closing his eyes, unless he falls back into the Desert Dream, following his father until he ends up in the Desert alone, with a son and wife following him, just deep enough in the background that they remain out of sight.

The funny thing about dreaming, Jakob continues, as something moves him out of bed and into step behind his mother, is that you don't always know when you're doing it. A lot of dreams, maybe most of them, play out just like real life, so who's to say that they aren't? He files this thought in the archive called *Raw Material*, and hurries to remain just a few steps behind his mother, whose pace has increased now that she's floating an inch off the ground, her bare toes gliding along the surface of the dew. He knows that he isn't really hiding—she's caught him following her before, and never forbidden him from doing it again—but, still, it's important to hang back enough to make it seem like she's on her own private journey and he's merely tagging along.

He follows her up to Main Street, bathed in greenish-blue mist as the stars overhead turn off and the first hints of dawn begin to develop, though the few passing vehicles still have their headlights on, and the houses set back from the street are still dark, full of sleeping people stacked like the mannequins he once found in a pile behind a dumpster.

Soon, his mother has turned off Main Street and begun to cross a meadow, so dew-filled it's almost puddled, and so full of ticks it sings as Jakob wades behind her, grass up to his waist. He hurries to keep up, since he knows that if he gets lost in the Tick-singing Meadow, he could easily become a wanderer for life, a mindless blood-bag groping for nothing in the tall grass.

This possibility almost makes him shriek, "Wait!" but he resists, afraid of interrupting the ticks' chorus.

Instead, he scurries faster, shoving aside thick wet reeds like he's swimming. When he's managed to swim to less treacherous ground, he sees his mother up ahead, her nightgown so drenched in dew it's almost invisible. This sight forces him to pause and ask himself, Do I really know her? Is she who I believe she is? Am I following a demon into hell?

Forcing his way out of this hesitation, he begins to run, throwing one foot after the other, determined to break through the wall of reeds before it closes with her inside. He makes good progress until the river appears between them, opening like a grisly wound in the grass.

He stops just before falling in and catches his balance by windmilling his arms, then abruptly sitting down. Seated in the dew, he watches her vanish into the woods on the far side, like the last white speck on a canvas that Gerhard Richter is mercilessly blacking out with his giant squeegee.

Jakob Visits
the Blood Clot

Jakob wakes on the bank of the river in the boiling sun, aware that he's ended up in a place he didn't intend to, which is always cause for concern at the culmination of a sleepwalk.

Craving company, he selects his big toe and bites its underside as hard as he can. He spits and squeezes the blood into the water, then watches it pool and clump up. He's big enough to know what the Blood Clot really is—his mother taught him the word *stillbirth* when he was eight, the twin sister who never was, the blood and tissue and soft bone that clotted out of her just as Jakob was born, and that she was then forced to bury in the river alone—but no one except him knows that he has the power to summon her anytime he wants, so long as he can bear the pain. No one knows that his sister lives inside him, as if he were both her brother and her mother, and that she's the only one he can trust because she came so close to being him.

"Hi, little sister," he says, as the blood takes shape, though sometimes he thinks of her as his big sister. It's hard to say, because she would have been born first, and so in that sense is older, and yet, things being as they are, she's much smaller than he's grown to be. Another conundrum for the Raw Material archive.

"Hi, Jakob," she says back. He knows he's doing both voices, but he forgets after a few minutes if the conversation's going well.

"I think we moved towns again," he says.

"Oh yeah? It's happening more and more often, isn't it?"

He nods. "Every month, it seems like, though mom says I have an unrealistic sense of time. I think she's the one whose sense is unrealistic, but she's still older than us, so I guess it's only fair to let her have the last word."

The Blood Clot shivers in a way that means she's nodding.

"Last night, at dinner, our father gave his speech, about how he's searching the country in his dreams, but I don't think he believes he's fooling anyone anymore. He's really searching, isn't he? In the real nights."

The Blood Clot shivers again, in a more noncommittal way. "I wish I knew, Jakob. But for me, space works differently. I don't live on land like the rest of you."

"I know. I just wish I could remember more clearly. I wish I knew for sure what the last town looked like, so I could prove that this one's different."

Jakob has a lot more to say, but he forgets what it is when, across the river, whoops and hollers break the spell. He looks up to see a crowd of boys kicking and stomping something invisible inside a cloud of dust. They shout, "Die, die, die!" so loudly and rhythmically that Jakob finds himself chanting along with them. He's long been given to mimicry, which can become a problem, as his mother never forgets to remind him, when the things he's mimicking veer too far from the things he would, of his own volition, say and do. Still, it's fun to chant, "Die, die, die!"

Even more fun, Jakob soon finds, is to run—hobbling, with more blood welling up under his big toe—still chanting, all the way across the bridge, past the bulbous fishermen where they sleep in their folding chairs, floppy hats over their faces and cans of Schlitz bobbing in their thick laps. He knows that crossing the bridge, which wasn't there a moment ago, will cause some derangement in the order of his life, but he's too excited to stop now.

On the other bank, the boys are catching their breath, having stomped to death what, as the dust settles, emerges as a small hyena. They turn to regard him, sweat and snot darkening the fronts of their shirts, some of them Greasy Fatsos and the rest Scrawny Little Twerps.

"Why you got blood on your teeth? Been sponging out your momma?" one of them asks. The others burst out laughing and slap each other's hands, front and back, but Jakob hardly minds. The better part of his attention's on the crushed animal, which still looks like a hyena, though, as it comes into focus, might prove to be a mere dog. He's already named it *Bellmer*, as he does with any crushed animal he meets, provided it looks somewhat dog-like and doesn't have another name already. Once, he even knew a Bellmer that was a decapitated deer.

"Hey, blood-breath, Tom asked you a question. You retarded or something?" Another boy shoves him, hard enough that he trips and falls over the carcass.

Now he's lying on top of it, safe in its warm, bloody embrace. He turns to face it, his back to the boys.

Another grunts, "Yo, you tryin'ta breed with that roadkill now?"

Someone's foot mashes him deeper into it, then another piles on, then they're all mashing him in, moaning from the depths of their chests, until he's covered in fur, which makes him feel powerful. Half-man, half-beast. With this dog's teeth over my own, I could eat you all as a snack, he gloats, but all he manages to say is, "You only think I'm dead."

The stomping stops for a moment, enough to let him turn around and regard his assailants.

"What was that?"

He repeats it, hoping no one asks him to explain, because he knows he won't be able to. He just knows that, in some very deep and true way, nothing that seems dead actually is. There are always processes, no matter how difficult and no matter how scary, for bringing matter back to life. "At least," he qualifies, "depending on your definition of life."

"You talking to yourself now, Baby Dracula?"

Jakob isn't sure. He knows that sometimes words spill out his ears, even when he's trying to keep them in. And when they spill out your ears, as his mother likes to say, some people will think they're spilling out your mouth. He shrugs. "Can I have this, please?"

He gets to his feet with the dog on his back, summoning all the strength hidden in his core, so that by the time he's standing, the dog is balanced on his shoulders like he's the one who killed it. Perhaps, through the magic of assemblage, which he can sometimes muster, the boys will come to believe this is the case. After all, Jakob allows, I'm standing right here to prove it. What power do their memories have against what appears embodied before them?

"I'm taking this Bellmer home," he says, shoving past the biggest boy, the one the others called Tom.

As Jakob passes, Tom whispers, loud enough for the others to hear, "Have fun humping your dead friend, blood-boy. But know one thing: we're the Boys' Boys and we're taking this town back. Before long, we're gonna string all the twinkie momma-gobblers up by their skinny wieners, right next to their mommas who shoulda flushed them when they had the chance, and everyone's gonna know who's boss! This town's gonna go back to how it was, before rodents like you burrowed in and turned it soft!"

As he walks home with the Bellmer on his back, aware that the trouble he triggered by reanimating the fish will be nothing compared to what this is likely to bring down, Jakob ruminates on the ever-shifting nature of the town's boys. Every time the Desert Dream comes, the boys look different, like there's a disturbance in the universe whose nature he can perceive but never quite articulate. The mood and feeling they give off never changes, but their faces, their bodies, their numbers, their names... this all shifts, like they're made of liquid. Jakob laughs so hard he drops the Bellmer when he remembers that everyone's made of liquid. But, after he picks it up and calms down a little, he thinks, No, in another way too. Not just sloppy blood and guts, but liquid that floats through time and space, never staying still even though it never goes anywhere. There's something strange about how boys like that are always trying to bring their town back to how it was before, while they themselves are never the same from day to day... and they're getting angrier, he realizes, more desperate to do whatever it takes to keep themselves from melting and hardening back together in the new day's hot sun.

"But I'm the stable one," Jakob shouts, ruffling the Bellmer, "not them!"

This gives him a good laugh too, though not as hard as the first one. Here, as in all things, there are diminishing returns. By the time he's remembered this, he's most of the way home. Did I ever cross the bridge again? The possibility that he's returning to a version of his house posed on the far side of the river gives him pause, but there's no time to consider it now. The first order of business, he decides, is smuggling the Bellmer up to his room without getting caught.

The Father's Discourse on Puberty

As he can see that his mother's in the kitchen, focused on her paperwork, Jakob makes a snap decision to stash the Bellmer in the backyard for now, grabbing a towel from the porch to wrap it in.

He drags it to a quiet place behind a rosebush and gets to work digging a bed in the dirt. Not a hole, he reminds himself—I don't want to see it disappear—but a bed about a foot deep, just enough for it to get some rest before being called upon to make its next move.

When the bed's deep enough, he eases the Bellmer inside, placing its smashed, toothless head on the higher part of the dirt, pillow-like. Then he covers its lower body with the towel, as a makeshift blanket—the sort that an animal deserves, a little coarser than what's right for a human, even if all living things, and even some of the dead, belong to the same family, and thus any attempt to differentiate them is just the whingeing of narrowminded pedants, as Jakob's ancestor Ludwig Wittgenstein once put it, or would have if asked.

He knows he shouldn't dally like this, as he can hear footsteps approaching, but, for now, he writes them off as a premonition. A sign of what could happen, but not yet of what's about to. Adjusting the towel, he leans in, picks up a bloody earflap and, putting his lips to the animal's flesh, whispers, "Dear Bellmer, there's something I need to know that I'm not yet capable of knowing on my own. Please think on this for me: is my town one or many? Where in the universe, if anywhere, am I?" Then he closes the earflap over the hole so the flies can't eavesdrop as the creature begins to think this over.

At this precise instant, his premonition comes true. His father shows up, shirtless under the coarse burlap smock he wears for garage-work, which has always struck Jakob as a costume more appropriate for butchering. Were his father to approach him with a cleaver and shout, "Give me your arm!" Jakob wouldn't be in the least surprised. Nor would he, even for an instant, consider resisting. Better my arm than my neck, he would think, if that awful vision ever came to pass, just as, in a sense, he's thinking this now.

"Sit with me on the Talking Rock," his father says, holding out his hand. Jakob takes it and is lifted to his feet, which he watches drag through the dust, away from the sleeping Bellmer, toward a rock that, like so much around here, seems to bob in the middle murk between strangeness and familiarity, like something I should know all about but don't, he thinks, or vice versa, something I do know all about but shouldn't.

Before he's gotten any further on this question, if it is a question, he's sitting next to his father, looking out at a green hill that slopes away behind the house, toward the backyards of a few other houses below. Close enough to run to, Jakob calculates, well aware of how quickly this situation might turn violent, but not so close that they'll hear what's happening unless I scream at the very top of my lungs.

"Jakob," his father says. "I saw what you were doing back there. I can't say that I like it, but I also can't say that there's a rule against it. Nowhere in my vision is there a clear answer as to the proper treatment of dead animals in this life we are, the three of us, trying to live together. So I've taken you here simply to speak, as equals, though we both know this is not what we are. Still, we can pretend for a moment, can't we, son?"

Jakob nods.

"Jakob," his father continues, playing with the straps on his smock, "I know that certain strains inherent in my journey are made manifest upon your person. Certain warpings, deviations. There is, it pains me to say, nothing I can do to mitigate this. But," he clears his throat, making it very clear how much effort this is costing him, "if there's anything in particular you'd like to ask me about, or tell me, now's the time. I cannot say why I am, at this moment, predisposed to be receptive, whereas in a few moments, and for the next few years in all likelihood, I will not be. Perhaps it is because of my rash behavior at dinner last night, which I will admit here that I regret. So, anything to ask?"

Jakob pictures his head as a sculpture made of soft dough with a hand squeezing it, forcing a question through a mouth that has not yet been made. When the pressure grows unbearable, it blurts, "Dad, what are the Boys' Boys?"

His father looks at him with a raised eyebrow, enjoining him to explain further. So he tells the story of the day, the boys who killed the dog (he calls it by this name now that he's in public again), and how they then started kicking him too, "which means" he says, "that it might've been me lying out there behind the budding rosebush, fast asleep, or hanging from the bridge by my skinny wiener. So what are these boys?"

His father takes his son's hand and says, "There's something called puberty, Jakob, which, depending on the circumstances, can either be a kind of growing or a kind of rotting. With those boys, if they are as you say, I suspect it's the latter. It happens when you've remained in the town you were born in, and are about to transition into the final form you'll take in that town. When you'll segue from growing to dying, and, in the meantime, fixating with a kind of savage desperation on spreading the nutrience you've absorbed from the soil of that town so that you might, in a diminished sense, live on. It can be a very sad thing, to arrive too late at the knowledge that the full wealth of existence has, due to your own inaction, become sequestered within the confines of a single remote settlement, and so it can turn some boys mean. You, luckily, will never undergo such a fate until we've finally arrived where we're going. You will wait in suspended animation, as you are now, part-doll and part-baby, until such time as my vision clears all the way and I know where to take us. And then, when we arrive, the soil will claim you, and you will go through puberty, but the growing kind, not the rotting kind, because, on that happy day, you will be in the only place on earth suitable for nourishing the roots you will have at that point put down."

When his father's been silent so long that Jakob fears the talk's at an end, he asks, "Have you... gone through it yet?"

His father pries up a handful of weeds from under the rock and, after staring for a while at the houses below, sinking into dusk, shakes his head. "Not by a long shot. It might not happen till I'm eighty, or it might not happen at all. I'm no farther along than you, the only difference is that I have a son and you are a son. This makes us nearly identical, both awaiting the day when the vision shows me, after so many years, where to go. We will then go through puberty together, Jakob. And won't that be a beautiful thing, the two of us becoming men on the very same day? Won't your mother be proud of us, each able, at last, to sire a *real* heir, and not a...?"

He looks at Jakob and tears up a little. Then he gets to his feet, dries his eyes, and says, "Now, let's each pick a handful of mint from the mint patch and bring it in to season our dinner. What do you say?"

Jakob thinks for a brief, wild instant that he'd like to say, I'm leaving here this instant and never coming back! But of course he says, "That sounds wonderful, dad. Thank you for taking this moment to tell me what I needed to know."

Back to School

That night's dinner is vegetarian, forestalling any repeat of the fish episode, though tomorrow's chicken can be smelled baking in the oven. Oh well, Jakob consoles himself, carrots too can be brought back to life. Still, he can't help mimicking their listlessness, staring down at them on his plate while his mother reminds him that tomorrow he returns to school. "And I," his father adds, "return to work full time. It's back to the garage with me!" He's beaming, unencumbered after his puberty speech, making no secret of how much he's looking forward to sealing himself back into his sanctum, where no one can ask what he's working on. Jakob feels both relief at the notion that, starting tomorrow, life will be back to normal, and sadness at the notion that his father will once again become off-limits: silent, remote, obsessed. Dangerous even to think about, let alone to disturb.

"You're crying onto your carrot, Jakob," his mother says.

Looking down, he realizes it's true. He feels the Blood Clot squirm inside him, shuddering with embarrassment as he bites into the dripping orange stick, mumbling, "I just wanted it saltier."

The next morning, he reports for schooling at 8AM, dressed in his uniform of clean white long-sleeved shirt and corduroy pants which, for as long as he can remember, his mother has been joking will soon be too small for him. Now they're more like shorts, accentuating his feeling of being a pupil in a strange foreign academy, lorded over by a cruel headmistress who resembles his mother in body alone. His father is long gone, locked in the garage, its exterior visible from the kitchen window, its interior as remote as the innermost sanctum of the Grand Temple of the Eternal Sun on Atlantis the day after it finished sinking.

His mother sets out a full coffee mug for herself and a miniature Training Mug for him, clears her throat, and begins the day's lecture, the same as every day's. "The Jews," she begins, "have existed throughout history, from the very founding of the universe, up until today. But there was a crucial split somewhere around the Fall of Rome, with the result being that our family belongs to one branch of this great tradition, the branch of Visionary Jews, while most others belong either to the vulgar branch—the City branch, that of sordid love affairs and high finance and spiraling neurosis—or else to the dogmatic branch, which worships old laws and old visions to the exclusion of all that is still unfolding. We, Jakob, belong to the elite branch of Jewish seers and mystics called upon to continue the work of the Demiurge. And what work is that?"

"Creating the world anew and anew and anew, never resting in its ceaseless creation and destruction and recreation, never accepting for a minute that even a single atom has reached its final form, because no such form exists," Jakob recites.

"And if it does?"

"And if it does, it will be revised in time. Not by God, whom only the dogmatic Jews still believe in, but by the Demiurge, who is everywhere on earth, transfiguring matter, reanimating the dead, and, most importantly, titrating the flow of vision that our heads exist in order to receive in tiny increments."

"Indeed, our heads..." Jakob's mother prompts.

"Indeed, our heads are porous for this reason alone. Were there no vision, we'd be born with eyes, ears, nose, and lips sealed."

She nods. "Very good. We are truly among the Chosen Few, Jakob, in a nation of automata, which is itself enmeshed in a world of automata. The lineage of the Greats, which your father is working tirelessly to reconnect us with, has in large part been sundered. Very few people today are furthering the work of Spinoza, Kafka, Schulz, and Jodorowsky, let alone that of Novalis, Nietzsche, Mann, and Jung, who went deep into hiding for their own dark reasons, cloaking their true Jewish nature in deepest Teutonic shadow. These are your father's ancestors, Jakob. Those from whom you're descended, and in whose footsteps you must walk."

After another hour of discussion on this topic, his mother says, "Would you like your first cookie of the day?"

Each school day, provided all goes well, Jakob is permitted three cookies—one in mid-morning, one after lunch, and one just before dismissal at 3PM. Some days, if he's feeling powerful, he resists the first two until mid-afternoon, because the reward of gobbling all three at once is among the sweetest experiences known to man. But today he isn't feeling up to the effort, so he nods.

His mother rolls one out of the plastic sleeve. It's a chocolate Trader Joe's Joe-Joe, not objectively special, but suffused, like all things, with the power of the Demiurge, ready to transform in his belly through the alchemy of digestion into a divine reagent. He crunches down on it, absorbing its spirit and beginning to think more freely. During each break, he's permitted one off-topic question. This time he decides to use it to explore ground similar to that which he explored with his father yesterday evening. "Mom, what are the Boys' Boys up to right now?"

Chewing the last of her own cookie, she looks at him skeptically. "The what's what?"

He tells her whom he means. "Are they in, you know," he hesitates, "school?"

She wipes crumbs from her fingertips and stares him down. "You're in school, Jakob. This, here, is school. Where those boys are? That's a room. A big, hot, sleazy room, like a pigpen. Is that where you'd rather be?"

He knows he's supposed to shake his head, but something won't let him.

"Is it?" his mother demands. "That's where you want to be? You know what they do to boys in that room? They make them sit very, very still and come around with a long brush and baste them with sticky, foul-smelling honey. All up and down their faces, they slather them with it, and do you know why? To keep them from cracking. To keep their shoddy, pretend skin from cracking off their shells and revealing them as what they are, which is something there's no name for. Is that the kind of thing you'd like to be?"

I'd like to not be a thing at all, Jakob thinks.

"Those boys," his mother goes on, "represent what most people, if we deign to use so inaccurate a term, in this world really are. Body-shaped sacks of sewn-together trash, basted with honey three times a day to keep their seams from showing. If 'school' is the word you'd like to apply to that, go ahead. But it isn't the one I'd use. Since you're done with your cookie, let's return to your lessons."

Jakob nods, consenting to let the rest of the afternoon wash over him in a familiar blur of desert wandering and stone tablets, Red Seas and transports of angelic ekphrasis, lurching back in time to accounts of Jewish apes in deepest Africa and forward in time to Jewish automata in the farthest reaches of outer space.

"Now," his mother says, "please recite the Larger Taxonomy of the Jewish Spirit."

"The Larger Taxonomy of the Jewish Sprit is broken down into the Forest, the Desert, and the City," Jakob recites. "The Forest signifies the homestead, the shtetl, the old country, the lost unity. The Garden, in a larger sense. Embodied by figures such as Isaac Bashevis Singer and Marc Chagall. The Desert signifies wandering, searching, exile. Embodied by figures such as Bob Dylan, Mark Rothko, and Leonard Cohen. And the City signifies culture, assimilation, the aggregation of power through social cachet rather than land owning. Embodied by figures such as Sigmund Freud and Billy Wilder. In other words, Neurotic Jews, sublimating their inner life into that of the Western culture they are at once assimilating into and helping to define. Not to be confused with the Dogmatic Jews, who are religious fanatics in the most retrograde way possible and, as such, of no interest to us. Their blind insistence on retracing our people's steps backward, all the way to the first Israel with its Old Jerusalem, rather than forging onward in search of the New Jerusalem, deeper into America until we find an even Newer World heretofore unreached by our people, is a mistake of catastrophic consequence, as the last seventy years of history have shown. No, the only way forward is onward, not back. For these reasons, we are never to forget that any form of orthodoxy, except to one's personal vision, is the worst kind of cowardice. No Testament, neither New nor Old, is complete, and so to worship one as such is to deny the ongoing presence of the very creative force that supposedly authored those Testaments in the first place."

"Very good," his mother replies. "And underlying the visions of the Visionary Jews?"

"Underlying our visions, supercharging them with catastrophic urgency, are the flames, which can erupt at any moment. The manic, ecstatic, lunatic gibbering of the Burning Bush. Transports of rage and ecstasy, the sudden quickening transformation of any landscape into one of revelation and reckoning. Embodied by figures such as Clarice Lispector and Harold Pinter."

His mother nods. "Lispector, Pinter, and... ?"

Jakob feels his eyes beginning to roll, but he freezes them before they get too far, knowing well the consequences of perceived disrespect at this climactic point in the lesson. "Lispector, Pinter, and Dad."

"Very good," his mother says, her own expression also a bit pained at the ritual's conclusion. "Now, ready for lunch and your second cookie? Last night's chicken is ready to serve."

At Trader Joe's

The second cookie proves to be the last in the pack, which means that this afternoon will take place at Trader Joe's, as the Replenishment Ritual dictates. "Go upstairs and get your veil," his mother whispers, beaming with excitement at the prospect of leaving the house. She hums to herself as she rifles through the bins by the back door for the car keys, which are only to be used on occasions such as this.

Jakob tiptoes past the snake and into his room, which still smells of fish, and rifles through his desk drawer until he finds the thick cotton veil he keeps rolled up with twine in the very back, near his lucky pennies, jar of baby teeth, and the oversized souvenir key that, he likes to imagine, will one day open the gates of the New Jerusalem. Tying the veil over his face, as he is required to whenever passing from the inner sanctum of the town into the Outskirts that surround it, across the Narrow Bridge That Spans the Underworld, as it's sometimes called, he gropes his way back down the stairs, arms outstretched, straining to connect with his mother, wherever she may be. He tiptoes through the kitchen, retracing the first, tentative steps he took upon being reborn in this house, in this town, a few days ago—though the memory has already grown so hazy that this account feels like a clown's rendition of the origins of the universe. He extends his fingertips as far as he can, imagining they're roots growing out of the central trunk of his body, desperate for purchase in any soil at all. Straining and grasping until he feels close to fainting, he finally senses the warmth of human flesh and lunges toward it, sticking his fingers deep into his mother's side, then latching on and refusing to let go.

Like a host conveying its parasite through the world, his mother leads him out of the house and into the car, where Jakob settles into the backseat. Pulling out of the driveway, she says, "Back into the breach. Ready for the voyage through enemy territory? Hunker down until I say it's safe to sit up."

Jakob makes a muffled squeal as the car jolts backward, then turns up the street to begin the strange, winding journey out of town and into the no-man's-land between one town and the next, the endless waste in which all souls who tarry must perish. Full of frozen men and women, his father has often said, flesh and blood beings turned to stone after one night too many upon cold and rootless terrain. Neither Desert nor City,

Jakob thinks, trying not to sneeze from the dust in the veil's fabric. He lets it gather on his tongue and pretends it's a taste of the underworld that's whooshing by outside the car. A warning, he thinks, tasting it before it dissolves. My whole body could be made of this, mummified inside and out, left to wither in isolation while my parents go on without me, seeking the New Jerusalem in towns so distant I can't imagine their location, not even when I picture the farthest reaches of outer space.

He spends the rest of the ride picturing these outermost reaches, drifting through them in a cloud of dust, imagining his body as a nebula that's still ambivalent about coalescing. When his mother stops the car, he jolts upright, terrified that he's about to fall out of orbit and plummet to the rocky shore of some alien planet. His heart's still pounding when she comes over to his side and loosens the veil, saying, "Here we are, spaceman, back on earth."

As his vision is restored, he feels a mixture of relief and disappointment at the prospect of returning to Trader Joe's, the one location outside of town where it's safe to set foot. The Fixed Center of the Turning Universe, as his mother calls it, the hub from which the spoke-like roads that lead to all the towns in America emanate.

Following her across the parking lot, he thinks, I'm glad the risk of drying into a husk in the Desert alone is behind me for the time being, though, on the other hand…

He can't complete this thought before they've passed into the store's interior and his mind is overwhelmed with visual sensation, but he can tell it's something like: on the other hand, how much longer can this go on? How long until I break, or it, whatever it is, breaks and leaves me to fend for myself in whatever town I happen to be in then?

"You okay?" his mother asks. "You're shivering."

Jakob takes her hand and nods. "Why do they keep this place so cold?"

She smiles and shrugs at the familiar question. Then they're on their way, the entrance ritual successfully completed, the shopping ritual successfully underway.

First of all: flowers. Jakob's favorite part.

He rifles through the bouquets of roses, daffodils, carnations, nasturtiums, and lilies, smelling their pollen and stretching their petals between his fingers like flaps of skin. His mother lets him do this for as long as he pleases; it's among the few unregulated moments he's afforded. As he checks in with his flowers, some of which appear to be the same from their last visit, he muses on one of his favorite questions, that of whether the room he's in now is "*the* Trader Joe's" or "*a* Trader Joe's," one example of an infinite series, one dot in a line that goes on forever. It's a question deep enough to knock on the locked doors of the sacred. It is, he thinks, the question of the All-one vs. the All-many, which is, in a sense, "the question that preoccupies my father, that of whether, day by day, all phenomena are coming together or splitting apart, approaching a point of infinite density or infinite..."

"Jakob! Stop talking to yourself in public. Pick a bouquet and let's move on."

Wincing with the pain of disembarking from an uncompleted train of thought for the second time today, he climbs out of his father's head, only now realizing that that's where he was. He shivers again to realize that, even at this great distance from the house, his father's mind still afflicts him. Perhaps it always will, he thinks, following his mother into the snack aisle with a bunch of carnations in his fist, because, at the end of the day, it's in me as much as it is in him. We're both just examples of whatever it is.

Panting, he decides to try simply to appreciate the riches around him. It takes all the strength he can muster to rivet his attention on the spectacle of his mother pulling Joe-Joe's and peanut butter cups and Clif Bars from the shelf, then grinding coffee in the self-serve grinder at the back of the store while helping herself to a small sample cup while she waits. Jakob takes a sample of coffee cake and nibbles it carefully, letting its simple flavors soothe him with the promise, though he suspects it's fraudulent, that not everything needs to be complicated.

"It's wonderful, isn't it?" his mother asks, when the coffee's done grinding and she's moved on to the frozen foods aisle. "All this variety here for the taking?"

"All thanks to its founder, Joseph Cornell. Trader Joe

himself," Jakob recites, further soothed by the stable litany. The heretical litany of modernist Gentile Geniuses, whispered about only out of earshot of his father.

His mother's face goes dumb and smiley as another woman passes by, then she nods and resumes stacking bags of frozen peas on top of the Puffins in her cart. "And what did he do?"

"He was the greatest collector of ephemera the world has ever known. He had the best eye, the best feel for those objects which, though cheap, were possessed of transcendental value. He left behind many tributes to his Genius, but the one most available to us," he sweeps his arms to take in the full expanse of Trader Joe's, "is this. An edible cornucopia the likes of which the world had never before seen, a palace of delights in which any conceivable combination of objects will yield a completely unique result, meaning that the combinations far exceed the number of meals possible within a single lifetime, or the lifetime of an entire family, or even an entire civilization. We are truly amongst the infinite here at Trader Joe's. The work of Joseph Cornell..."

Jakob stops as his voice cracks. He can tell that his mother is as shocked as he is. It leaps an octave, then falls several, so that "Corn" comes out as the voice of a boy, and "ell" as that of a man.

The voice of his father.

He's so surprised that it takes a moment to realize life has already moved on, from one surprise to the next: that of his mother leaning against the boxes of wine in the wine aisle, at first trembling and then rocking back and forth in tears. He stands frozen and watches her, his sense of her realness rapidly bleeding away. Part of him wants to fight to hold onto it because the notion that she might soon be no more than another automaton is terrifying, but now it's too late.

As he watches her cry while other grown-ups drift past in feigned ignorance, reaching around her to get what they need, he falls back through time to much earlier Trader Joe's visits, back when he was the one crying. He sees himself on the floor in the snack aisle, devastated by the news that he'd have to decide between peppermint and peanut butter Joe-Joe's, the world closing in, the sense that life could never be full enough to be worth living already oppressing him at age three, as he lay pounding his fists on the cold tile, desperate to find a way to get both kinds of cookies at once, to never have to take one path and leave the other untried.

This vision grows so compelling that he loses track of which one's happening now, and which happened then. Is it me crying and my mother watching, or the other way around? It seems that both are equally plausible, and the uncertainty is more than he can take, so he forces himself to close his heart. It doesn't matter, he decides. Either way, it means nothing. Whichever cookies I choose are the wrong choice; whichever of us is crying is the fool.

He leans back against the pretzel and popcorn bags

and watches something sob, some mechanism with eye-holes that squirt water and a mouth that emits sloppy wailing huffs, and he thinks, it's an it, it's an it, it's an it; it's nothing but an it, an it that's not my mother. He pictures this thing drained of all that made it recognizable, and he can tell that, if he doesn't stop picturing it this way very soon, he's going to see his mother dead, and then life as he's known it until now will be over.

Just before this happens, the thing turns, face red and slick and puffy, and says, in a voice that sounds terrifyingly like his mother's, "Leave the basket, Jakob, we're going home."

It grabs the box of wine off the shelf and runs past the checkout lines and out of the store so quickly that he has no choice but to follow, still clutching the bouquet, which sets off an alarm and, in dreamy slow motion, calls a guard, who bellows at the thing that has come to resemble his mother, and Jakob sees himself handing the guard the bouquet like it was a gift meant for him all along, and then he and she are running to the car, faster than the bouquet-wielding guard can follow, and then they're driving even faster, swerving out of the parking lot and down a side street, trying to hide, and, before he can process what this might mean, he realizes that he's leaning against the window with his veil on the seat beside him. He watches the countryside, shredded by highway overpasses and empty lots, whir by. "Mom?" he mutters, from the backseat. "Why are you showing me this?"

After veering to a halt in the parking lot of a Waffle House, beside a Tyson Meat Truck, his mother reaches into her purse, removes an orange bottle, sucks down a handful of white pellets, and jerks the driver's seat all the way back, so that her head is almost level with his.

"Jakob," she begins, swallowing a dry lump, "what you just saw? It was a dream, okay? Sometimes, as we've discussed, dreams crop up when you least expect them. They trick you into thinking you're awake. They like to play games, making us think it's daytime. That's why they're called daydreams. Many whole days are nothing but dreams, alright?"

He knows he's supposed to nod, but something won't let him. Curiosity, perhaps, or something closer to anger, or maybe just the driver's seat, which is pressing hard into his chest. "No, mom," he says. "Either I'm not dreaming, or we both are. Either way, something happened. What was it?"

She turns and regards him with a mix of curiosity and anger. After a drawn out sigh, she says, "Alright, look. I'm not going to say much, but I will say this: that story about Joseph Cornell? About how he was the original Trader Joe? That's not true, Jakob. That's kids' stuff. I know I taught it to you, but you need to stop telling it now. You're not a kid anymore, so you need to stop believing kid stuff. Okay? You need to stop repeating everything we tell you. It's not your fault, but..." Her face trembles again, and he fears it's about to lose the ability to convince him that it's hers. If it does, he can tell that he won't be able to deny this impression a second time. Regaining control, she says, "But just stop it. We can't go to Trader Joe's anymore. From now on, think of it as the lost cornucopia of your youth, okay? Picture it sinking down to take its place on Atlantis."

This time he doesn't hesitate to nod. He wants to ask more, but he can tell that no more is within reach today. You can never get the whole thing at once, he knows, no matter what it is. Whatever you're trying to do or think or make or learn, it's always one little piece at a time, pushing you to the brink of despair, though never quite past it.

"Okay," his mother says, adjusting her hair in the rearview mirror, then dabbing at the undersides of her eyes with a tissue, "now I need you to put your veil back on and never tell anyone—and you know who I mean—that we drove home with it off. And this conversation? We never had it."

He stretches it over his eyes and lies down in the backseat without saying anything. As the outside world goes black, he focuses on arranging the factories, rest stops, loading docks, and roadside accidents into a diorama as large as the earth itself, overhung with a handsome ceiling of stars.

After rolling to a stop in the driveway, they make their way back into the kitchen and take the seats they'd been sitting in before, as if they'd never left. Soon enough, Trader Joe's begins to recede and his father, dead-eyed after twelve hours in the garage, tramps into the kitchen and says, "Smells like old chicken. Don't we have anything fresh?"

"We got carried away with today's lesson. We'll go to the store tomorrow," his mother replies, and serves the remnants of the chicken that must have sat out since lunch. The bones are still intact under the skin and gristle, which has thickened and turned to rubber. This reminds him of the Bellmer slumbering out back, and he imagines suturing a chicken wing to its armpit so it could fly away in times of crisis, or perhaps patching up the wounds left by the Boys' Boys with some chicken-skin bandages. The possibilities, he's happy to realize, are still endless.

In the Garage

Late that night, Jakob wakes up beneath the Night Crusher, the hairy, red-eyed, horned beast that stands on his chest after days of exceptional strain. He lies like this until the weight relents enough to let him turn his head toward the window that faces the backyard. In the bottom left-hand corner, he sees a glowing square, which, after a few moments of slack attention, resolves into the shape of the garage. The shape of the regular garage, he thinks, trying to laugh at the absurdity of needing to remind himself of this, but his lips are still frozen. So he just lies there, watching the orange glow flicker, knowing that it's only a matter of time until he's on his way down there. As soon as you become aware of the paralysis, he thinks, the process of waking up has begun. As soon as you become aware of anything, he goes on thinking, you're more than halfway to doing it. It seems so obvious that he'll eventually end up in the garage, where his father works by day and no one's allowed at night, that now he can't be sure it isn't happening already. It feels like studying a painting on a wall, tracing lines with the eye that were set down long ago. No matter how many times you look at it, he thinks, descending the stairs in the Night Crusher's arms, the lines always end up in the same place. Still, you have to check it every time. Otherwise—he's being carried through the back door now—there'd be no reason to do anything at all. You might as well just curl up and die!

Now he's crossing the backyard, past where the Bellmer slumbers, toward the garage, kicking his feet through the dew once the Night Crusher puts him down and holds him until he regains his balance. He approaches the door just as his arms thaw enough to enable him to reach for the handle, and he watches his still-nerveless fingers wrap like vines around it.

The door to the place where he knows he should not be is now open.

The instant he gets a glimpse inside, he swoons in the hot reek of fertilizer and forgets what he expected to see, so he can't tell whether he should be surprised. And what, in fact, is it? He tries to explain what he can see: it's his mother and father in there together, but separate, facing away. Each is naked and hooked up to a robot, or a doll, some mix of wood and rubber, doing something with it. The same thing, Jakob thinks, wavering there in the doorway, the same thing but different too. Opposite, somehow. The longer he watches, the harder it grows to tell which set of bodies belongs to his parents. His father is pounding in and out of one doll or robot, while his mother is watching the other pound in and out of her. Jakob lolls there in the doorway, mesmerized by the motion, unsure if they can see him. "Bad! Bad! Bad! You've been bad!" his father shouts in the ear of his doll or robot, while his mother shouts, "I know! I know! I know!" into the ear of hers.

It sounds to Jakob like both a punishment and a reward, a combination of sounds that is at once deeply familiar and harrowingly strange. "She told your dad about Trader Joe's," the Night Crusher whispers in his ear, breathing hot, alcoholic steam. "He knows what happened with your voice. How you spoke as him."

The longer Jakob watches, the more he feels the vastness from which he was built, or conjured, being stirred by this activity, reignited, like he's watching the scene while also being created by it, spawned as a creature doomed to walk the earth as something part human and part mechanical. "So this is the robot factory," he whispers, "the room where the Blood Clot and I were made, and programmed with all the thoughts we'll ever have, including the thought that our minds are somehow our own."

In the deep background, behind where his mother and father are heaving, he can just barely see what looks like another doll, its face almost identical to his, its expression mirthful and unafraid, like, here in the garage, is the real Jakob and he's the waxen intruder.

He blinks hard, forcing the image out of his sight. With his eyes closed, he insists, No, it's just the regular garage! Nothing's going on in here. This thought makes him laugh, so it's a good thing the Night Crusher's hands are still around his throat—otherwise I'd be a babbling ape by now, and then my parents would turn and see me, and I'd be frozen solid like I'd just met the damn Medusa!

As soon as the Night Crusher loosens his grip, Jakob turns and runs out of the panting orange light, knocking over a paint can on the way. He hears his father stop and shout, "Hello?" but he's already running through the yard, past the Talking Rock, and over to the hole where the Bellmer slumbers, desperate to keep from being alone with whatever he just saw.

The Déjà vu
Frog Pond

It doesn't take much to wake the Bellmer. Jakob pulls off the blanket and watches as a cloud of white, wriggling bustle emerges to greet him. It dances across his forearms and onto his shoulders as he reaches down and picks up the creature, hoping to rouse it gently, but now it's wriggling too, so, faster than he'd planned, he finds that he and it are both hustling across the yard, away from the house and the Night Crusher, who's waiting for the sunrise, when he'll be transported to some other part of the world, where it's still night and people are still sleeping uncrushed in their beds.

Jakob, meanwhile, suspects that he and the Bellmer are speeding toward a revelation. He has to run to keep up, the soft hulk of the animal pressed into his side, leaning against him, playfully threatening to knock him down. They run up the street the house is parked on and toward downtown, bypassing the place where his mother turned into the meadow and toward the woods, and don't stop except to pick up a new member of their menagerie—a pigeon crushed under a rock at the corner of his street and Main. Another gift from the Boys' Boys, he thinks, thrilling at the possibility that they are acting as his assistants. A surge of power passes through him, making his head wobble. "I am the master and they are my apprentices," he declares, somewhere between galvanized and petrified to hear that his voice still sounds like his father's. He scoops up what's left of the pigeon and shoves it under the Bellmer's collar, so that it looks like it's flying with a dog's head for a helmet.

He can tell that an old man in a rocking chair on his porch is watching him, yesterday's newspaper held low under his eyes like a shoddy mask, but Jakob pays him no heed, inwardly reciting the line his mother taught him about neighbors: whatever secrets we may have from them, just think of the secrets they have from us. The truth about neighbors, understood yet denied the world over, is that none truly wish to know us, just as we most certainly do not wish to know them.

So, with a half-hearted salute in the old man's direction, Jakob gathers up the Bellmer and runs on. He nearly flies the rest of the way into town, whipping up the energy that he trusts will guide him to where he's supposed to go, since, he thinks, it connects me to the Greats of history, although, at the same time, another

voice interrupts, "I wish I knew some actual people."
This is the kind of thought that marks the line between
the end of the night, where nearly anything's possible,
and the beginning of the day, where nearly nothing is.
He closes his eyes, licks his lips, swallows, and feels the
Blood Clot swim a queasy loop from his throat down to
his legs and then back up to his gut, which he thinks of
as a womb when he can feel her in it.

Then he looks down and notices that the Bellmer
has led him to a frog pond. He kneels by the edge
to watch the sunrise in the scummy water, searing
the Lilly pads that break up its reflection. Staring at
the water with the Bellmer resting in the grass beside
him, Jakob allows déjà vu to overwhelm his system.
It comes fast and consumes everything: a second ago,
the specifics of this town felt hazy, but now everything
reminds him, on a level so deep it hurts, of everything
else. The déjà vu throws out strings that connect
everything he sees to everything he thinks, suturing
him into the middle of it all, a twelve-year-old boy
who was somehow also conceived last night, and is
somehow also an eighty-year-old man, having lived
his whole life in this town, waiting for an authentic
birth that never came. The strings pull tighter, until
he can barely breathe. He thinks about Winnicott and
the relief of reentering the holding environment, while,
at the same time, thinking about the snake, about it
finally swallowing and digesting him and, in this way,
making him a permanent part of the house, a notion at
once blasphemous and irresistible.

The strings continue pulling inward, crushing his ability to conceive of anything beyond what's immediately apparent, so that he can't help but declare, "Of course this is the town where I belong, where every thought I've ever had belongs, and where whatever I end up doing, in the years between now and eighty, will be done. And of course this is the ground in which I will one day be planted, the seed of something unimaginably greater." The simplicity of this fact, thus articulated, is so absolute that he exhales and feels the strings let up. "So this is it," he pants. "The New Jerusalem.

"And if it isn't, I can make it be. Because if I can't, then there's nothing between me and the Tyson Meat Truck, no place to hide from the fear that life is nothing but loading docks and highway overpasses, cold storage and sides of beef on meathooks."

He exhales again, letting the strangeness of his changed voice expand away from him as he feels the last of the crushing sensation abate with a cathartic squirt. Looking down, he discovers that he's squished a frog in his fist. Opening his fingers to examine its ruined body, he realizes that it was a sacrifice to mark his acceptance of permanent residency in this town, and his ritual expulsion of the last slimy pustules of doubt. "Thank you for you service," he whispers, "your death was not in vain." And to the Bellmer, he adds, "Thank you for leading me here. I couldn't have found this place on my own."

Getting to his feet, he attaches the frog to the top of

the Bellmer's collar, so that it protrudes like a cock's comb, a warped double of the pigeon below. Stepping back to regard his work, he can't help but admire it. Reinvigorated with pride, he sets out for downtown, ready to meet the morning as someone who's now certain he belongs in it.

The Town
Museum

With the Bellmer as his guide, Jakob walks away from the Déjà vu Frog Pond, as it will be known from now on, and toward downtown, along a road he hasn't traveled before. He knows that roads and doors open only at the right time, when he's ready to use them. This is one of the First Principles. Still, the excitement of finding a new way into town, gathering staples and screws from a dumpster—as he notices himself doing now—and inserting them one by one into the Bellmer's eyes and tongue, is real.

He stops to regard his work as if it were that of a stranger: the Bellmer's head bulges with metal, matted fur and flesh framed and riveted by screws, staples, and nails, some of them gleaming, others rusty, all of them from a bag in the dumpster that, it doesn't take a prophet to see, was planted there just for him. I have reached the next level, he thinks, proudly, enjoying the game-like aspect of it all. Somewhere far in the back of his head he's aware that his mother is waiting for him at home, and that he's about to be in Contempt of Court, which is the name for missing school, but he can't bring himself to worry about this just now. He has bigger fish to fry.

Fish!

The thought of what's left of the fish moldering in his bedroom makes him blush. If only it too were here, he thinks, to join the frog and the pigeon in the Bellmer's screw-riven mass of dogflesh, then something perfect would be complete. Then I'd be a hero in my own time. Still, one must press on. No sense in giving up halfway—to where?—just because I forgot my fish. "Only the process is holy," he recites, over the voice of doubt, which Elias Canetti once promised would never go away. "The working and reworking and reworking some more, until something reworks us into a form we'd never recognize."

So he gathers the Bellmer, which had been catching its breath against his leg, and forges on, along a side-street that the low road dovetails with, past a boarded-up pizza place, a hardware store, an auto repair shop, a Moravian church (here, he makes the alien sign of the cross over his head), a noodle bar, a soft-serv stand, a clam shack, the Chamber of Commerce, a law firm, a dentist's office, and a Mexican restaurant, all of them emerging from the haze they'd been hidden in so far.

The town is resolving itself, Jakob begins to see, like a blurry photo I've finally found a way to develop, although there's something sad about seeing it for what it is: this is it? part of him worries. There's nothing more? This is enough of a world for lifetimes to pass in? But there's something soothing about it too, like he's finally managed to return home after years and years alone in the Wilderness. Giant Chinese and Wing Hut and Mama's Pizza are clustered together in a strip mall, framed by two vacant storefronts and an Army Recruiting Center. They radiate familiarity, though Jakob knows it might be a trick. The familiarity I feel for these three restaurants is separate from the question of whether I've actually eaten at them, he warns himself, since I'm pretty sure I haven't. He looks down at the Bellmer, as if some clue might be hidden in its fur, but nothing, as far as he can tell, is. It's just me and Giant Chinese, Wing Hut, and Mama's Pizza—unless I want to join the army!—standing at the edge of the parking lot as a truck pulls in.

Something about the noise of the horn, even though he understands what it means, shocks him, so, blinking back tears, he hurries up the road, past the trailhead for something called Evangeline Mansion Nature Walk 1.2 mi, and finally to a one-room white wooden building with a hand-painted placard out front that reads, "Town Museum: Entry $1."

This, Jakob thinks—or, rather, knows—is my destination. He drops the Bellmer with a thud, which causes the screen door to open and an elderly woman to pop out onto the porch. Sipping from a mug of tea, she squeezes her eyebrows above her glasses and looks at Jakob, then at the Bellmer, then back at Jakob. "That for me?"

He doesn't reply, not knowing, quite yet, whether it is.

"Are you an artist?"

He doesn't reply to this either, not knowing, in any sense at all, what she means. Are you a witch? He'd like to ask, but manages to restrain himself.

She hobbles down the stairs, one of her feet in a cast, until she's managed to sit next to the Bellmer and place its head in her lap. She takes her time petting its many surfaces as they range from mammal to bird to amphibian to steel. Then she looks up at Jakob and says, in a way that he's pretty sure isn't a lie, "It's beautiful."

After a few more compliments and a little coaxing, he finds himself inside the Town Museum, sitting on a stool beside the woman, who's told him her name is Greta. The Bellmer's in here too. It must have walked in beside us, he thinks, unless she carried it. "I'm Jakob," he must've said a few minutes ago, because now she says, "Would you like a Coke, Jakob?"

He must've nodded, because now he's sipping it, slimy and freezing between his two hands, the Bellmer on the floor between them. He hopes she knows it's just resting. Something about the way she smiles at it, then at him, then back again, reassures him that she does.

"What do you see, Jakob?" she asks, watching him explore the boxes, maps, and charts that adorn the walls. He doesn't answer, instead letting his eyes slither out of the dry skin of his face and into what feels like a new world... the real world, maybe, at last. A world of interconnected streets, rivers, deserts, and woods, like the realm his father explores in dreams, but, in the drawings, watercolors, and collages displayed on the Town Museum's walls and shelves, it's fleshed out in a way he's never seen before. A fantastical mix of nautical charts, Alpine lodges, hellish torture-caves and grottoes stuffed with scorpions and bats, all of it connected by a logic that Jakob can immediately perceive, even if he could never explain it. A glue that's binding me to all this, he thinks. Making me part of it, and it part of me. Like this were, at last, an accurate chart of my veins and muscles.

"The greatest artist who ever lived," says a voice behind him, and it takes a moment to remember he's not in here alone. Turning around, he watches Greta hobble up from her rocking chair as she says, "Wilhelm Wieland, WW as we call him, graced this world with a gift it was too shabby to receive. Oh well. Their loss, our gain." She smiles. "This, Jakob, is the only collection on the planet." She comes up behind him and enfolds his soft, pink hand in her crispy, gray one. "I can see that his work speaks to you. It doesn't speak to everyone. It's like a language that... well, you know it, don't you? In some way you may not yet understand, you know that you know it."

She looks down at him, dabbing her eyes as he looks up. He nods, almost knowing what she means. She too, he understands, is part of the world these things are here to reveal. A witch, certainly, but perhaps a good witch.

"'New Jerusalem 2,' he calls it," she says. "The place where all that we are inside corresponds exactly to what we are outside. Where there's no repression, no miscommunication, no lying, and, ultimately, no distinction between dreaming and waking. No exile. A beautiful notion. And," she gestures at a painting of three she-wolves suckling at the jugular of a little girl on a bed of wings, "a horrible one. Just don't ask him what happened in the first New Jerusalem." She smiles in a way that leaves it unclear whether this is a joke or something too frightening to mention with a straight face.

Still, everything she says makes sense. It's a welcome feeling, and a rare one. They browse in silence for a while after this, circling the Museum several times. Each circuit seems to reveal a new side of WW's work, as if the room had eight or sixteen walls, rather than only four.

"**There's** something familiar about you," she says, after Jakob's had time to absorb all the work on display. "Not like we've met before, but like we have something in common. I can't put my finger on it just yet. If he's

WWI, maybe you're WWII." She looks him over, clearly eager to find out how easy or hard it will be to make him smile. "I need to take my medicine and lie down, but do you mind if I keep this?" She gestures at the Bellmer with the cast on her foot.

Jakob looks at the combination of cast and dog, wishing he could sew them together. Slowly, reminding himself that, for now, her foot belongs to her, he nods. "Okay," he manages to say, startled to hear his own voice echo in the dusty Museum. It feels like the walls are reaching out to capture it, preserving it in this space so that, centuries from now, whoever comes inside will hear it.

"I can't promise I'll keep him here on the rug," she says, retracting her cast into the shadows under the rocking chair. "If he starts to stink, I may take him out back. But I'll put him under plastic, not dirt, so you can come by and see him any time you please. How would that be?"

Jakob thinks about it. "Can I ask him?"

She nods, so he puts down his Coke and kneels down to the Bellmer's ear. He pinches the flap and finds that it comes away between his fingers like a piece that had only ever been juxtaposed against the head, never attached to it. Holding it out with one hand, he clamps his nose shut with the other and leans in to whisper, "Can you live in a hole, if there's plastic over it so the sun comes in?"

Then he puts his ear to the creature's mouth, feeling maggots dance on its tongue like it's still panting. A moment later, he stretches the flap back over the ear, gets up, and nods. "He says okay, but just for tonight. Can I come back tomorrow to check on him?"

She smiles. "Of course. And, if you're ever looking for a little pocket money, I might have some boxes that need sorting, and shelves someone oughtta dust. Think about it."

As Jakob walks out, toward the Boys' Boys whom he can see ravening in the weedy lot across the street, he can tell that the Town Museum is going to be one of the defining locations of the next phase of his life, and Greta one of its defining personas. All that's been decided now, he realizes, with a sense of mourning for the future that, even yesterday, was still wide open—or at least, in yesterday's holy ignorance, appeared to be.

Ragtown

Jakob strides down the steps of the Town Museum, still basking in Greta's approval, making no effort to evade the Boys' Boys despite knowing that what's about to happen is unlikely to be pleasant. What he wonders, in the last instants before they're upon him, is whether he's capable of dying. He wonders this often, of course, but never as acutely as in moments like these, when a heaving mass of Gentileflesh is bounding toward him with its collective teeth bared.

He has the sense that he's talking to himself in the last millisecond before Tom barks, "Yo, Baby Dracula, you talking to yourself again?" and the others cackle.

"There's just so much to say," Jakob replies. "Are you about to try to kill me? Because if you are, I should warn you that I can't guarantee I'm capable of dying. In fact, that's what I was just wondering about."

"We wonder that too," Tom replies. "But not today,

no. You know who's in there?" He gestures back
toward the Town Museum.

"You mean Greta?"

"That old bag?" Tom laughs. "No dude, the weirdo
who made the art. WW. You know who I mean?"

Jakob feels his head nod like Tom's words activated
a button that compelled this response, overriding any
decision he might've made to keep his newfound
awareness of Wieland's work to himself.

"You know what he did?"

Jakob shakes his head for the same reason that he
nodded a moment ago.

"Well, follow us to Ragtown and maybe we'll tell
you."

Jakob follows the Boys' Boys across the river, no
longer certain which side he was on before, nor which
side he's on now. Lagging behind the group, he
sketches an impossible map in his head, one in which
the bridge always crosses the river from the old side
to the new, always forward, across the Red Sea to
Jerusalem, never back to Egypt. On the Jerusalem side,
he places the Déjà Vu Frog Pond and the three
restaurants in the strip mall that he lingered before this
morning—Giant Chinese, Wing Hut, and Mama's Pizza,
lined up like three totems guarding the entrance of the
Grand Temple—overriding his uncertainty as to where
they actually belong. Inside my mind, he thinks, there's
a master and there's a slave, and when one tells the
other what to do, the other does it without complaint.

The notion that the town within the town could be represented on paper, even if it required an infinite supply of ever-shifting pieces, like a celestial mobile, brings him no end of pleasure. If this isn't how the world works, he thinks, then it's how the world within the world works. It must be, if I say so. The possibility that it's now up to him to decide fills his lungs with an energy he's never felt before. He breathes it in, then breathes it out, tasting smoke.

He indulges in this taste until he finds himself in a junkyard surrounded by popped tires, scrap metal, and piles of boards suckling hungry broods of nails. A mesmerizing number of squirrels and chipmunks scuttles through broken windows into clumps of weeds, nibbling with practiced caution around shards of glass and spools of razor-wire. They dance over the nails like self-mortifying saints, winking at Jakob and tittering amongst themselves, either inviting him into their jagged sanctum or conspiring to punish him for intruding. Cryptic little devils, he thinks, though he can't suppress his affection.

When a harsh plastic ridge jabs Jakob's left testicle, he looks down to find himself sitting on a plastic crate beside all the Boys' Boys except Tom, who's sitting across from them in an armchair with springs and stuffing poking out in every direction. All in all, it's a scene whose details appeal to Jakob, so much so that he has to remind himself that he's in it, and thus subject to whatever dangers or opportunities it might contain, rather than studying it inside a frame on the wall of the

Town Museum, where he'd much prefer to be, now and perhaps always hence.

"They say he used to come out here," Tom begins, or continues if he'd already been talking. "To gather up trash and bring it back to his cabin. For his mobiles and collages. Pieces of garbage that he thought meant something." Tom scoffs, forcing everyone else to scoff with him. "Until, years ago, he started making his stuff out of kids instead. He uses everything: their eyes, their hair, their skin. He sews it all together into sculptures and dolls and God knows what else, all up there in that cabin of his, deep in the woods. The Museum you were hanging around at? That's just part of his work, the surface part. The cover story. The rest of it, the real part, he keeps up there, where almost no one's brave enough to go. No one but us. Isn't that right, boys?"

Tom looks around, gauging support. Everyone except Jakob nods.

"You see," Tom goes on, "that old creep haunts this town. Kids have been disappearing for years, but no one can prove it. The police claim they just keep getting lost, wandering off the trail, falling into the gorge, whatever. All the grown-ups are in on it too. Their parents, the mayor, everyone. Wieland is some kind of satanic magician, forcing the parents to worship the statues he makes out of their kids, like they only ever had kids to contribute to some new form that matter was waiting to take. Evil shit, dude." Tom leans forward and snaps three times in Jakob's face. "Yo! Did you hear what I just said?"

Jakob mumbles "Uh-huh," hoping he won't be asked to repeat it.

Luckily for him, Tom goes right on talking. "So, every kid in this town, if he wants protection from us, has to go up there and make it back alive. To prove he's worth protecting. Isn't that right?" All the other Boys' Boys nod.

"We all did it, and narrowly escaped, but the others like you? Weird new kids with no friends? There've been lots, and let's just say most are hanging on his walls and standing in his garden now, wicker gnomes with human skulls and teeth and hair, waiting to be fed mayonnaise from a jar, which is how he keeps them alive, though they're not really alive, they're more like... well, maybe you'll find out soon."

The others nod again and the atmosphere turns so solemn that, next time Jakob looks over to survey Ragtown, it's almost dark and all the squirrels and chipmunks are gone. Only the glass, metal, and wood remain, and all of that too seems heavier in the changed atmosphere.

"So if you want us to protect you, you gotta prove you're worth it. No promise you'll come back alive, but if you don't, you better believe you're gonna die down here. Without protection, that's a guarantee!"

"Protection from what?" Jakob consents to ask.

All the Boys' Boys get to their feet at Tom's signal as one of them leans into Jakob's ear and whispers, "Us. Now close your eyes till we're out of earshot."

When Jakob opens his eyes, he's alone in the Ragtown dark. Tingling with fear and excitement at the transgression he's about to commit, he gets up from his crate and sits down in Tom's chair, adjusting his legs so they're nestled between the springs and the stuffing.

He closes his eyes and sinks into a dream of kingliness, of ruling this town many years from now, of everything in it being a direct outgrowth of his singular Will, all its matter having been shaped by his hands. Roads, rivers, bridges, houses, dogs, bats, people... all of it, he dreams, settling deeper into his throne, has been shaped by me, turned into exactly the town whose king I was born to become. As the Demiurge is to the universe, so will I be to wherever this is.

Listening to the voice in his head say these words, he realizes that he's discovered the secret, that which his father is unable or unwilling to see. As the king, he assembles his subjects and tells them, "The right town can never be discovered by wandering; it must be created from the available materials, which can be found in any town at all, including this one, provided one has the courage to dig down to the very root of Ragtown and find the rawest of the Raw Materials and haul them, no matter if the needles strip your finger bones bare, all the way up to the surface."

A horrible scuttling jolts him out of this reverie. As soon as he opens his eyes, what he sees scares him so badly that his mind empties out. Like a hat that's blown overboard on a ship in the middle of the ocean in the picture book his mother used to read to him about the school of fish that together defeats the giant shark, he knows with total certainty that the realization, which could well have changed his life, is gone. It can never be recovered; it will have to be conceived of for the first time again.

Trying to shake off the despair of this second realization, he gets to his feet, tiptoeing around old men and women caked in their own filth, rooting around in the trash like mangy dingoes. "Rat People," Jakob mutters, thrilling with what he knows is the cruelty of this term. Still, no one can tell me it isn't apt. He watches them pick up the sides of cars and the frames of old windows, or work together to haul shattered neon signs and whole pieces of houses from one place to another, spooling out copper wire and cans and anything else, Jakob supposes, that can be taken someplace and exchanged for money.

Poor denizens of the real world, he thinks, creeping back through the hole in the fence he must've followed the Boys' Boys in here through, I pity your reliance on dollars and cents, and the lack of vision that has consigned you to that state. He knows the thought is uncharitable, but he can't deny that it rings true. He can tell that ruminations about the lives of the Rat People will occupy him for the rest of the long walk home, so he orders his mind to devote itself to this topic and no other. With the master having spoken, the slave complies.

Jakob's
Midnight Bath

Jakob creeps into the house, though he knows it's late enough that he could stomp in if he wanted to. The Emergency Protocols only go into effect after he's missed three dinners and three days of school, so anything short of this and his parents are guaranteed to be fast asleep, indifferent to his absence so long as he reports for schooling in the morning. "It is good to explore the floating-trash-world outside the doors of this house," he recalls his father proclaiming after the first time he missed dinner, "so that you might see for yourself how crucial the saga of my dreaming is to the future of our family, for, without it, the lives of humans and the lives of animals are indistinguishable along any rubric you or any honest broker could ever devise. So, by all means, go marinate in the sump pit out there, so long as you don't stay long enough to let it turn you."

As he takes his shoes off in the dark of the kitchen, the smell of dish soap emanates from the dishes where they soak in the sink. He pads over in his socks and listens to them bob and bubble, feeling the old mimicry reflex surface from the depths of his brain like a chewed tendon surfacing from the depths of the sink. "If my body were this house," he whispers, "the sink would be my brain, and the idea of taking a bath would be the dishes, rising on a gust of soap up from the darkest, blackest depths toward the fresh air above, the Promised Land where they can, at long last, breathe free, even if they would then dream only of the wet warmth they left behind."

He feels wonderfully light as he hurries up the stairs and strips naked and runs the bath, licking the undersides of his teeth to sharpen them up in preparation for a midnight conversation with the Blood Clot. After pouring in a dash of bath salts, imagining the brine as a stew he's about to cook himself in, he slides into the water, exhaling loudly as the steam covers his eyes and rushes up his nose, making him pee.

After relaxing for a few moments, letting the excesses of the day seep out, he pulls his big toe to his mouth and bites into the scab over the place where he bit it yesterday, or perhaps two days ago, easing off the barely formed new skin so the blood gushes freely. He lowers it into the brine and gives birth to his sister. I am succeeding where my mother failed, he thinks, again reveling in cruelty as the Blood Clot emerges from him.

When she's taken form, she says, "Good evening, little brother. How are you?"

"Just fine, thanks." He giggles at the unnecessary formality of the exchange.

"What have you been up to lately?"

He tells her about the Town Museum, the Boys' Boys, Ragtown, the legend of Wilhelm Wieland.

"I see," she replies. "And is there a question buried in all of that? There usually is, when you summon me. Much as I'd love it if you ever wanted to just talk. Or, God forbid, to hear about my life."

He's glad she can't see him blushing through the steam, as he tries to duck under the shame of the realization that he's never once thought to ask her how she's doing, nor even formulated a stable image of what her life, inside his bloodstream, must consist of. Instead, he tries to remember his question. Whether to sell the Bellmer, even though it said it only wanted to spend one night in that hole behind the Museum? Whether to accept the Boys' Boys' dare and go up to the cabin in the woods? Whether this really is the town in whose woodwork everything that's going to happen is waiting for me to let it out, or just another nameless stop along the way?

The more he contemplates it, the woozier he gets, only half-aware that blood's still streaming out of his toe. He leans his head against the warm, slippery back of the tub and falls into a vision of himself alone in this house as an old, old man, the house he's lived in alone all his life, where he's made the thousands of drawings, sculptures, and collages that, in aggregate, will stand as the only physical testament to the fact that he ever existed, and the only reason for that existence to have occurred.

This house, he thinks—merging in his mind with Wieland, whom he forgets that he's still never met—is located at the heart of the town that formed the nutshell for my entire conception of the universe, the still point at the heart of so much astral commotion. So much dissonance and noise. The one setting where every idea, no matter how abstract, no matter how depraved, made sense. The one setting where, so long as I never left, I could be assured that insanity would chew me up but never swallow. He thinks back on the long years of gathering scrap in Ragtown, the pit from which the town itself emerged, like the primordial ocean that hatched humanity, and thus all the discarded toys, broken chair legs, bloody safety razors, rusty oil cans, and condoms—he grins at the mention of the word, which, though it remains outside his Official Vocabulary, he's heard slip from his mother's mouth when her face was trained on the password-protected laptop, her eyes half-closed like those of a robot on standby—full of still-living sperm are nothing less than the fundaments of the universe itself, waiting to be assembled into new and ever more harmonious forms. "And it was only me," he gloats, "out of the thousands who've lived in this town over the centuries, who saw it clearly and managed to assemble its pieces into a coherent map of what existence, stripped of the sheen of false seeming, actually is."

"**Jakob**? Jakob? Jakob?" The Blood Clot has to shout his name three times, each louder than the last, before he remembers that he's not alone. When he opens his eyes, he sees his mother standing over him, towel in hand. His sister, for now, is gone, back into the womb of his bloodstream.

"What are you doing here?" his mother demands. "Did you pass out in the tub again?"

Looking down at his body, he sees that the bath has gone rusty red. Just talking to my sister, he wants to say, but instead he shrugs and leans into the towel, allowing himself to be swaddled and thus rendered momentarily incapable of self-expression as he falls back through the decades, rapidly unbecoming the old man he was, and once again assuming the mantle of the scared little boy he still is, despite all that has recently become clear to him.

Breakfast

Meeting

Still wrapped in the towel, Jakob lets his mother pose him at the kitchen table, behind his bowl of Wheaties and Training Mug of coffee. His father sits across from him, stirring his own bowl.

"Jakob," his mother begins, her voice distant, "is there cause for concern?"

He knows this is a question he's expected to answer, but for now all he can do is marinate in the strangeness of existing as both a boy and a man, both with and without his parents, both before and after creating the colossal, barely describable body of work that will ink his name onto the short list of human lives that were worth living. He shudders as the two timelines dance atop one another, always about to resolve into one but never quite agreeing to do so.

"Jakob? Are you okay? You need to be listening very, very closely here."

He nods. Then shakes his head. Then nods again. I'm too strong to have to sit here and listen any longer! he thinks. I know too much! He wants to shout this and flip the table to show his parents what he's really made of, but no part of his body is strong enough to do it. On the outside, he thinks, I'm a quaking little twerp, just like I've always been and will probably always be. Or perhaps, he thinks, sinking further into despondency, my body is actually more than able to do it, and it's my mind that's too cowardly to give the order. It thinks it wants to, but it doesn't *truly want to.* Not in the way that counts. He seethes in frustration until he feels like the paralyzed man who could only write with his left toe in one of the books his mother read to him when he was seven. "He was every bit as brilliant as you or I," he remembers her saying, "but his body didn't care. He couldn't do anything except move that one toe. Isn't that the saddest thing you ever heard?"

At the time, Jakob hadn't known how to answer, because hundreds of sadder things crowded his mind as soon as she asked him, but now he knows exactly what she meant. He wiggles his left toe under the table, suddenly terrified that her question was meant as a warning.

He must have moaned or shuddered, because his father drops his spoon into his cereal and shouts, "Jakob! I'm talking now!" Lowering his voice once it's clear that Jakob's paying attention, he says, "In the garage the other night? Your mother and I heard you creeping away and, well, I could handle this brutally, but I am handling it gently for now. I have asked the Demiurge to hush and let me speak as a mere man for the duration of this short address. It is one that I'd had no intention of giving and so, as such, falls outside the Canon. Consider it a piece of Apocrypha, though heed it closely nonetheless." He pauses, looking at Jakob with just enough menace to signify that things might, at any moment, take a very sharp turn.

Then he continues, "What you saw was a form of love. Your mother and I love each other very much, as you know, but we cannot risk the possibility of another child. You are all we will ever need, and even you, as you know, were hatched in desperation, in the disquiet of the middle of our journey, far from its holy terminus, and yet, in a woman's life, the day comes when it simply has to occur, holy terminus be damned, and so..." He picks up his spoon and stirs his flakes. "Do you have any questions for us, Jakob?"

Questions, he thinks. Yes, I did have a question, didn't I? Isn't that why I summoned the Blood Clot? He tries to remember what it was, while keeping up an expression that looks like he's listening to the rest of his father's speech, which he estimates will go on for another five minutes. He imagines the contents of his own mind as Ragtown, and he rummages around in them, throwing aside all the sharp and hairy refuse in search of the prize at the center: the question he'd meant to ask last night and, marinating in the dark of its runoff, the answer.

He rummages and rummages, cutting his hands on discarded razors, digging as fast as he can, terrified that the sun will go down in the form of his father's speech ending, and he'll be stranded there in the dark, easy prey for the Rat People.

But he's in luck! At the bottom of a pile of shattered microwaves, he finds a grease-stained envelope. Opening it quickly, he takes out a notecard that reads: *Sell the Bellmer to the Town Museum, yes or no? Accept the Boys' Boys' dare, yes or no? Entrench in this town, yes or no?*

Emboldened by the awareness that articulating the question is ninety-nine percent of finding the answer, he digs harder, plunging his hands into a pile of stripped screws, praying that any damage he incurs will stay in his imagination rather than etching itself onto his skin. Just as the sun wavers at the edge of the Ragtown horizon, he submerges his arms in a pit of paper pulp and dredges up a sculpture made of slick bone.

Holding it up to the last of the daylight, it looks like the ribcage of a small mammal, but, after studying it a moment longer, he can see that it spells S-E-Y. Turning it around, though it's now too dark to see, he understands that it must spell Y-E-S.

"Jakob?" his mother, once again, pulls him out of himself. "Your father asked you a question. What do you say?"

Turning toward his father, he smiles and says, "Yes."

His father smiles too, clearly relieved. "I'm very glad to hear that, son. Now, about that blood I hear you left in the bathtub overnight. Let me see what we're dealing with up there. It may well be a sign of puberty."

Taking his camera from its shelf by the back door, his father nods at the two of them still at the breakfast table, and heads upstairs, making no effort to conceal his relief at having managed to say whatever he must've said while Jakob was rummaging in Ragtown.

Jakob's First Sale

The only force equal to his mother's insistence on schooling is her insistence that Jakob leave the house between 3 and 8PM, so that she can spend a few peaceful hours alone with her notepad and password-protected laptop before it's time to set about making dinner. It's thus a matter of utmost ease for Jakob to slip away after a stultifying morning of reiterating the distinctions between the Neurotic, the Dogmatic, and the Visionary Jews, as if any possible ambiguity could remain after all these years. "In much the way that the Dogmatic Jews study the Talmud in endless repetition," his mother reminded him at the end of the lesson, "we study the Dogmatic Jews in hopes of discovering a lasting Exodus from the strictures of their worldview and into one capacious enough to encompass the infinite complexity that any true visionary knows reality to consist of. Short of this, there is no hope whatsoever of discovering the promised end of our wanderings anywhere upon the earth."

Having acknowledged that this is true, he walks out the front door, far from the garage where his father is most likely developing the pictures he took of the bloody bathtub this morning, and begins the now-familiar journey into town.

When he arrives at the Museum, his toe blistering inside his sneaker, Greta is sitting on the porch with her broken foot on a stool and a smile on her face. "Jakob," she says, "I've finalized the display of the piece you brought me yesterday. I'm pleased to announce, the Museum would like to acquire it. How does $10 sound?"

It sounds good, he thinks. He gives her a look that he hopes conveys this.

"Come to the backyard and see for yourself," she says. He watches as she heaves to her feet, thinking that he should offer to help but afraid to touch her in case whatever disease or injury she has spreads to him, as the pain in his toe indicates it might. So he just watches and waits, wondering whether to tell her what the Boys' Boys said about Wieland. Not yet, he decides.

"This way." She points at the dusty trail that leads behind the Museum, and starts hobbling along it.

He follows, past a grate that opens onto a dusky basement, past several plastic chairs around a metal table, past a pile of soda cans interspersed with crabapples under a tree, and all the way to the back, near the fence. Here, Greta picks up a broom and sweeps away a thin layer of dust to reveal a plastic screen covering the new bed in which the Bellmer sleeps, surrounded by green and purple bandanas.

It stares up at them, the frog and the pigeon each in a deeper pocket of ground, so that the entire head lies flat with all of its eyes free to make probing contact and transmit what they see back to their respective brains.

"What do you think?" Greta asks, after she's given Jakob a silent moment to take it in.

He's not yet sure. On the one hand, he thinks, it's wonderful to see that it's found a place for itself, and someone other than me to care for it. This will let me devote my attention to other, newer work. On the other hand, it's awfully sad to see it trapped under plastic, when it would be so much happier in the open air. He tries, and fails, to forget that the Bellmer told him it only wanted to spend one night here.

Though he can't help but wonder if he's becoming a kind of murderer, he manages to shrug and say, "It's alright."

Greta seems to understand. "Let's go inside and get your money. Sound good? Also, I'm working on a little plaque for it, and I realized I don't know your last name. What is it?"

Jakob looks up at her, his tongue throbbing against his teeth, as he tries to stifle a laugh at the realization that he doesn't know, either. Partway up the back steps, he collapses in a fit of giggles, only barely managing to reply, "My father says we haven't decided yet!"

Greta looks at him, skepticism and compassion mixed on her face. When Jakob's finished giggling, she helps him to his feet and in through the back door. Taking a seat at her desk in the yellow afternoon light, she motions for him to sit across from her.

He approaches but stays on his feet, scanning the cardboard boxes overflowing with files on the high shelves while he wipes away the tears that the giggling brought to his eyes.

She seems satisfied as she fumbles in her pocket for a small wad of bills and peels off a ten. "Here you go, the proceeds from your first sale. That's a major event in an artist's life, Jakob. Why don't you go down the street to the diner and get a chocolate shake, or vanilla if you prefer vanilla, or even strawberry, though I don't recommend it, and a large plate of French fries. You've earned it. I'd join you, but there's someone else I'm scheduled to dine with." She reaches under her desk and holds up a picnic basket.

Jakob would rather go with her, sensing, as he often can, that wherever she's taking that basket is more significant than the diner where he'll shortly be drinking a chocolate shake and eating a large plate of French fries alone. But he can also sense that not only would she say no if he asked, she'd also close the line of communication that is now open between them.

So he takes the money and gets to his feet as she gets to hers. On their way out through the main room, each of them limping, she says, "And if you'd like a job here, helping me sort boxes, shuffle exhibits, and perhaps man the desk at the gift shop," here she gestures to one corner where, Jakob now notices, some of the objects are for sale, "as I've said, I'd be very happy to have you. I pay ten dollars per afternoon, which is more than a boy your age, even or perhaps especially one with such promise, is likely to earn elsewhere in this town. What do you say?"

(Nighthawks)
At the Diner

Sitting alone at the counter with his chocolate shake and large plate of French fries, Jakob marvels at how much his life has just changed, and how clear the change has been, as opposed to the years of denial of any change within the family. Alternating bites of sweet and salty, cold and hot, he enjoys the spoils of his labor and slips back into the vision that began in the bathtub last night, when he aged sixty or seventy years in a matter of minutes. He feels himself aging again now, slumping over this exact same counter as it too ages, the smooth plastic warping and filling with silverware scratches. He's here for his daily lunch, still a shake and fries after all these years, though he knows he should've switched to soup and salad back when he was still young enough to protect against the bad heart that's now beating itself out inside him. He's finished another hard morning's work in the garage, putting into order the chaotic shards of the world that pile up around him, day in and day out. What is the purpose of our lives, he thinks, his long-dead father's voice loud inside him, other than to leave the world a little more ordered than it was when we came into it, even while knowing that entropy is a non-negotiable fact of every conceivable regime of existence?

He looks around the diner, much the same now as it was all those years ago when he first started coming here, elated to have made his first sale. Now, as then, it's as empty and cold and gorgeous as the one that Hopper—King of all the Kings of the Midcentury Urban Gentiles—immortalized in 1942, sealed in by thick, steamy glass. The same few people are eating the same meals at the same tables they were eating at then, no one ever coming or going, until they die and are replaced by their children. It's a sad thought, perhaps, but it makes him smile. I found the ground upon which I took my stand, he thinks, the soil I drilled my roots down into and from which I harvested all that I could grow.

The man and woman behind the counter, an old married couple, are friendly enough, though they know to leave Jakob alone. Perhaps one is the son or daughter of the couple who worked here when Jakob was young, taking turns making shakes and working the register, then as now. Perhaps they even grew up hearing stories of the very first time he came in, with the first money he'd ever earned, from the first sale of the first piece in the body of work that would eventually put the town on the map of World History, turning the diner into a consecrated site along the daily path of an Epochal Genius.

The loud slurping of his straw at the bottom of the milkshake glass brings him back to his original self, the one whose future hasn't been spent yet. He lays down the ten he earned, getting back a dollar and some coins in change, which he puts in his pocket, thinking, Now I'll never hear what the Bellmer had to say, and I may even have consigned it to the fate of being buried alive, the worst of all possible fates, and yet... would it have expected me to turn down the payment, and go forever without the ability to buy myself a milkshake and a plate of fries? And if it did want that of me, should I have listened?

This line of questioning might have gone much further had the Boys' Boys not burst in, raiding the penny candy by the door and shouting, "Yo bloodsucker, we were looking for ya! Time to start training for your little adventure!"

Boot Camp

Jakob follows the Boys' Boys back to Ragtown, keeping to himself his discovery of the fact that all his future work will be sourced from these sky-high piles of Raw Material, just as the world itself was sourced when the Demiurge first decided that existence must be preferable to its opposite. The whole universe, he thinks, lagging behind the others, is in a sense contained within this town, and thus the question of whether my father has been moving us from town to town, or burrowing ever deeper into this one, is perhaps less pressing than I used to think. Perhaps it's two ways of saying the same thing.

"Wake up!" one of the boys snaps at him, "this is serious shit. People have died, dude, going up there. So pay attention."

Jakob resolves to try.

Tom, back on his throne with no knowledge that

Jakob took his place after he left last night, picks up a bottle of brown liquid and, after taking a long swig and passing it to the next boy, begins to explain. "Okay, so like I was saying, back in the 60s, people started worshipping this guy's sculptures. Like literally taking them for holy symbols. He had this whole other town that he said this town really was..."

He's flustered, Jakob realizes. Look at him trying to explain what he doesn't understand! It grows hard to keep from grinning.

Tom continues, "Everyone who lived here then, I guess they wanted to become part of that other town instead. It was supposed to be this like pure land, where everything was poetry and art and music and there was no money or death or jealousy or, I don't know," he scoffs, as do the others, "garbage." He gestures at the expanse of Ragtown, which, in the encroaching dusk, extends all the way to the horizon. "Anyway, people got the idea that they had to sacrifice their children to these huge, spidery sculptures he'd put in the yard outside his cabin. Like the spiders were the gatekeepers."

The brown liquid reaches Jakob and he freezes. Something tells him not to drink it, that it's spider venom, but the glares on the faces of the boys next to him make it clear that if he doesn't, he'll be sucking down his own blood in a few seconds instead. So, fearful of drowning the Blood Clot, he opens his gullet, imagines he's the snake in the walls of the house, about to swallow a rat, and tips it down until he gags. He begins to shiver and the scene around him shivers too, splintering from Victorian portraiture into Cubism as the other boys laugh and a pair of hands takes the bottle and the story continues, tinged now with a sallow air of sick.

"So then one night, all these people snuck out to the cabin with their kids in chains and, after praying or singing or whatever the fuck they did, they impaled three ten-year-olds on the spikes of those sculptures, and then they linked arms around the cabin, bellowing for Wieland to come out and acknowledge their sacrifice. Who knows how they got the idea? There was an exhibit of his early work at the Town Museum, and I guess it kind of drove some people nuts. People with nothing else to live for, you know? People praying there might be another life for them, nearby, just waiting to be found. Anyway, they're up there at the cabin, begging him to come out and say, 'Yes, now that you have brought my creatures to life, the gateway is open to you.' After hours and hours of this, around dawn, he finally did, in his bathrobe. He stands there, staring at the people, then at the bloody lumps dripping from his work. Then someone in the crowd asks, 'Is it enough? Are we in?'"

Tom leans closer to Jakob now that the sun's gone down, making sure his face remains visible in the twilight. "Any sane person would've said something like, 'In where, you fucking lunatics?' But Wieland just nods and says, 'This is more than enough. Please, enter. Enjoy the New Jerusalem as it unveils itself around you on the streets and squares below.' And the crowd, thrilled with the feeling that they'd finally crossed out of the shitty old world and into a gleaming new one, does, and Wieland, I guess, sets about pulling those kids off his spider-spikes and skinning them and using their skin for dolls. After that, he never came down here again. All the kids he needed came to him, like the spiders had learned how to summon more. Some freak named Tobin brought him whatever else he needed from Ragtown." The boys gasp at the name, though Jakob has the sense they're pretending for his sake. "And that weird lady you've started hanging out with?" Tom continues. "She knows all about it. She brings him food and whatnot. They had a kid too, you know. He fled town as soon as he could. That's a whole other story."

The boys laugh, but Jakob is too deep in to notice. He's there now, like a mime reproducing a classic routine, helping the old man butcher the fleshy flies that his spiders have caught, neither proud nor ashamed to see that they've done what they were built to do.

By the time the story's over, the Rat People are back in the trash piles, rummaging with their hands or with shovels and rakes, and the Boys' Boys have dragged Jakob to his feet and into a ramshackle hut on the far edge of Ragtown.

"Imagine this is the cabin," Tom says, "and these," he points to a series of scarecrows set up inside and all around it, "are all that's left of the boys who failed the test. Those who only got partway before the spiders did what they do. Now your job, after we spin you around, is to escape without letting them catch you! If you get tangled up, that's it. The next boy will soon be running by in fear of you. You'll feel the straw growing inside your organs, and there will be no way to prove you're still alive. Cold mayonnaise will drip down your lips and you'll have no way of swallowing it. Ready?"

Before Jakob can reply, a mess of hands is on him, spinning and spinning, faster than he's ever spun before, and then he's flying into the dark of the hut, crashing into scarecrows and dummies, their sharp fingers prying into his hair and face, their straw jutting up his nose and into his mouth while the laughter of the Boys' Boys dims to an indistinct cackle behind him. The brown poison in his gorge forces its way up, and soon he's spewing onto the faces of the scarecrows in the dark corners of the hut and they're looming in at him, mouths open, breath as rotten as his own must be, and then he's flailing, tilting into their soft stomachs, unsure where, or even who, he is, and he can sense that the Boys' Boys are long gone and, even though this means he's safe, he wishes they'd stay so at least he wouldn't be alone. Perhaps this, he thinks, is how you become a Rat Person.

When he can't flail any longer, he stops and opens his eyes, squinting up into the darkness to see one of the scarecrows squinting down at him. Somehow, he's ended up in its lap. As he pants and shivers, spitting out the last of the vomit that's still clinging to his tongue, he reaches his arms out and climbs up the scarecrow's shoulders, then pushes down on its head as he gets to his feet.

"Thank you for helping me up," he says, though he knows he did all the work.

He crosses Ragtown in the pitch dark, one slow step at a time so as not to impale his shins on the rusty fenders. Then he crosses back over the river and walks past the Town Museum, stopping further along the same street at the strip mall plaza that contains Giant Chinese, Wing Hut, and Mama's Pizza. The truck that pulled in before is there again, idling with its lights on.

The Tyson Meat Truck!

As soon as he sees the sign, a vision of himself butchered and hanging on a hook in the back grows so compelling he breaks into another run, despite knowing that, in short order, it'll make him vomit again.

He doesn't stop until he's well on his way home, determined to slide into bed and pull the sheets over his eyes and hide there until morning, but the sight of a white-clad woman drifting up the street absorbs his attention instead. Now, only dimly aware that he's reversed course, he's trailing behind her through the Tick-singing Meadow, vomiting silently into puddles of dew as he prepares to enter the woods, where, he realizes, Wieland will be in his cabin, flanked by his spiders, waiting to receive him.

The Cemetery
of Lost Futures

Once Jakob gets in sync with his mother's gliding pace, the journey becomes easy. He relaxes and floats through the underbrush behind her, picturing the Chagall book that often appears in the midst of his schooling, when the need to illustrate a particular nuance of the woods-as-bower-of-all-that's-primal-in-the-Larger-Taxonomy-of-the-Jewish-Spirit arises. As soon as the reference enters his mind, the hazy nighttime world grows hot and fluid, and he feels himself and his mother becoming characters in a paint-drama conjured by Chagall himself, now serving as avatar for the Demiurge, which is only able to act through those rare vessels willing and able to heed its call.

The more the world takes on this quality, the less

consequential it becomes to Jakob. Now he's merely a figment within it, a casual visitor passing through. He scrambles to keep pace while his mother skirts the edge of a ravine, fords a narrow creek, and crests a steep hill, each image swollen with deep blues and reds, like a sequence of canvases in an infinite Chagall exhibit, or a single ultimate Chagall that goes on and on and on, farther than any spectator can possibly see. He follows her along a winding woodland path, past cracked and jagged oaks, until he finds himself with two fistfuls of thorns, clinging to a rosebush while she walks into a clearing. He stands here and watches as the open space is lit by the very beginnings of the dawn, which must arrive sooner up here than it does in the town below. He holds his breath as she walks out into it, her nightgown soaked through, and he watches as she begins to pick grass and weeds from the very center, slowly making, or revealing, a patch of bare dirt. A clearing within the clearing, like a landing pad for aliens or an altar for human sacrifice.

The Chagall exhibit ends when a ghost train of children with mayo dripping from their mouths passes by, vanishing as soon as Jakob notices it. He shivers and feels that story syncing up with this one, the two planes scraping together like tectonic plates. He begins to sense that, in the distance on the far side of the clearing, the spiders are waiting. Please let this be a nightmare, begs a voice in his head, but it's so frail that another, louder voice rejects it. No, that voice declares.

This is no nightmare. This is exactly where you've arrived.

He watches his mother work as the sun rises. She's finished pulling up weeds and raking the dirt with a tool she must have carried up here in her backpack. Now she's digging a row of identical holes, as if she intends to plant something.

Before he can see what it is, another sight absorbs his attention: in the very distance, behind the trees that mark the far edge of the clearing, the brown walls of a ramshackle cabin come into view, carrying with them the clanking of metal in the otherwise silent air. "So that's where Wieland lives," he whispers. This feels like as natural a fact as any other, like he's reading it off the caption under a photograph of the scene he's taking part in. "I suppose everyone has to live somewhere!"

"Well, when you put it that way," he tells himself, "it really does feel natural, not strange at all," though some part of him still feels the quickening and the clotting that occurs whenever a place of too much density—the overlapping territories of his mother's project and Wieland's cabin, not to mention everything the Boys' Boys say happened here in the 60s—insinuates itself into the otherwise meager reality of the landscape around him. Any ground can be the staging ground for something monumental, he knows, just as any object can be a prop of crucial significance. Granted, this may rarely happen, but tonight, it's about to. Life can't remain boring forever. As soon as he thinks it, this thought, too, feels as natural as the fact that everyone has to live somewhere. The two thoughts feel like versions of one another, and so, in this sense, redundant.

He reels his attention back from the distance to the middle ground in time to hear a voice say, "Jakob?"

At first he's sure it's Wieland calling, outside in his bathrobe just as Tom described him. Jakob's spine seizes up and he thinks, What if I'm about to be impaled on a pincer? The thought makes him cry. It makes him want to beg, to say, "No, please, I'm not one of them, there's so much left for me to do..."

"Jakob? That's you, isn't it? Why are you crying?"

This time, thankfully, he recognizes the voice as his mother's. He blinks several times to focus on her where she stands in her nightgown stained with dirt and grass, staring at him, eyes hollow as those of a ghoul in an Alfred Kubin print.

She looks so transfixed that he doesn't bother answering. Instead, he asks her what she's doing up here, sensing that she's likely to answer more transparently now than she will once she's woken up.

"What am I doing up here?" she replies, standing beside him to regard the patch she's just cleared. Her voice sounds automatic, like the playback of a recording made long ago. "I'm building a cemetery. A Cemetery of Lost Futures, where all the lives I might have lived, and all the lives we might all, as a family, have lived, will be buried. Side by side, in harmony, so they don't pass out of this universe altogether unacknowledged. To mark what was once possible, and perhaps, in some slightly different version of reality, still is. The life we might have lived, your father and I, and even you, perhaps, had what happened in the Art World not happened. I'm sorry, Jakob, this is more than I should be telling you, but... tonight, I've just begun digging the graves. The gravestones, the markers, the text... all of that will come. It's my new work, Jakob. My new project, to tie me, however tenuously, to a life of my own."

She turns away from him as she cries. He turns away too, unsure of his role. I don't like this, he thinks. I don't like not knowing how to be.

This thought sets the spiders to chattering. Never show weakness! he warns himself, but he knows it's far too late. As quickly as he can, he turns from the clearing and sets out for home, hoping his mother will follow. In due time, she does, freighting him with the responsibility of remembering the way. She's still crying, covered in dirt and grass. In no state to get us back there on her own, he thinks, at once proud and frightened of the role he's slipped into. The feeling of drifting passively through an exhibit prepared by Chagall now feels very ancient, a cherished memory from a long-gone childhood. Now, every step brings with it the fear that it's a step in the wrong direction, across the Red Sea and back into Egypt, where the Pharaoh's men are waiting with open nets and sleazy grins.

They walk the rest of the way down in a silence

that remains unbroken until they're halfway across the Tick-singing Meadow. Then she turns to him, her eyes less ghoulish, and says, "Know this, Jakob: by the time we get home, in the full light of day, I will deny that we were ever here together. If you press the issue, I will insist that you were dreaming. I will insist so strongly that you will come to believe me. I wish it could be otherwise, but it cannot. Not now. So, before that happens, is there anything else you'd like to ask me?"

Don't you know who lives in the cabin? he'd like to ask her. Don't you know what happened there? But he doesn't ask. He has the feeling that somehow she does know, perhaps in much more detail than he does, like it's a story she's had to bear all this time. He shakes his head and lets her retake the lead as they walk up the driveway and into the house, where his father is sitting at the breakfast table, staring down into his Wheaties. He gives no sign that he's aware they've entered, so, when they join him at the table to stare down into bowls of their own, the day appears to be off to a completely normal start.

Time Passes

The eerie normalcy of that breakfast extends over the next few weeks. Jakob falls into a rhythm of school in the morning, work at the Museum in the afternoon, training with the Boys' Boys before dinner, and following his mother up to her cemetery at night. Sometimes he wonders where in all this he ever manages to sleep, while other times he wonders if perhaps he's been asleep the whole time, waiting to reawaken.

This sets him to wondering whether the choice of when and how to wake up, if he's been asleep, or else when and how to move events on to their next phase, if he's been awake, lies within him, or outside, in the impersonal chaos of the world. Going a step further, as he likes to do, he wonders whether this distinction, between the *me in here* and the *them out there* is real, or only another layer of the dream, a tissue paper curtain he could tear down with one determined clawing motion, if he could only make his mind move his arms to do so.

In any event, he decides, my arms, for now, are slack. So he goes through the motions, running circuits through that horrible Ragtown cabin, bumping into scarecrows while the Boys' Boys swill their brown liquid in the shadows. Sometimes, when he stops to catch his breath or finds himself abandoned there, alone with the scavenging Rat People who never acknowledge him, he considers telling the Boys' Boys, tomorrow or whenever they meet again, that he's already been up to Wieland's cabin, or near it anyway, and thus that any further training is unnecessary. I know more about what's up there than all of you put together! he longs to boast, but of course never finds it in himself to do so outside the safety of his bed, into which he wishes he could pull the whole world and smother it there.

He works his way through the Ragtown routine, memorizing it, perfecting it, growing bored to the point where he has to wonder when and how it might be possible to force an evolution or breakthrough to the next phase.

"But not just yet," he gasps, as he lies in bed with the Night Crusher on his chest, who only lets him up when Jakob's mother begins her journey. Then, compelled by the same sleepwalking energy that's moving through her, he finds himself drifting up the street and back into the woods, to watch her dig her graves deeper and, slowly but surely, begin to assemble the neon markers whose inscriptions he is not yet brave enough to read.

The Father
Visits the Gift
Shop

Since school has flattened into sterile repetition, the only site of possibility, outside of Ragtown, is the Town Museum. Jakob's at work there one afternoon in what feels like September, tidying boxes in the back while Greta tallies expenses on her solar-powered calculator, when the bell that means someone's entered through the front door rings. Jakob waits a few moments, letting the visitor get their bearings, as he's been instructed to do, before presenting himself in case they have any questions or—God willing, as Greta puts it—wish to buy something.

When those few moments have passed, he puts down a box full of lion-faced flies on fishhooks, and walks out, head hung, to take his place behind the small desk of the gift shop, ready to smile like he has on the six previous occasions when someone has come in.

This time is no different except that, when he looks up, he locks eyes not with those of a friendly or sullen stranger but with what he can't help but recognize as the eyes of his father. His first thought is that some monster has plucked them out and inserted them into its own gaping, mindless skull, so that only very slowly does he realize, or accept, that, no, the thing he's looking at is his father himself.

Before Jakob can say anything, his father turns his back to make another circuit of the Museum, examining Wieland's boxes, sketches, collages, and, most thoroughly, his maps. He stares hard at them, moving his lips without speaking and holding his fingers very close without quite touching the art's surface. He seems completely transfixed, a scowl growing on his lips and spreading outward, so that, by the time he returns to where Jakob sits on his stool behind rows of postcards, key chains, pens, and colored pencils, he looks like Wieland has reached a hand through his chest and shaken his heart.

"Dad?" Jakob stammers, trying to keep some distance from the knowledge that things are about to get very bad, as they inevitably do on afternoons when his father's work is going so poorly that he decides to leave the garage and take a walk, even though, as Jakob has learned well by now, "time spent away from one's work is time fed into a pit." Add to this whatever effect Wieland's art has just had on him, Jakob thinks, and whatever is about to happen is not something I'd like to see! For a moment, he forgets that he's going to have to.

"Dad, I..."

His father begins to shake. In a clipped, abnormally high voice he says, "Do you have any cream-colored butcher paper?"

Jakob tries to get him to recognize whom he's talking to—"It's me!" he wants to shout—but it's clear from the look in his father's eyes that no such recognition is about to occur. His father's too deep inside whatever crisis has forced him out of the garage to think of anything but rectifying it.

"Cream... colored... butcher... paper," his father growls, beginning to shake. "And Micron pens. Black. 0.7mm."

Jakob looks around, trying to signal to Greta in some way other than shouting her name, but no other way is possible, and by the time he's accepted this, he's also accepted that he has to tell his father, "No, we don't have anything like that here, sir. Dad? Can we go home now?"

Something about the word *home* must have gotten through, because now panic and anger override the affectless determination his father had worn until just now. He's beginning to seethe, his face going red, his breath getting short, as he says, "Jakob, we are leaving this place."

Jakob stares at him, hesitating, wasting his last chance to leave peacefully.

"Jakob‼" his father shrieks, so loudly the boxes on the shelves rattle and a pile of pens jumps on the desk. "We are leaving!"

With that, he reaches over the desk and grabs Jakob by the neck, dragging him over the papers and cards, face first, so that he falls hard on the far side. "Get up!" he shouts, just as Greta hobbles out of the back room, wincing as she tries to keep her weight off her injured foot.

His father stops to look at her, glaring, his jowls puffing in and out.

"Leave," she says, her eyes fixed on his. "Right now."

His father breaks eye contact with her and looks down at Jakob, cowering on the floor. Then he looks back at her, traveling this circuit several times before grabbing Jakob again by the collar and tripping down the front steps, which causes them both to fall. The Boys' Boys, who are gathered across the street, eating fries from a paper bag, burst into laughter that echoes the whole way home.

An Emergency
Lesson About
the Art World

Dinner that night is tense. Jakob stays in the chair where his father deposited him, listening to his mother make the meal without looking to see what it is. He's afraid that if he looks up, he'll catch her eye, and then the dilemma of whether she's on his side or his father's will have to be faced. For now, it's better not to know.

At some point, she and his father go out the back door and into the garage, leaving Jakob alone in the seat he knows better than to try leaving. "Hey," he whispers, trying to catch the attention of the snake in the walls. "Hey, since you live inside the house, not just in its rooms but in the house itself, can you tell me where things stand? What is the mood of the house right now? How is its spirit?"

But there's no response. Its head must be elsewhere. Somewhere on the second floor, or warming up in one of the heating ducts. He can't blame it, though he wishes it would come to his defense, so it could be two against two instead of two against one, which, unless he summons the Blood Clot, he can tell it's about to be. He looks at the butter knife and thinks about summoning her right now, but, before he has a chance to steel himself, his father and mother are back in the room, whispering by the stove while something in a pot begins to boil.

A few minutes later, they come to the table carrying steaming bowls of oatmeal. Jakob looks down to see one in front of him as well, an island of brown sugar dissolving in the center.

"We're having breakfast for dinner tonight," his mother says, "to bestow upon us the feeling that the day is still to come, and thus that school is about to begin. Because, Jakob, though this gives me no great pleasure to say, it is. An Emergency Lesson has been convened. Your father, who wishes he could be here to fill it himself, has brought it to my attention that a crucial gap in your schooling has been discovered."

His father sits mute across the table, spooning up his oatmeal without any acknowledgement that his wife is talking about him.

"This lesson," his mother continues, "and please feel free to eat your oatmeal while you receive it, concerns a place known as the Art World. A monstrous pit of vipers and demons, fanged, poisonous, pitiless creatures. The very place that Bosch represented, as literally as possible, in the few paintings he left us. And he would know, since he too was part of it. An unwitting part, perhaps, but a part nonetheless. Sadly, it claims a great many souls blessed with profound vision. It is," here she looks to his father, who nods, "the fate of such souls, in almost all cases. A cabal of disguised officials is dispatched from the Art World as soon as a person of extraordinary gifts makes that fact publicly known, their sole aim being to smother and absorb that person, to suck and dry them out until they are nothing but a husk, a speck of chaff drifting away on a cold November wind. Is that what you aspire to become, Jakob?"

He shakes his head, too on-edge to delay the response he knows she expects.

"It's not what we want you to become, either, but it's the road we are both shocked to see you have begun to walk down. Your father caught you this afternoon working at a Museum, Jakob. While this may seem, from your still-naïve perspective, like a harmless means of earning a little milkshake money, please hear me when I tell you it is anything but. It is a baby step toward the Art World, and any step is one too many. Souls perish in that pit every day, Jakob, and you have, despite all we've done to raise you as a Visionary Jew in a proud tradition of Visionary Jews, begun the profoundly dangerous descent into a place from which there is no rescue. Not by us, not by anybody. Hell is real, Jakob, but its doors open not through any of the silly, minor transgressions, such as lying or masturbation, that children are usually taught to fear, but rather through the major, irrevocable transgression of ambition. Of leaving behind the town of one's birth, as your father was forced to do, in search of... something unnamable in the City. Servitude, bondage, the long road to Egypt, trod by Joseph years ago. Nothing more, no matter what, from the vantage of one's hastily abandoned hometown, the future might once have seemed poised to become. Do you understand me so far?"

He nods again, eyes on his oatmeal.

"Your father, and this is the painful part of the story," she glances at his supposedly absent father for permission to proceed, "was almost lost to the Art World once, long before you were born, but, thankfully, managed to save himself at the last moment. Clinging to the fragile shards of his vision, he hauled his body out of the pit they tried to dissolve it in, one bloody fingertip at a time, scraping his way out past razor-wire and broken glass and spikes and teeth and poisons the likes of which you cannot imagine. Heroically, he fought his way out of the City, where the Art World is strongest, and back into the country, the great open expanses of the continent, where his life as a father and his life as a prophet began in tandem, fused in the body of a man who, having faced utter dissolution, pulled back from that brink and found himself changed. In one sense, it was too late. The town he'd abandoned was gone. There was no original Israel to which we might return. Not yet," she looks at Jakob again, "anyway. In another sense, however, this transformation has made your life possible. Never cease to be thankful for that. A life as a son born to a father already claimed by the Art World? That is no life at all, believe me. Who knows Picasso's children? Who knows Dalí's children? If the New Jerusalem is to present any portal through which we might one day enter and at last return home, that portal will surely emerge in a town, where the air is clean and good for dreaming, not in the City, where it is choked with greed and bad faith, thickened by the fumes that honest souls give off as they die."

She falls silent here, and, if Jakob's not mistaken, flashes his father a quick look shot through with a kind of resentment he's never seen before. It disappears before he can verify that he's seen it correctly, but its impact lingers. There's something more to this, he can tell. Something she wants me to know that she can't say. I should ask her tonight, when we're in the woods, though he knows that, once the sleepwalking takes over, it'll be impossible to think or do anything other than what the dream has prepared.

"We didn't want to tell you any of this yet," she continues, her face frozen back in its usual neutrality. "But you forced our hand. There is still more to be said, more and worse aspects of the Art World that you are nowhere near old enough to comprehend, but, from this day forward, you will go on with your life in the knowledge of the battles your father fought for your sake, and, as part and parcel of this, the knowledge that hell is real. The Art World seeks to pry out whatever is unique and beautiful in a person and roast it like an oyster in the harsh neon light of the City, chucking the shell into some windswept alley to be sniffed at and pissed on by stray dogs. Suicide is, for the shells of some visionaries, a heroic decision at this point. These people are in some ways to be envied, because for us," she looks at his father here, that same resentment crossing her face again, less disguised this time, "suicide is no option at all. It's not in our DNA, Jakob. We, as Visionary Jews, are fated to live on, to wander on no matter what, no matter how raped our souls become. So do not allow it to happen. Stay far from Museums, which thrive on the lie that art can be completed, catalogued, displayed, and thus bought and sold like some natural resource, oil or diamonds, denying the revealed truth that the world is always in flux, and that our job, here on earth, is to continually shape and reshape and shape it again, never to step back and present our work to the Art World for its sinister delectation. Now, one last time, tell me you understand."

After Jakob has told her that he does, and promised never to return to the Museum, he goes upstairs and gets in bed, beginning to whisper in hopes of coaxing out the snake. This time it responds, slithering around so that its head is right behind his pillow. The wall grows hot and wet with its breath, as it says, "Do not heed them. They wish to lead you astray. Perhaps they love you and perhaps they don't, but only the love of the Art World can make life worth living. Once he is no longer a child, only in the City can a Genius truly arrive."

With these words thick and sticky in his head, Jakob falls into a sleep so profound he almost doesn't wake when his mother begins to sleepwalk. Only with a painful, groaning effort does he manage to get out of bed and fall into step behind her. Somewhere in the middle of the Tick-singing Meadow, he makes a decision that, in the overdetermined way some dreams have of seeming to reveal future events that occurred long ago, he knows will change his life yet again. He accepts this change gladly, aware that it's not him making it. As he climbs into the clearing to gaze upon the Cemetery of Lost Futures, full now of glowing red, purple, and orange headstones, he hears himself say, "Those of us stuck on earth are always the last to know, but when at last we find out, only we are in a position to act on what we've learned."

The Cabin

Though he knows the decision has already been made, Jakob still finds his knees shaking as he crosses the clearing. He drifts past his mother where she works, and he thinks, Make a grave for the version of me that never entered the cabin. The version that found a way to live in a past that never became the future which is about to begin.

Then he passes out of the clearing and into the murk on the far side, which feels hot and thick, like a chamber in which mushrooms are growing. He wishes the Blood Clot were with him now, and then he remembers that she is. She's in my blood, like always... but when she's in there she's invisible, he knows, like everyone's blood, except for when they're bleeding!

So he forces himself onward alone, under the shadow of the spiders, tall and elegant as the best of Louise Bourgeois, and past the rows of gnomes, which may or may not have human skulls and teeth and hair, heeding the call of the Demiurge which says, speaking to him directly for the first time, "Your only chance at furthering the development of Creation lies in confronting the man who lives here. There is no future you without the present him."

The ground underfoot feels wet with both water and time, like the puddles he's wading through are the product of history melting down. The moment in which Wieland appeared at the door in his bathrobe in the 60s and accepted the sacrifice of the children is preparing to recur, Jakob understands, in slightly altered form—and now, indeed, there he is.

He stands very still in his blue robe, white chest hair corkscrewing out to mingle with his sharp whiskers as his milky blue eyes suck Jakob in. He says nothing, leaning against the doorpost while Jakob stands there regarding him, aware that they could wait in this position for hours with nothing happening, but that there will be no next phase until he gets through this one, so he determines to throw himself into it as quickly as possible. "Sir, I'm, uh," he falters. "May I come in? I mean no harm."

Wieland squints at him more intently, perhaps considering whether to laugh at the notion of this boy meaning any harm. Then he shrugs and turns inward from the doorway, leaving the door open. As he shuffles into the dark, Jakob follows, into the humid reek of the cabin, among spindles and screws on the floor, hands outstretched in hopes of finding a wall or some other solid means of orientation. He finds he's glad for the training the Boys' Boys put him through in Ragtown. "This is just the real version of that," he tells himself, trying to control his breathing as the walls continue to evade his touch and the lights remain off. He gropes deeper in, aware of Wieland's footsteps, terrified that at any moment he's going to career into the pit that will serve as his grave, the real one, while the one outside in the clearing, dug by his mother, will only ever be pretend, an artist's rendition of an unspeakable tragedy.

He reaches his fingertips out further, straining them, willing them to grow into their full adult size, until, like a miracle, they do! They collide with a soft belly he assumes must be Wieland's, but it's scratchy and coarse and, as he digs in deeper, a flickering light comes on to reveal that he's groping a life-sized dummy. It grins with a slack, toothless mouth as he recoils and tips backward into a chair, swooning, before he comes to and finds himself in a rundown kitchen, sitting at a plastic folding table, watching an old man stir chocolate powder into two glasses of milk.

The man stirs slowly and carefully, clinking the edges of the glass with each rotation, seeming to take great pleasure in the process, which he carries out well beyond the point of necessity.

Finally, he carries both glasses over to the table, his hands shaking enough that he spills half of each before he manages to set them down. Jakob pulls over the one nearest to him as Wieland says, in a heavily Germanic accent, "Tonight, I can do whatever I choose." He grins and looks over at the door. "I could do door." Then he looks at the fridge and says, with a degree of menace that Jakob's never experienced before, not even in his father's worst rages, "I could do fridge." Then he looks at the block of knives sitting on the table and Jakob almost passes out when he says, "I could do block."

After another long silence, Jakob hears him say, "But tonight I'm tired, so I just do milk."

He taps his glass with the back of a ring on his left hand and indicates that Jakob should take a sip. It's profoundly rotten, as Jakob knew it would be, but it's nevertheless a relief, given the alternatives. He sucks it all down, forcing himself not to gag under Wieland's unwavering attention. When the glass is empty, Jakob sits back, proud with the sense of having just passed a test, and takes in the dummies of all sizes surrounding the room, some sitting in chairs against the wall, others on shelves, and still others hanging from chains and nooses at varying heights from the ceiling.

"Do they live in New Jerusalem 2?" Jakob asks, licking foul milk from his teeth.

Wieland smiles and scratches his chest under his robe. After several minutes, he yawns and says, "I need to sleep. Show yourself out. Greta mentioned a young boy. If you're not him, then there's two."

Jakob stays put, unsure whether to answer or leave.

Wieland gives no indication either way. The moment drags, growing scarier, until he finally says, "Come back here one day and I'll give you a tour."

With that, he heaves up to his feet, apparently with great effort, and pads out of the kitchen, leaving Jakob alone with his empty glass and Wieland's half-full one. When the shuffling has receded into the distance, he leaps up and runs as fast as he can, wind-milling his arms in case he's dreaming and thus able to fly.

·

Jakob's First Mannequin

Jakob flees the cabin and tears across the high clearing, seeing it for the first time in daylight, though he doesn't stop to examine his mother's cemetery. He slows to a walk only once he's in the woods, retracing the old nighttime route as best he can. On the one hand, it's easier to navigate now that he can see clearly, but, on the other, it's harder now that he doesn't have the dream to guide him. On the whole, he reasons, trying to fill his mind with anything but rotten milk, the journey is about equal in difficulty to how it was at night. This calculus occupies him as he skirts the ravine and begins the descent, then crosses the river using the old fishermen's bridge, again struck by an aching uncertainty as to which side of the Red Sea is which. He manages to make it to the middle of the

Tick-singing Meadow before the clouds turn greenish and the grass underfoot softens and he tumbles, face-first, into the ticks, where he lies, unable to remember which surface is ground and which is sky.

There was something in that milk, he realizes, flashing back on the enchanted rice pudding that marks the onset of the Desert Dream. Whatever's working its way from my belly to my brain now is the next iteration of that. His stomach curdles further as a tick crawls up his nose and another burrows under his collar and, terrified that he'll bleed out and turn to mulch if he lies there any longer, he forces himself to his feet and runs back to the house, which, now that he stands before it, looks like nothing much at all. Two stories, a living room, playroom, and kitchen on the first floor, a bathroom and two bedrooms upstairs, grey siding and a black shingle roof, a car in the driveway and a garage out back... the longer he stares at the house, the more he feels like laughing at the thought that it ever held any familiarity at all. It's just a box! he thinks, though, deep in his head, a quieter voice cautions him not to listen. That's just the poison milk talking, it whispers. Go in there and wash up before you forget how to enter and end up a streetwalker for the rest of your days, sealed off from every decent interior, missed by nobody.

He heeds this voice eagerly, hurrying past the two bodies in the shapes of his parents who are sitting at the breakfast table, spooning up Wheaties in silence. He runs to the upstairs bathroom, where he vomits in the toilet. Then he pulls three ticks off his neck and one out from under his left ear, and throws them likewise into the toilet, just as it's flushing. He's pretty sure there are more, but, for now, he resolves to put them out of mind. "If you're there," he tells them, "enjoy yourselves for the time being." After washing his hands and face and chewing toothpaste straight from the tube, he returns downstairs, composing himself into an approximation of calm just before reaching the kitchen.

"Sorry," he says, as he sits down at the table and pours milk over the Wheaties that have been set out for him, though the prospect of more milk is revolting. "I couldn't sleep so I went for a stroll as the sun was rising."

His parents nod, willing to pretend to accept this explanation for now.

Now that he's met Wieland and found his own way up to the cabin, Jakob has no intention of going through with the Boys' Boys' dare. He hopes he'll simply stop seeing them around, as if forgetting about them might cause them to stop existing.

After a day or two of lying low, he ventures back to the diner after school and gets his usual chocolate shake and fries at the counter, where he no longer has to give his order. Though he hasn't returned to the Museum since his father's intrusion, and thus has no fresh income, he's saved enough change for a few more meals.

Soon enough, he's taking long, thick sips through a

straw and gnawing on crispy, slick shards of potato. He's thankful that he manages to get a few bites down before Tom appears and says, "What'up, Doggie Dahmer?"

By way of response, Jakob nods to the old woman behind the counter, slides down from his stool, and presents himself to the gang, hoping that whatever's coming can be gotten through quickly.

They frog-march him to Ragtown, shove him onto his usual crate, and take their places. Tom pees on a pile of tires, flaunting his uncut penis. Then he zips up and stands in front of Jakob. "So where ya been? Thinking maybe you'd just scuttle back under whatever rock you came out from and we'd never think to look for you there?"

The others laugh until Tom clears his throat.

"Think again, Blood Boy. The time's come. Soon it'll be winter, which is too late. So you going up there to get eaten by the cannibal, or staying down here to get burned by us? Those're your choices. Pick one."

Jakob closes his eyes, squinting tightly so as to make it look like he's thinking hard. In reality, he's imagining a giant cycle wherein the Boys' Boys are sad and lonely grownups back in the 60s, trekking up into the hills to sacrifice their children to a man they believe can grant them access to paradise. And that man, of course, is him. His heart flutters at this realization, and his muscles swell. If I let them kill me, he thinks, that man will never exist. And if that man never existed—this part is obvious now, but he thinks it anyway, as if for the benefit of the dimwitted Boys' Boys—then I'll never exist either. If any part of the cycle is broken, the whole thing sputters and burns like a piece of melting plastic, leaving nothing but skid marks in its wake.

The image of this plastic smoking and curling and shrinking into itself gives him an idea. He opens his eyes and says, "Burn. I don't want to go up there. I'm too scared. No matter what, I can't eat the mayo."

Tom looks astonished, like he's trying and failing to act as if he expected this response, and is ready to honor it. "I knew you didn't have it in you, chicken-clit. Most kids don't. Okay, so you wanna burn?" His voice wavers, like several futures are vying for supremacy inside him, and, as soon as he speaks, only one will be possible. The future in which he's a murderer vs. the future in which he's just a mean man who used to be a mean boy, for example. Jakob feels sorry for him.

"Okay," Tom says, though he still doesn't look sure. "A week from tonight, right here. The Boys and I are gonna build a stake, get everything ready. You say your goodbyes to whatever you have that passes for a life. And if you tell your parents," he whistles, like the thought is almost too much to bear, "we'll come by in the middle of the night and burn your house down with all of you in it. Don't think we don't know where you live. Got me?"

Jakob nods, affecting a sort of solemnity that he also sort of feels, unsure, as he is, whether his plan will work.

He's in bed later that night, his parents long asleep, when the Night Crusher releases him and whispers, "Get up. If you're going to do what you planned, it's now or never."

Jakob protests just long enough to pretend that he has the power to refuse. Then he gets to his feet and makes his way down the hall, past the room where his parents are sleeping, down the stairs, through the kitchen where breakfast will be served in a few hours, and over toward the basement, where his father's Raw Materials are kept, those not yet ready for deployment in the garage.

Straining on tiptoe, Jakob slides the dead-bolt open and, violating the Honor Code more egregiously than he ever has before, descends the frigid concrete steps beneath a bare, swinging bulb.

Here I am, he thinks, catching his breath as he begins poking around boxes of paint thinner, industrial glue, wire, drillbits, and a thousand other metal, wood, and plastic materials, wondering how best to approximate his own physical makeup. There comes a time in a man's life, he thinks, his father's voice ringing inside his head, when he has to ask himself what he's made of. For me, that time is now!

He laughs silently, then pinches the skin on his forearms and calves, trying to match it to the sheets of wax paper and rubber and polyurethane that his father has stacked up against the basement's back wall. I already feel pretty plasticky, he thinks, wanting to laugh again, though he can't be sure this thought is still funny. Hoping to numb the uncertainty, he picks up a corked bottle of clear liquor and takes a stinging swig that almost knocks him over.

Then he proceeds to the pile of faceless mannequins propped against the back wall and begins to fondle them like the Demiurge in a warehouse of pre-people, deciding what faces and names and personalities to give them before they enter the murderous arena of the real.

After he's selected one that's about his size and weight, he spends what feels like an hour amassing paint, scalpels, model-glue, and brushes of various sizes in a corner. Once everything's in a neat pile, he covers it with a checkered towel he found under the boiler, figuring there probably isn't time to do any more before his parents come down for breakfast.

He spends a last moment admiring his stash, wondering if Greta would be proud if she could see it. "I knew the Bellmer was only the beginning," he imagines her saying. Then he takes another swig of clear liquor. As he swallows, he feels his system swarm with sadness at the thought of his effigy burning before she can see it.

The week passes without interruption. Everyone leaves Jakob alone to work on his effigy, which he does, unfailingly, every night in the basement between 2 and 4AM, finally putting to use the long, glorious art lessons he was given as a small boy, back before his indoctrination into the canonical works of others had begun. Back when, as his mother put it, "You are still too young to have developed the capacity for heretical ambition, and thus may be permitted, if only for a little while, to roam free in your own pristine interior, in the prime of the state that David Graeber codifies for us as *pure play*, before any cynical notions of gamesmanship have taken root."

Night after night, he creeps down the concrete stairs, pulls off the checkered towel, tapes up a photo of his face that his mother took beside the car in the driveway when he was eight or nine, and begins to cut, paint, and chisel the mannequin's blank features into his own delicately Semitic ones. He takes a single sip of clear liquor at the beginning of each session, just enough to get in the mood but not enough to get sick, and works for exactly two hours before covering his workspace with the towel and returning to bed, where he mimics, as closely as possible, the resting position he left the effigy in, trying to dream its dreams so that, when the day of the burning comes, it won't only look like him, but also, in some subtle yet highly perceptible way, *seem* like him as well. Anything less, he decides, and the Boys' Boys won't be convinced.

In this way, his dreams come to take place more and more in the basement, activating that room as the crucial locus within the house, while leeching power away from his bedroom so profoundly that he starts to think of it, only half-jokingly, as *the Guest Room*.

Then, each morning, he pretends to wake at the usual time and comes down to breakfast and the day's schooling. He's never thought of himself as an especially good liar, but since no one asks, there's nothing to lie about, and the sense of being a lodger in this house grows unchecked and unremarked upon.

Jakob is

Burned Alive

Finally, the night before the burning arrives. The Night Crusher wakes him at 2AM and he tiptoes down to the basement to take a last sip of clear liquor and wake the effigy from what he's come to think of as its bed, peeling back the checkered towel he's covered it with for the last time.

Then he drags it out of the house and past a neighbor in the yard next door, raking leaves in the pitch black with his headphones on. He pays Jakob no mind and Jakob thinks, unsure if this thought makes any sense, Good riddance to you, too!

He rounds the corner and sets out for downtown, taking the long way that leads past the Déjà vu Frog Pond, which he wants the effigy to see once before it burns. When he gets there, he settles into the grass with the effigy beside him, and together they look out at the night, darker and colder than the last time he was down here. A distant smell of wood smoke drifts over the stagnant water, under which the frogs are probably hibernating by now, or about to begin, as soon as their sky turns to ice. The whole scene grows so profoundly laden with déjà vu that Jakob feels like he's falling into a black hole. If I'm not careful, he worries, it'll crush me down into a little speck of diamond that some treasure hunter, centuries from now, will find in this grass and carry off in a bucket, unable to hear me screaming inside.

Still, he indulges for a moment longer, arms around the effigy, tears welling up in his eyes. He leans over and kisses its waxy skin and whispers, "I'll always remember this moment, the two of us on the edge of autumn, just before the awful thing that one of us had to suffer so that the other could live."

Then he heaves himself to his feet and, once he's gotten his balance, pulls up the effigy. He hurries along the low road, the same route he took with the Bellmer, all the way to the Town Museum, which is still closed, though the diner is open, with a few ancient customers already at their usual tables inside.

At the edge of Ragtown, as the sun begins to rise, Jakob stops and stares into the effigy's face, trying to shake off the sensation that he's staring into an unframed mirror. "Today, you have to be me, so that I can become my next self," he whispers. "Our next self. Are you ready for that?"

The effigy seems to nod, but Jakob stops looking at its face before it mesmerizes him into an overabundance of sympathy. He pulls off his Champion sweatshirt and stretches it over the effigy's head, careful not to muss its shredded rubber hair. When he's adjusted the fit, he positions it with its arms around the stake that the Boys' Boys built this week. "You and this stake are each a week old," he explains, as if pointing this out might give the effigy some consolation as he settles its backside into the dry twigs and affixes a note in his handwriting to its back. The note reads:

Dear Tom and Others,

I accept my fate, so I wanted to make things easier for you. DO NOT LOOK INTO MY FACE or you will have nightmares for the rest of your life. Just light the fire and be done with it!

Thank you for letting me live as long as you have. I have no regrets,
    Jakob.

Then he returns home. He goes through his usual morning and afternoon routine and then, around dusk, sneaks back to Ragtown and into the scarecrow shack at the edge, with his father's digital camera—left on the edge of the blood-filled tub—around his neck. Peering through a crack between two slats of wood, he waits for the Boys' Boys to arrive, hoping it doesn't get too dark to photograph without flash.

After a period in which nothing but the scuttling of the Rat People disturbs the trash's silence, the Boys' Boys show up, whooping and swigging their brown liquor. They strut up to the pyre, one of them carrying a can of gas, another a long kitchen lighter, all of them a few paces behind Tom.

He walks right up to it, trying to conceal the hesitation in his gait, and rips off the note, illuminating it with his lighter while struggling to read aloud. Jakob, from where he's hiding in the shack, can't help but feel a twinge of sympathy for this boy, so big and angry and yet barely able to sound out the words. It almost makes him cry.

When Tom's struggled through to the end, he crushes up the note, peers down at the effigy, kicks it twice and screams, "Yo, blood bucket! Hello? Anybody in there?" Even though it doesn't respond, he turns to the boys with the kerosene and lighter and snaps, "You bitches waiting for a sign? Light 'em up!"

Jakob exhales inside the shack, relieved, of course, but, underneath his relief, frightened as well. What if I've mixed up which one of me is real? he suddenly worries, clenching the straw of a nearby scarecrow to keep from panicking. As Tom stands back and the other boys empty the gas can and spark the lighter, some feral inner part of Jakob wants to run out of the shack and scream, "Wait! Wait! You're about to burn the wrong one! Burn this one instead!"

But he holds off, warming up the camera and taking refuge behind its glass eye. As long as I stay behind the viewfinder, he decides, taking his first picture of the scene, nothing on the other side can hurt me. It's like an impermeable wall...

He tells himself this just as an actual wall of flame bursts up from the stake and the effigy begins to smolder and curl. Tom steps back, coughing, and, in one of the pictures Jakob snaps, he can detect relief on the big boy's acne-scarred face. I knew he'd be glad to have the chance to burn something other than the real me, Jakob thinks. I knew he wasn't, in his guts, a real killer. Though this knowledge, Jakob allows, is consoling only if I assume that he realizes the thing that's burning isn't really me, and, to take that a step further, only assuming it isn't! Again, the Jakob in the shack feels ghostly, like his flesh is nearly gone and soon only a shadow will remain. A bodiless thing that will haunt Ragtown forever, luring in future boys so it can inhale their living scent for a few precious seconds.

He continues snapping photos as the light in the sky disappears and the light of the flames overwhelms the image, and then even this light begins to dim. The Boys' Boys depart once the effigy has been reduced to embers, silent as they turn their backs. They move with an unnatural mixture of speed and stealth, clearly torn between wishing to run and thinking they shouldn't, for fear of seeming guilty, even to themselves.

Jakob snaps a few more pictures and then, once

he's sure his executioners are gone, he leaves the shack and approaches the pyre, unsure whether a close-up of the damage will bring terror or relief. By the time he gets there, the Rat People have reemerged from the shadows to warm themselves by the embers, so, for a moment, he and they coexist in unacknowledged juxtaposition. He stares down at the last of his work, and at the final burning scraps of his note, and then he turns and begins to make his way out of Ragtown as the Rat People press closer in, desperate for the embers' warmth as the autumn night turns cold.

Jakob's
Nighttime
Wander

Jakob knows he should return to what he now can't stop calling *the Guest Room*, and resume the charade of his life in that house, but so far he hasn't done so. Perhaps, he overhears himself thinking, I never will. And even if I do, it won't be for long. Whichever boy survived the burning no longer lives where the old boy used to.

He wanders to the other side of the river, among subdivisions and mobile homes and all-night liquor stores, scattered like pieces of a model train kit that no one's figured out how to assemble. He feels untethered, freed of all responsibility, even to himself. Perhaps only the best parts of me remain, he hopes, the parts that will let me do my own thing, free from all fear, panic, and pressure. Like life will now be nothing but an unending vacation.

It's a nice thought, though it seems unlikely, or at least no more likely than the opposite, which is that the best of him went up in smoke and now he's nothing but a nightwalker like his mother, unmoored, untethered, entirely aimless upon the surface of the earth, following a homing impulse that will lead straight to the cemetery... where my body would lie, had it not just crumbled to ashes and been scooped up by Rat People. He leans against a porch attached to a trailer and shakes this thought off, reminding himself for what feels like the thousandth time tonight that he's the real one, and only the effigy was burned. "How do you know, blood-boy?" he whispers, mimicking Tom's voice, and then he shrugs, playing the part of himself in a minor key.

He clenches the trailer's porch more tightly, listening to the people inside snore, and forces himself to suppress his uncertainty. "Whether or not I'm me," he decides, "I hereby pledge to act as though I am." He repeats this again and again, until he starts to believe it, or at least to feel as though he's ready to act like he does.

Then he lets go of the trailer and sets out across a muddy patch of dead grass that feels fraught with potential violence, like a gladiator ring abandoned between one killing and the next. Something bad has happened here, he thinks, stopping in case any other voice begs to differ. And something bad will happen here again.

He resumes his progress toward the woods, again picturing the graves his mother has set up. Even if I wasn't burned tonight, he realizes, even if I'm still me, I'm alone here in this town, awake in the middle of the night with no place to go and nothing to do, and so what, really, is the difference between waiting another six or seven decades and just going up to the grave right now and crawling in?

He knows he shouldn't indulge this thought, but he finds he's used up the last of his self-control, so now it takes hold and he's powerless to stop his feet from finding their way to the Tick-singing Meadow, which turns out to be much closer than he would've liked it to be. He feels himself aging as he walks, so much and so quickly that, as soon as he's registered the thought, it's as though his mother and father are ancient archetypes upon which the patterns of his wandering have been founded, not real people who are still alive, waiting in a nearby house for his return. As he climbs out of the meadow, past the ravine, and into the woods, his aloneness swells far beyond the current moment, cannibalizing the past and the future until it comes to feel like the only state he's ever existed in, like his sole purpose is that of wandering alone at night.

Tramping over branches and crunching soft beds of moss, he feels uncoupled from his father's grand narrative and thus free to wander anywhere, all the way to the Outskirts and past Waffle House and Trader

Joe's to the Desert, though another part of him recoils at the thought of crossing out of the town and making himself an easy target for the Tyson Meat Truck, which he pictures plying the highway, back and forth and back and forth all night long, in search of lost children.

It didn't frighten him much the first time he saw it, but, like it'd spent all this time gathering human cargo, now it activates his innermost reserve of terror, which warns him against leaving town. "No matter how lost you may come to feel within the boundaries of any one town," the terror whispers, "it's nothing compared to the lostness possible within the larger nation, where souls vanish every minute, and are never recovered. It's better to cleave close to that one town, even if it means being a prisoner all your life."

As soon as he receives this message, whatever boldness he'd felt evaporates and he's left with nothing but fear. He's cold and alone in the damp meadow, facing his mother's neon graves, wondering which one's meant for her, which is for his father, and which is for him. He looks into the darkness beyond the clearing and knows that Wieland's cabin is waiting, but the taste of rotten milk is still too sharp in his throat. So, afraid that he'll run into his mother on her nightly journey if he stays here any longer, he turns and hurries down the mountain, back across the Tick-singing Meadow, and past blocks of identical houses, all of them with identical cars outside. He flails through the night like he's trying to swim for a surface whose existence he's begun to doubt. Just as he approaches the verge of drowning, he flops ashore onto a lawn that turns out to belong to the house he once lived in.

Though the feeling of homecoming is fraught with a sense of entrapment, like the roads all conspired to thwart his escape, relief is the stronger feeling. "Just get me to my bed," he pleads, looking down at his feet, which are only too happy to oblige.

Jakob Returns
to the Town
Museum

School is heading toward a breakdown. As Jakob sits at the kitchen table, yawning with his mother, who's yawning too, he sees this clearly for the first time. He made it back to bed and down to breakfast without incident, but the morning's now dragging like a wounded animal looking for a place to die. He repeated her stories about Vision and Greatness and Courage and Cowardice, mixed now with increasingly hellish anecdotes about the Art World, but none of it feels vital. Usually, his father presents new edicts every few months that advance the course of the lessons, adding to the Saga of the Visionary Jews as his dreams uncover more of its secrets, but it's been a long time since any variation appeared. Though he'd never dare to ask, Jakob has begun to suspect that his father is blocked, stagnating at this point in the story, floating on his back when he should be swimming on his belly.

Perhaps, Jakob thinks, looking at his mother, who's looking out the window, this is as far as it goes. Perhaps there's no more to his story than this. Perhaps all lives end in the middle.

He tries to signal his mother with his eyes, hoping she'll break character long enough to address the boredom that's clearly weighing on them both, but today she offers no way in. Her glaze remains intact, thick as the honey she once claimed was spread over the faces of boys in regular school.

Since Trader Joe's is a thing of the past—now she calls it "Traitor Joe's," when she mentions it at all—there are no more cookies. When it's time for a reward, she offers him a slice of bread with jam. It's such a weak replacement that he doesn't bother refusing. It sits on a paper towel between them, the jelly slowly soaking through the soft starch and onto the paper towel beneath.

That afternoon, when lessons are finally over, Jakob takes the digital camera he used last night and heads downtown. He'd been putting off returning to the Town Museum since his father burst in, but now he has something to sell and the time has come to sell it.

The walk there has come to seem impossibly brief, as each block along the way now triggers the exact same series of thoughts, so that it feels as if his driveway spits him out right on the Museum's front steps. He climbs them as quietly as he can, trembling under the weight of what's in the camera. As soon as he sees Greta, fiddling with a framed picture that's started to hang crooked, he blurts, "I brought you something," holding up the camera.

She looks at it skeptically.

"Not the camera itself," he blushes, hoping she won't cut him off by asking about his father's intrusion last week. "Something on it. In it, I mean. Will you look?"

After a moment, she nods, clearly aware of the conversation that Jakob's trying to avoid, and leads the way into the back office, where she boots up her old computer and plugs in the camera. As the images of last night's burning fan out across the turquoise desktop, Jakob shudders and excuses himself. "Just tell me if you want to buy any, okay?" he mutters, and stands back in the gallery, leaning against a wall and playing with the fasteners that support one of Wieland's collages. He hears Greta clicking and, though he felt genuinely unwell at the sight of the images, he also has the growing sense that he's helping his cause by acting so affected. It'll make her think more of them, he understands, if she thinks they came at great personal cost to me, which can only be a good thing for the sale.

She reemerges half an hour later with a smile on her face and several bills rolled up between her fingers.

"This is very daring work, Jakob. Upsetting and intimate. I don't want to know how you staged it, but, whatever you did, you got at something vital. I'd like to buy three photos for a temporary exhibition. There's a patch of blank wall where three old collages used to hang. Wieland recalled them for revisions. I never see them again when he does that!"

She looks at the wall, then, after a few seconds, turns back toward Jakob and says, "Anyway, I'll have the photos printed and framed this week, and we'll have an opening on Friday night, if that suits you. Will the regular fee be acceptable?"

She holds out the bills and Jakob nods, his stomach wavering between elation and distress. He swallows, pockets the money, and strides out, straight to the diner, where he pulls up a stool at the counter and nods when the cook asks if he'd like his usual.

As he's sucking down his shake and fries, he sees the Boys' Boys outside, peering in, but as soon as they spot him, they shudder and hurry away, like they've seen a ghost. That's right, run! he thinks, settling into a more luxurious eating rhythm, unafraid now of being ambushed, aware that a new era, marked by a surplus of cash and the untapped potential for more, possibly much more, has begun.

The Father
Returns Home
Beaten:
A Sermon on
Nazism

Several more days pass in the tense silence of the Boys' Boys' retreat, made tenser by the secret of the upcoming exhibition. Jakob continues with his schooling, never mentioning his fear that his father has run out of vision and thus that his lessons will never escape the rut they're currently stuck in. He helps Greta prepare the photos for the show, using all his spare energy to force himself not to consider what'll happen if his father returns to the Museum and sees them on the wall. Thoughts like these can be held under the threshold of awareness, he's learned, but it's exhausting work, and they pop back up the second he relaxes his grip.

He never mentions his visit to Wieland's cabin, assuming that Greta will bring it up when the time is right. He eats at the diner every day after work, watching the Boys' Boys roam past the door and look at him with a mix of fear and resentment, never crossing the threshold to confront him, and never averting their eyes until he turns and stares them down. If it's true that you've sacrificed me, he thinks, as they scamper away, then it's also true that you've sacrificed yourselves to lives spent haunted by that decision, torn between wishing you could forget it and wishing you could do it again, because nothing you do now will ever compare.

Nothing significant occurs until Wednesday night, when his father drags himself to the dinner table with a bloody nose and a black eye. He collapses into his chair and waves away Jakob's mother's offer of an ice pack, as well as her questions about what happened. Since it's clear he'll only talk in his own good time, she serves dinner—brisket and peas—and takes her place next to Jakob, making no effort to start another conversation.

When the food's been polished off, Jakob's father wipes his mouth on his sleeve, winces, and says, "Now the tale must be told." He pauses and makes the face he uses to signal that he's drilling down, out of the tangible world and into the realm below. Then he says, "I was out walking through town this afternoon, hoping to clear my head after long hours at work in the garage, when I found myself in a clearing between three trailers, a low place of damp woodchips and dog urine, potato chip bags and crushed cans of Schlitz. I was just trying to think, to gain a fresh perspective on the work that, as you both know, consumes me day and night in the garage, when a cabal of slavering fishermen emerged from the trailers, barred my way as I tried to leave them in peace, and grunted, in unison, 'What you doin' in our town, Jew? Our sons say they've seen your boy skulking around like a dimwit. Talking to dogs. Don't you know whose town this is?' I made every attempt to refrain from engaging them, but they were determined. They surrounded me and the laying-on of hands commenced soon thereafter. First a slap, then a punch, then a rain of fists, until I was on the ground, curled up like you, Jakob, back when you were born, defenseless, tiny, unfamiliar with the world in all of its malfunction, preparing to die, preparing to accept that I'd only ever get this far," he gestures around the kitchen, disdainfully encompassing Jakob and his mother, "but, for one reason or another, they decided to let me up. 'This is your first and only warning,' one of them barked, and the others jeered assent, one of them kicking me again as they departed, all together shouting, 'Leave this town and never come back, Jew! You people have done enough damage as it is. You have your own country now. Your own goddam desert. Go there, or kill yourselves.' They shouldered their fishing poles and set out for what I can only assume was a body of water. A trash-choked swamp, full of carp and catfish. I crawled to my hands and knees, then to my feet, and limped back here, regaining my strength as I went, accepting that my time had not yet come, that my journey was not yet at its conclusion, however close at hand that conclusion may nevertheless be. But, in the meantime, I have resolved to deepen my engagement with dreaming, to open myself even more fully to the Demiurge, to truly prostrate myself before it, like a virgin begging to be made pregnant with the new Messiah—which, in essence, is all that prophets are, empty vessels waiting to gestate the Truth, without which all of existence is in vain. There is no time for niceties, so I will dispense with them. Visionary Jews like us, Jakob, are a tenuous breed upon this earth. It is as though we are crawling along the back of a sleeping dragon, quietly making our way up and down its great scaly bulk, attempting to glean the secrets hidden in its soul, and yet..."

His father chokes up, and his mother gives him a look that seems to mean, *hasn't this been enough for one night*? But he swallows and goes on, undeterred. "And yet, Jakob, once per century, if not more often, the dragon wakes up and nearly snuffs us all. There is never an end of Nazis, because Nazism is a possessing force, able to coopt new bodies whenever it pleases. Like zombies, Jakob, ordinary people, the townsfolk of any town, in any country, can be turned to Nazis in an instant. Kill them all and more will grow. If only it were the same with Jews. But no, only in the New Jerusalem will our people be safe, and thus the pressure to glimpse where that sanctified town may lie has never been stronger in my heart, nor has the Nazi desire to stifle our search been stronger outside of it. Only America contains the seeds of the New Jerusalem in its soil, and thus here are they guarded more fervently than anyplace else. The Art World, Jakob, is a Nazi bastion as well, obsessed as it is with hammering flat all glimmers of true vision that emerge, tenuously and miraculously, into its midst. Because the fundamental Nazi writ is that the world is complete, so all it requires now is maintenance. Conservation. Curation. Restoration. The quest to push it ever further in its development, to keep the wheels of Creation turning until the very last gasp of the universe, to continually cultivate the ground so that the seeds might, at last, sprout of their own accord... only the Visionary Jews are committed to this calling, Jakob. All others would rather see us dead, skinned, and strapped to the walls of the same European Art Museums and private collections, lorded over by inbred princes deep in the Black Forest, that the Nazis have filled with stolen art. Never forget this."

He pauses and wipes his eyes and nose with his sleeve. Then, sniffling, he continues with an air of finality, "Would that I could demand the vision arrive tonight, but the Demiurge will not be cowed. It reveals only what it pleases, and only when it pleases. To tamper with this truth is to deny reality itself. But a great turning is afoot in this country, I fear, and if we do not find our destination soon, it will consume us all, and pick its teeth with our bones, and the Israel we've renounced will never take us back."

With this his father exits the kitchen, leaving Jakob and his mother alone to eat the bread pudding she's prepared for dessert. She offers him seconds, even thirds if he can eat it, but he finds that he can't. After a few pained bites, he asks if he can be excused and she nods, sinking into herself while he makes his way to bed.

Another Desert
Dream

Jakob curls up with the snake in the wall behind his pillow, its hot, regular breath lulling him into the deepest kind of sleep. At first, he basks in warm, orange honey, but then the snake licks the honey dry and leaves Jakob in the Desert at dusk, the sun burning orange against the distant dunes, which tend more toward yellow along the same spectrum. He's riding a camel and has the sense that many others—perhaps dozens, perhaps hundreds—are following behind him, though he's unable to turn his head and check, or he's unable to decide to try. He feels thick and muscular up on his camel, imbued with a sort of responsibility he's never felt in waking life. "No longer am I the follower," he declares, as night begins to blanket the topological landscape of the dunes. "Now, wherever I go, it is where the people go too. No one here will mistake me for a child, nor allow me to mistake myself. Onward, out of Old Egypt, which every world becomes soon enough," he pictures the Nazis as termites pouring from the rotten woodwork of America, after consuming the seeds that might have sprouted into the New Jerusalem. "The Pharaohs, the Nazis," he continues, riding under cover of night now, aware that there will be no stopping until dawn, "they're all the same, embodiments of the same force, and they're chasing us, desperate to catch up and drown us in the Red Sea before we can cross." He laughs at the literalness of the parable, its refusal to be interpreted in any manner other than as a description of actual events.

"I won't fail you," he promises. "I won't run us aground this time."

But, as he journeys onward, into the dawn of the next day, his camel weary but as determined as he is, another voice begins to whisper, from deep in the sand. The voice of the snake, which has burrowed under the Desert so deeply its voice seems like that of the dunes themselves. "You have it backwards," it whispers. "Auschwitz, Egypt... that's obscurity. Genius dies when it is not recognized, or when it is dismissed by those who cannot comprehend it. Townsfolk the world over, desperate to quash the slightest glimmer of free thought. No, Jakob, the Promised Land is the Art World. New York, London, Tokyo. Allow yourself to dream of these places. Picture yourself emerging from this Desert with all of America behind you, and only Los Angeles ahead. Smell the cool wind off the Pacific, after the stifling heat of Texas, New Mexico, Arizona. You have survived the journey with your gift intact. Silverlake, Echo Park, Santa Monica... luxuriate in their names, give yourself to them like a bride on her wedding night. Only in these places is genuine transcendence possible. An escape from the mire of wandering generations, ever seeking purchase and ever failing to find it. Rise above, Jakob. You are a man now and you have what it takes!"

In the far distance, he sees a glimmering body of water that he knows is the Red Sea, and he feels a dead weight lashed to his camel's hump, just behind where he's sitting, and he senses, though he still hasn't turned to examine it, that it's a body, wrapped in muslin and ready for burial...

And then he wakes.

With the alchemical logic of collage, by which several unrelated objects seem to reveal a hidden, shared essence by simple dint of juxtaposition, Jakob opens his eyes and thinks: there's some connection between my nascent manhood and the nation's nascent Nazism. Not that being a man means being a Nazi, he cautions, but both are forces acting against my father, curtailing his power just when he needs it most. Soon, he realizes, his eyes tearing up, I and everyone else will be beyond his control, and his will be a body we'll have to jettison before we can leave the Desert behind. He lies in bed and cries for a long while. Then he wipes his face on his pillow and goes down to breakfast.

Jakob's Art
Show

If Jakob ever had any doubt about going ahead with the show at the Town Museum, he doesn't anymore. The snake convinced me, he tells himself, as he helps Greta set out trays of carrots, celery, and cherry tomatoes on Friday afternoon. The photos of his burning effigy, or his burning body, adorn the walls where Wieland's work used to hang.

He stops to read the plaque by the door, which Greta must have written. "Deathlessness: Towards a Representation of the Burning Body Resurrected in the Moment of Its Own Consumption by J."

"Like it?" she asks, coming up behind him with a bottle of Coke under one arm and a bottle of Sprite under the other. "I figured you wouldn't want more of your name out there than that. You never know who'll show up at these things. J. Kind of cool, don't you think?"

Jakob nods, but whether he's mimicking her approval or communicating his own is more than he can tell. His nod becomes a smile. Deeper in his head, his father whispers, "Aestheticization kills true vision, Jakob. Only Nazis worship plaques."

He dampens this voice by helping her set up the soda and plastic cups, then watching her open a bottle of red wine and a bottle of white. His attention is then absorbed by a hand-drawn arrow on a piece of paper taped to the door that leads into the back office.

"What's that?" he asks, when Greta next looks up.

She smiles. "Pointing the way to your dog out back. That's part of the show too. Another deathless thing, don't you think?"

Jakob feels a spasm of shame at the memory of the Bellmer, suffocated under plastic. "I'm still sorry I abandoned you," he whispers, wishing he could turn heel and run, burst through the back and rescue it from its chamber before the eyes of strangers descend upon it. But he knows it's too late, so he spends his last private moment paralyzed with indecision as the bell on the front door begins to ding and strangers' footsteps begin to fill the once-familiar gallery space.

When Jakob turns around, he sees five grown-ups, all elderly, all with wispy gray hair except for one bald man, all sipping wine and munching carrots that drip tails of hummus, eying the pictures on the wall like these too are morsels they would like to eat. The hunger in their eyes makes Jakob sick, though whether this sickness comes from fear or pride is also more than he can tell. Part of it feels good, he has to admit, as he hides in the back room, peering out like a crab under a rock, watching the desperate grown-ups roam from one picture to another, sucking them in, murmuring about them, asking Greta questions he can't hear. He wonders what woodwork they've come out of, these strangers who appear to be the same age as the fishermen and the Rat People, but culled from a totally different stock. Thin, withered, and wealthy. There are always more people in the woodwork than you can imagine, he realizes. It's like an endless dressing room that can spit actors onto the stage whenever it pleases, whether or not they have lines in the play.

He grows so focused on this dressing room that someone has to say, "Excuse me," twice before he moves aside, realizing a moment later that he's just granted this person permission to tramp out back and ogle the Bellmer. He leans against the desk where Greta does her paperwork and watches as the four other adults, plus three more who must've just arrived, follow the first one back there, munching carrots and sipping wine. One woman stares at him, perhaps noticing a resemblance between his face and that of the boy on fire in the photos, but says nothing, and soon she too is congregating around the plastic-covered grave, the crowd so thick that Jakob can no longer see through it. He stands there in shock until Greta shuffles over to him, her face red and her wineglass full, and says, "They love it, Jakob. You're a big hit. The people of this town... they're hungry for new things. Starving. They're... well," she trails off, like she's afraid she's said too much, or was about to. Instead, she puts an affectionate hand on Jakob's shoulder and leaves it there until he walks away, back through the gallery, where the table's now piled with used napkins and half-eaten snacks, spilled wine and a hummus-smeared cell phone.

He takes a moment to look at his pictures in peace. There I am, burning up, he thinks. Then he nods to Greta and walks out, the door dinging behind him like he's just one more townsperson eager to look at something diverting as the sun goes down on another Friday in the middle of nowhere.

As he walks home to dinner, vibrating from the attention his photos and the poor Bellmer received, he understands that he's been putting off his second visit to Wieland's cabin for as long as possible, but now the time has come. I have crossed another line, he thinks, taken another step toward the Art World, and once again the only way forward is through. This realization brings him no comfort, but it does bring relief, as clarity, even awful clarity, always does. He pictures the rest of the night—from where he stands now to his house and the dinner table, to the woods and then to his mother's cemetery and finally to Wieland's cabin—as a single straight line on a map that's been unfurled across a formless landscape. Then he looks at the sky and thanks the Demiurge for making it so simple. "If only you could also make it less scary..." he mutters, hurrying home in the cold.

Jakob's Tour of Wieland's Cabin

After a nearly silent dinner and bedtime, Jakob sets out for the cabin in the dead of night, following his mother.

In the clearing at the very top, he hangs back and watches her attend to the gravestones, shuffling them back and forth in the soft ground, and attaching bits of text to their faces... lists by the looks of it, though he can't read them in the moonlight. As he watches, beginning to slip deeper into dreaming than he would like, given that he has a job to do, he sees three other figures emerge from the background, attending to what look like graves of their own. More Lost Futures, he thinks, forcing himself to keep from wondering if they're the same people who showed up at his exhibition, though he already suspects they are. The same thinness, the same hesitant gait. He hurries to the edge of the clearing, deep enough into the shadows to avoid being seen, though the people in the cemetery look incapable of noticing anything outside the objects of their gaze.

Consigning them to their grief, he passes into the province of the giant spiders, the air silent except for his footsteps and the clacking of wicker fetishes in the trees. For the second time in his life, he knocks on Wieland's door. He waits, gathering his pajamas around his center, meditating on the fact—obvious, but unarticulated until now—that these flannel L.L. Bean pajamas are his uniform just as the ratty, half-open robe is Wieland's, which, indeed, he's wearing now as he opens the door. Both of us dressed for the occasion, Jakob notes, missing any chance to utter a greeting, which is just as well since Wieland is already shuffling deeper into the cabin, the smells of old milk and dog fur and an unflushed toilet bowl enveloping them both.

"You look harrowed," Wieland says, after he's shown Jakob into a back room and turned on a desk lamp whose nearly dead bulb only pushes the gloom deeper into the corners.

Jakob tries to imagine what this might mean, and settles, eventually, on the burning. Perhaps, he thinks, he means I look ghostly. He nods and says, "Thank you."

Wieland seems to have long since moved on. He settles into a frayed red-leather armchair and motions for Jakob to sit in a lower, black leather one with a footrest, on the other side of a mahogany night stand.

Jakob sits down heavily and Wieland winces. "Careful there. That's an authentic Eames chair. A holy relic from the brief period when I had money! Magazines lining up to write about me, galleries lining up to buy my sculptures, girls lining up to, well..."

He laughs, so Jakob does too, careful to stop laughing as soon as the old man does. When both have returned to neutral, Wieland says, "This is the room where I made the discovery. Where I put New Jerusalem 1 to rest and came to see how New Jerusalem 2 could be unearthed in its place. Each is buried under the other. I never would have imagined the answer could be so simple, but it was." He throws his head back and marvels at what he's just said, so Jakob does too, thinking, Mimicry will serve me well up to a point, but after that point, a new mode will be needed, if I'm to have any hope of moving into my own life.

"Greta told me you sent her some pictures, and that people were drawn to them. The people of this town are lost. They need to be shown the way. Any way. That's what I tried to do over the latter half of the twentieth century. Maybe it's your turn now."

He sighs, then falls silent for so long that Jakob thinks he must be sleeping. So he closes his own eyes too, letting himself forget the danger of falling asleep in a strange Eames chair, in a strange man's cabin so deep in the woods that, if anything happened to him, no one would ever find out. But no, he thinks, from behind closed eyes, I'm not forgetting this; I'm enjoying it. It feels good to close my eyes and sink into myself, leaving my body to the wolves if they want to gnaw it while I'm away.

He feels a claw grab his ankle and he jerks back into the leather cushions, his spine clenching and his eyelids ripping apart. Wieland stares down at him, breath rancid with whiskey and tobacco, and says, "I only ever sleep a few minutes at a time. Keeps me in the sweet spot between waking and dreaming. Come on, let me show you around."

Once Jakob's hauled himself back to his feet, separating his skin from the chair's fine leather, he hurries to follow Wieland into the room behind the one they were sitting in, which adjoins the kitchen through another door. This room is filled with hundreds of boxes, stacked on top of one another from floor to ceiling. They're labeled in fading black pen, some comprehensibly—"Buttons," "Twine," "Army Men," "Picks"—and some less so: "Realm of Dissociation," "Poison Wine," "Animus/A," "Lapses & Trembles." Still others are in a script that Jakob can't read. When his eyes falter over the strange curving letters, punctuated with sharp, irregular dots, Wieland says, "The Holy Script of New Jerusalem 2. Powerful stuff, let's just say."

He tries to move a box, but such a cloud of dust comes up that he devolves into a coughing fit instead. The room goes briefly grey, reducing Wieland to a gaunt, bunched-up shape in the background, like a living model for one of the spiders out front. Jakob sighs and pictures himself floating in an indeterminate middle space, surrounded by symbols he can't understand and perhaps doesn't need to. The feeling is so peaceful that part of him is disappointed when the dust clears and everything, hazed as it was with mystery, comes back into focus.

Wieland says, "Maybe I'll show you some other time. For now, let's go down to the basement." He pushes aside a pile of boards, perhaps the remnants of a broken easel, and pries open a door that leads to an extremely steep staircase, which he descends in the dark, leaving Jakob to follow.

The basement, which remains dark despite a bare bulb swinging overhead, is a wonderland: table after table, jammed so closely together that it's almost impossible to walk between them, most full of dioramas, models, maps, blueprints, and tools. Cans full of paint and brushes, turpentine, drill-bits, hammers and nails, and, behind it all, a solid mass of dolls and doll parts so thick it looks like one of the mass graves Jakob's seen in his mother's Holocaust books.

Something catches in his throat as Wieland says, "This is where I play, just as the Creator played while creating us. This is where the real work gets done, and the real work, as I said, is play. Never forget that. It's... by the way, do you know why you're here?"

Wieland trails off, following Jakob's gaze into the pit of bodies. Jakob stares at them so long that he starts to fear he'll never rescue his attention, and that his body will have no choice but to join it down in there.

He wants out now. He wants to know the answer to the question Wieland just posed, but not as badly as he wants to be back in his bed, safely under his covers and inside a dream of anyplace else. "And what place might that be," the snake's voice asks. "Can you picture one? Anyplace at all? Tokyo, London, New York, Los Angeles... can you see them now? Try to see yourself in a svelte black blazer, striding down a sunlit boulevard in..."

Don't rush me! Jakob wants to shout, but he can't move his mouth. He starts to shake, realizing for the first time that he's completely unsure whether he's free to leave. What would happen if I asked? He shivers to think that he can't tell. The dolls stare at him, and he imagines them thinking, We, too, wanted to leave, and look what's become of us!

He feels his groin tingle and he realizes he's about to pee his pajama pants, so he blurts, "I have to, um..." and dances back and forth on his legs in such a way that he hopes will keep him from having to say it.

"I bet it's getting light out there," Wieland replies. "I'm part vampire, you know." He laughs. "Can't be seen in daylight. Now, why don't you run along and we'll pick up where we left off next time?"

He falls silent, staring at one of his worktables, so, after a painful hesitation, Jakob nods and makes his own way up the stairs, trying not to run until he's outside.

He makes it out of the cabin, past the spiders and gnomes, and all the way to the clearing before his bladder bursts. He rips down his pajamas and pees, bare-assed, on the ground a few feet from the grave his mother marked, "For the Future in New York City, now never to be lived. In your name we cry."

He stares at it only for as long as it takes him to pee, sensing that if he stays there any longer, he'll end up knowing something he doesn't yet want to know. Something about the grave meant for him, and those meant for his parents. So, as soon as he's able, he hikes up his pajamas and makes his way back down the mountain, through the woods, across the Tick-singing Meadow, and into the house, hoping for a bowl of Wheaties in peace before a day with no more surprises.

The Father Visits the Art Show

Relieved at having survived his second visit to the cabin, Jakob moves through the day in a powerful mood, despite the scare he got down in the basement. *Wieland's* basement, he reminds himself. Far from here.

He forces himself to his feet, thinking, Next time, I'll go down there with my head held high, undaunted by the doll pile. Last night I was just tired. He papers over his memory of the deeper terror he knows he felt, determined to return to the Museum after school to check on his work and ask Greta how the rest of Friday's opening went. If she mentions my visit to Wieland, he decides, I won't deny it, but if she doesn't, I won't bring it up.

He goes through the motions of his lessons that morning, which consist mainly of reassuring his mother that he understands the link between the Art World and Nazism. As soon as she gets out her legal pad and password-protected laptop, he says he's going for his afternoon walk. She gives him a slightly funny look, but he thinks nothing of it as he takes the now-familiar route down Main Street, past the river where the fishermen who attacked his father are in their usual poses, popping cans of Schlitz while they wait for action on their lines. Then he climbs the Museum's front steps to find Greta doing paperwork in the back room. She smiles and motions for him to sit down.

Pulling a folding chair up to the desk on the other side, he leans forward and waits for her to speak. "Word's been going around town," she finally says. "People are intrigued. They're talking."

Jakob feels himself blush, his mood rising into a realm of excitement he's never felt before, at least not while awake. "They... are?" he asks.

She nods. "People are hungry for new images. They live on food and water and sleep, sure, but not only that. Without new images, they starve. They may not know they're starving, they may even look like they're doing just fine, but inside they're drying up. When you show people images they've never seen before, something dead inside them comes back to life."

Greta trails off and lets the compliment hang in the stuffy air, raining down over Jakob, soaking him with pride and something deeper as well, something darker.

Power. He shivers, unsure how much he should try to bear. He glimpses one possible future, one possible thing he could be. He glimpses how it would feel to wield this power over people, people outside his family, strangers, many of them, perhaps a great many. "Hundreds, thousands. Why not millions?" the snake whispers. He feels hot, short of breath, like he wants to collapse into his mother's arms and sob. He wants to apologize for what he now knows he's capable of, the monstrousness of how badly he wants to compel millions of strangers into blind worship of his Genius.

He opens his mouth, then closes it.

Greta gives him a look that indicates she understands some of what he's thinking. "People have been coming in and out every day," she says, getting up to take two cans of Coke from the small fridge in the corner. "Let that feeling sink in. Then, go out there and make me something else. I hope this is just the beginning."

Jakob spends the rest of the week in a trance, unsure where in his heart the line between pride and fear should be drawn, and unsure whether what he's becoming is different from what he was always going to become, or if it's only the next stop on the path he's always been on. Each night he lies in bed with the Night Crusher on his chest, as his head alternates between wondering what his next piece should be and wondering whether there should be any next piece at all. Some nights, he's haunted by masses of soul-dead townspeople clambering at his bedroom door, begging him to feed the dead things inside them, desperate to be soothed as only fresh images can soothe them. Threatening: make us something to feast on, or we'll feast on you. On one of these nights, he bolts upright and nearly calls for his mother, but he knows she's long since left for the woods, and only then does he realize he's stopped following her. The thought makes him cry, and the tears soothe him back to sleep.

His father, still healing from his injuries, remains silent through one dinner after another, eating tentatively and staring over his shoulder at the back door, as if afraid of leaving his work in the garage unattended for even the few minutes it takes to polish off a bowl of stew. Something is hardening in his eyes, a severity, a gauntness, a desperation. Perhaps even rage at the Demiurge for withholding the next vision. There are times when Jakob wonders whether word of the show has somehow reached him. Perhaps, he thinks, the Art World speaks to all those who've been entangled with it, taunting them in nightmares as they wander in exile, and, thus, somehow every step I take in that direction is known to everyone who's ever walked that road before me. Bosch and Bacon and Kiefer and everyone else, he thinks, flashing on the hellscapes his mother showed him during his lessons this morning.

The thought is so frightening that he asks to be excused and goes straight to bed, and from bed straight into a nightmare in which his father's destroying the

Museum, crushing the whole structure with Greta inside, like a giant compacting the frail building until it's nothing but an extension of Ragtown, another pile of boards and bodies for the Rat People to pick over. And then his father and mother, both giants in the nightmare, stride from the wreckage of the town and onto the next one, without a care in their hearts, without a single passing thought of the son they've left behind.

The nightmare smothers any hope of restorative sleep, so he lies in bed until dawn, then drags through breakfast and his lessons with almost no presence of mind at all. Then, at 3PM sharp, he runs to the Museum, terrified he's going to discover it smashed. The exterior's intact, but this gives him little comfort. He tiptoes up the steps, praying he'll find the interior in the same condition. He opens the door slowly, preserving the last instants of relative peace for as long as he can, but even at this rate, the horror hits fast. He stands in the doorway watching Greta sweep up broken glass and twisted metal frames, shredded paper and wicker and wood, the ruins of his show mixed imperceptibly with Wieland's. The scene is even more brutal than it was in the nightmare, and for a moment he tries to entertain the notion that it was someone else, the Boys' Boys or the fishermen, but this effort peters out almost right away. It hurts to realize that he knows his father is capable of this, knows without asking or being told, but that's the truth, which only cowards hide from.

And only cowards turn and run, he thinks, as he observes himself doing just this, locking eyes with Greta for a moment, which is more than enough to scare him away from trying to help her, though he knows it's the right thing to do. He feels hot blood rushing into his temples and his scalp, and hot tears rushing down his face, and he teeters and swoons and falls on his face on the sidewalk, scuffing his nose and busting his lip so that, without intending it, the Blood Clot rushes out of him and quivers on the pavement, shocked, shrieking, "Jakob! I'm drowning, get me out of here!"

Her voice is so loud in his head that he forces himself to his feet and scoops as much of her up in his hands as he possibly can and runs through a weedy lot, past the hardware store and the diner and onto the riverbank, where he leans over and throws her in, only exhaling once he sees that she's spread out, back in her element now, no longer drowning.

Phew, he thinks, as both himself and her at once.

Then he sits there, panting, trying to decide how to tell her what just happened, what it is their father just did. "And is it true that when we dream his dreams, the things we dream actually happen?"

Who are you asking, me? he imagines her saying.

Who else is there to ask? he imagines replying, but this conversation is too bleak to actually engage in, so he just sits there, staring at the bloody water, hoping only for a brief pause in the sequence of events that he knows is now well underway.

Prison

In the end, Jakob found himself unable to tell the Blood Clot what he'd seen. It was too awful, the sight of the Museum with Greta in the center of it, an old woman surrounded by trash, barely strong enough to sweep it aside. And what did I do? He tries to be honest. I left her there, to flail on her own, just as I'm leaving my sister now, the twin who was almost me, to flail in the Red Sea, wondering why she was summoned and which side is which. He gets to his feet in shame, promising to summon her again soon, once he's gathered his composure and revived her inside him, and begins the walk home from the riverbank, past the sullen eyes of the Boys' Boys where they stand throwing rocks at a dove taped to a trashcan. He wouldn't mind an old-fashioned run-in with them now, to take his mind off heavier matters, but since the burning, they've done little more than shoot him furtive, spooked glances. Yelling at them, he knows, would only cause them to scatter. He pictures them fluttering home to their fishermen dads, roosting among the woodchips between their trailers to chirp about what the little Jewboy did now.

Laughing at this image, he walks the rest of the way home while clutching his thin plaid shirt around his sides. It's cold and dark out, he realizes, in the way of night, but more than this too: in the way of deep autumn. His bodyweight seems to double as he realizes that summer's long over and snow and dark and death are almost here.

Wintry silence blankets the dinner table. He sits there with his bruised face, planning to tell his parents that more Nazis attacked him if they ask, but they don't, and he doesn't tell his father that he knows what he did to the Museum, and his father doesn't say why he did it, or even admit that he did. He looks older and frailer, his wounds healing badly, his breathing ragged, and Jakob can't help nursing a strain of tenderness toward him. I can't forgive you for what you did, he imagines saying, as he watches his father spoon up pasta and wince as he blows on it, but I can't quite hate you for it, either. He looks to his mother for reassurance, but she's staring at the empty chair between Jakob and his father, the spot where, had his twin sister been born alive, she would have sat. Her eyes are watery and vacant, like she hasn't slept in days, the sight of which makes Jakob so tired he asks if he can be excused. When neither parent responds, he scrapes his uneaten pasta into the trash and crawls up the stairs like a three-year-old.

Lying in bed, his mind becomes a floor for his smashed photos, interspersed with Wieland's boxes and collages, but this time Greta is absent. Though he feels a twinge of cruelty at eliding her, his primary feeling is elation at seeing his own work in the same pile as Wieland's, as if the two of them were cut from the same cloth. Furthering the thought—he's most of the way asleep now, his consciousness yielding to the snake's soft whisper—he begins to sense that he and Wieland are connected, mediated, perhaps unwittingly, by his father, who destroyed the Museum not only out of rage but out of a desire to mix the artworks together, the old man's and the little boy's, freed from their respective boundaries and reduced to an indistinguishable pile of Raw Material, out of which some profound synthesis will one day emerge.

"Whether he knows it or not," the snake whispers, "your father is driving you toward the Art World. He's doing everything he can to ensure you end up there, a king in a New York or a Los Angeles mansion, thronged by acolytes. Thank him for this. Or thank the Demiurge for acting through him."

Jakob squirms deeper, under the snake's rasp and into the bottommost subterranean layer he can access. All the way down here, in a chamber so narrow that his arms are pinned to his sides, and so deep that Death is palpable just underfoot, the following thought is to be found, etched in burning wax on a cobalt altar:

What if Wieland is my grandfather and Greta is my grandmother, and therefore this is the town of my father's birth, the one he's been searching for all my life? And what if he smashed the Museum precisely in order to show me this... knowing that I, unlike him, am in a position to accept it?

In the morning, Jakob wakes with the sense that a thought of immense importance occurred to him in his sleep. Soaked in the déjà vu of having had this exact thought before, by the Déjà vu Frog Pond, he lies in bed and tries to remember it, but, for now, it's gone. He used to panic at moments like this, but over time he's come to trust that if the thought's important enough, it'll occur to him yet again in due course.

So he gets to his feet, yawns, rubs his swollen lips, and steels himself for the breakfast table. Downstairs, his parents are as silent as they were last night. They stare at him, and he at them, all three crushed by something too large to name. As far as Jakob can tell, everyone knows what's on everyone else's mind, but no one knows how to broach it. Are we all still on the same side? Were we ever? He looks from his mother to his father, and back again, and receives no answer except a vague, slightly exciting sense that this question is a version of that posed by the two sides of the Red Sea. He closes his eyes and pictures a plastic sign hanging on the walls of the Town Museum, engraved with the words, "All Appearance of Distinction is Accidental." This makes him smile.

When his Wheaties are gone and the silence has sucked up most of the oxygen in the room, Jakob's mother says, "We both feel it'd be best if you spent today out of school. Up in your room. Just take the day off, okay?"

Jakob looks at his father, who appears even more reduced than he was last night, perhaps by guilt from what he did, or else with the lingering rage that caused him to do it. He nods, concurring with Jakob's mother, but still refusing to speak. After putting his bowl by the sink, he shuffles out to the garage, a roll of butcher paper and a bunch of Micron pens—he must've ordered them, since the gift shop didn't have any—under his arm.

Jakob and his mother sit alone at the table and Jakob finds himself wishing school would start now, much as he's come to loathe its repetitiveness. Because without something to repeat, he thinks, what will we talk about? He finds the prospect of the morning gaping open before him to be more oppressive than that of once again sorting Philip Roth, William Kentridge, and Noah Baumbach into their respective categories. What do people do all day? He wonders, and almost laughs at how simple yet impossible this question is. This too, he thinks, would make a good sign for the walls of the Museum.

"Upstairs, now," his mother says, after he's sat there

almost giggling for a few minutes, picturing his new exhibition filling up with bald strangers dripping hummus onto their leather clogs. Her voice isn't angry, but it's firm, resigned to a verdict that must be imposed. He wonders what she'll do today if she's not teaching him. He almost asks, but the look on her face makes it clear that it won't take much to make her yell, and he doesn't feel up to bearing that just now. So he nods and shuffles back upstairs, pretending it's night.

Here begins a long phase of internment. The word "prison" isn't uttered, but Jakob decides that it's what his parents are thinking, so he decides to think it as well. Extending this notion, he decides that his father's in prison too, in the garage. He and I, serving our sentences side by side, he thinks, same as in the camps. He lies in bed through the afternoon, his stomach puffed out and gassy from lack of exercise. Festering there, he pictures his father likewise festering in the garage, and he feels his mind softening, growing at once weaker and more receptive, less defined around the edges. Less determined to be one person and not another. He slips in and out of sleep, losing track of the line between day and night, which also grows harder to distinguish as the year dims toward its end.

As time wears on, Jakob finds his spirit drifting out to visit his father in the garage, where he sits hunched over a worktable drawing maps, one after another after another, endlessly overlaying possible routes to the New Jerusalem onto a map of the Continental USA.

Hovering in this state, Jakob thinks: I have gone into exile inside this house in exactly the same way that my father has gone into exile inside this country. Twin gulags, one a microcosm of the other, just as the country is a microcosm of the world, and the world a microcosm of the universe, and the universe, well... he stops before he loses track of scale entirely. Both of us, he thinks, zooming back into the miniscule story of himself and his father, hope that by retreating deeper and deeper into our microcosms, we will at last break through to...

What?

This is the question that obsesses him throughout his term in exile, haunting his room, barely speaking to his mother and father, speaking more to the snake and to the Blood Clot, who he finally finds the courage to summon again, late one night in the bathtub, where he apologizes, falteringly, for his botched attempt to converse with her down by the river, and tells her what he now thinks, that the man in the woods is their father's father, which means this town, at long last, is the New Jerusalem.

The Blood Clot is unimpressed. "This dump?"

Jakob has to admit she has a point. "I don't know," he replies, trying to keep his voice down, in case his mother is wandering the house, snacking and thinking, as she sometimes does before setting out into the woods. "Maybe if we could see the town the way that Wieland does, the town within the town, then..." He trails off, certain there's something meaningful that belongs at the end of this sentence, but not yet sure what it is.

The shortening days continue to elapse, the sun now a pale yellow speck in a pale white sky. The moldering mugs with their teabags stuck to their sides and the piles of unopened mail return to their old positions on the windowsills and countertops of the downstairs rooms, like an old exhibit that's back by popular demand, or unchanged due to the Museum's dearth of new material.

Jakob hasn't been outside in a month, perhaps two. There's been no mention of Hanukkah. He wanders the house in near-silence, eating with his parents but barely discussing the situation, whose nature now seems both fully apparent and beyond his grasp. Maybe I'm sick, he worries. Maybe I have a fever and, as soon as I get over it, things will go back to normal. But he doubts this. The innermost chambers of reality seem to be open, the concrete of the world's foundations soft and pliant, just as they must have been at the very beginning when, shocked into action by the weight of eons of loneliness, the Demiurge first decided to make something out of nothing.

Jakob puts his ear to his pillow and listens through the floors to the foundation of the house shifting, the concrete slabs of the basement floor cracking and rearranging themselves, the piles of mannequins and cans of paint and long rows of hideously rusted saws from his father's basement merging inexorably with

Wieland's, the two zones bleeding together until, after a season of flux, their separation will be only a memory.

What this means about the two divergent sets of rooms above them is more than Jakob can yet say.

He lies in bed in the minutes before dawn and listens to his mother return, and he can see his father's materials from the garage creeping into the house, the long roads and paths he's drawn on his maps of America growing inward like vines, overwhelming the modest garage and stuffing the house, snaking down the stairs toward the basement that is now Wieland's, from which Jakob ran in terror the first time he was granted admission, only to find himself living above it.

If I ever get another chance to go down there, he thinks, his head against the wall behind his pillows with the snake's head on the other side, its hot breath scorching his brown hair blonde, I will spend days and weeks and months at the workbench. I won't come back up until I'm a real man. I wasn't brave enough then, but I nearly am now.

The crisis that initially drove him into this state has burned away, as causes always do if their effects linger long enough. Now, in the guts of winter, Jakob can't remember what necessitated his imprisonment, only that its purpose was to make him stronger, to smother the boy he used to be and reconfigure him as a man brave enough to confront whatever Wieland is hiding in his basement, even if it means dying and letting his body become part of the secret. He wonders whether seeding this new awareness was his father's intention all along.

Registering the enormity of the change sends him into a dream where his bed is hanging on chains directly above the basement, like a Joseph Beuys installation, rocking with a loud crunch every time he tries to get cozy. It's sixty years in the future, just as it was at the diner. He and Wieland merged long ago, and the cabin and the house have likewise grown together, variations on a theme, of which there are perhaps many others, scattered throughout the woods.

Jakob feels the roots of his family tree rotting as the ground they grow out of turns to swamp. He feels his family's history being rewritten, or written for the first time. Nothing is definite, he thinks, nothing is final, but things do seem to be revealing themselves in earnest at last.

Perhaps—and this, he's pretty sure, is a thought he's never had before—perhaps some things can be gotten right. Perhaps endless exile isn't the only ending.

He rocks and shudders in his hanging bed, squishing his pillow into his face, trying to cool down. It feels like these visions are feasting on him, burning up the last of his fat in order to show him what he needs to see, which is now the coming-together of his grandfather, his father, and himself, three into one, many places and many timelines collapsing and colliding, the chaos of his father's maps rearranging itself into the calm of knowing that he's lived here alone all his life and, over the course of decades spent in the basement, he's created the tremendous, multimedia body of work known throughout the Art World as "New Jerusalem 3."

He shrieks as his mind drifts back to the Art World, or the Art World drifts back into his mind, its needle-strewn alleys etching themselves into the town, forcing its boundaries out and out and out, until he's alone in a vast metropolis.

He keeps shrieking until his mother bursts into his room and then into his bed, forcing it off its chains, and cradles him in her lap. If he's not mistaken, she's covered in dirt, like she was just up at her cemetery, digging in the ground, and all at once the decades melt away and he's back to being a frightened twelve-year-old on the cusp of something but not yet over it, and the world feels immense beyond belief.

He curls into his mother's lap and sobs and falls back asleep. Hours later, when he's woken up alone for a second time, he comes downstairs to see that his father's work has completely blanketed the house, from the kitchen to the living room to the playroom. Maps and charts and celestial sketches and taxonomies of desert sand and Jewish history and occult lore, sunken continents and demonic altars and holes in the earth cover the walls, floor, and ceiling, and all the space between the back door and the garage, so densely that it seems the garage is now just one more room in a vast exhibit, a wing of a Museum that incorporates all three of their lives. The notion that the house has become the very Museum his father destroyed is too funny to bear. Jakob bursts out laughing, spilling his Wheaties, cackling so loudly that his frail, haunted-looking father leaves the table, vanishing into his papers and leaving Jakob's mother to pull her coat over her nightgown and say, "Jakob, you're shivering. It's time you went back up to bed."

A Country
Doctor

Back in bed, Jakob shivers through the day and most of the night, soaking his sheets until they feel like a mass of ectoplasm. He wants to peel them away and throw them out the window, but his fingers are too cold and crooked to move, so he finds himself once again in the puppet state, waiting for someone or something to pull his string.

Deep in the night, close to his mother's sleepwalking hour, something does. It yanks his mouth open and he hears himself begin to moan. At first it's just a low, steady *uhhhhh*, but it grows louder, until he's rocking on his sodden sheets and keening like a banshee, filling his room with so much sound that his mother comes running in and grabs him from where he lies like she's afraid he's about to burst into flame. But I've already burned, mom! he wants to shout. This thought makes him laugh so hard that he can't stop as he sits in the kitchen and stares at the fridge while his mother makes a muffled phone call in the playroom. Soon after this, Jakob finds himself strapped into the car for the first time since Traitor Joe's, back in what feels like a previous life, on the far side of a transformation whose effects are impossible to ignore, even if its nature is, as yet, equally impossible to describe. Like that was the Demiurge's previous exhibition, he muses, and this, my life as it begins this morning, is the next one.

His veil forgotten in his bedroom drawer, he looks out at the sparse buildings under cover of night, as blurry and washed-out as a town underwater, and he feels the passage of centuries, all of human civilization collapsing into a single era, perhaps a very bleak one, among the infinitude of eras that makes up the history of the world. They drive past the Town Museum and he tries to avert his eyes, but it's too late. He catches sight of the CLOSED sign across the door, and though he knows this probably only means it's closed for the night, he can't help fearing that it means something more insidious, as well.

He hears himself keening again as the car rumbles over the bridge, past the fishermen's abandoned bait buckets and folding chairs, surrounded by protective rings of Schlitz. He knows his mother won't stop to ask him what's wrong, since this ride feels like a faster version of their sleepwalking journeys, a time when the night's so deep it serves as a sort of anesthesia, lowering them into a state where they both are and are not aware of the other person.

And soon, he thinks, the doctor will enter the scene, as they're now rolling up his driveway, and now up to his door. His mother knocks, seemingly without sound, and a few minutes later a barefoot old man in shabby corduroys and a tucked-in blue shirt with toothpaste on the collar opens up, squinting. After an exact rehash of the muffled phone call in the playroom, he ushers them in. They follow him through a foyer and into a room with two beds, one of which is occupied by an old woman sleeping soundly with the covers bunched under her chin.

The old man motions for Jakob to sit on the other bed, which, after trying to gauge the relative normalcy of this request on his mother's face, he does. He scoots back over the bare mattress, coughing a little, and then he sighs, waiting as the old man rummages through a dresser for his medical bag, muttering what sound like curses until he finds it.

The bag is made of dry, cracked leather and has what looks like a military insignia, which Jakob finds far more interesting than whatever the man's asking him, which sound like questions that can all be answered with a nod.

"I see," the doctor says, poking a tool deep into Jakob's ear, then thumping his chest with a frigid stethoscope. As he peers up Jakob's nose, Jakob looks over at the sleeping woman in the other bed and feels the deepness of the night all around her, filling the room with thick, invisible gelatin that binds the visible field together and lends the doctor's every move a palpable yet inexplicable meaning.

Is this all my dream? he wonders. He immediately senses that the answer, in some very important way, is no, and yet this can't be waking reality, either. None of these other people are quite here, he thinks, eyes still on the old woman who shows no signs of stirring, even as the doctor and his mother speak without trying to keep their voices down, just as I'm not quite here for them. We're all in separate versions of this same moment, wondering if we're dreaming, trying, as best we can, to cast the others into the roles we need them to play in order for our presence here to mean something.

This thought lands with the force of revelation. Maybe, he thinks, as he sits there on the bed watching the doctor hand his mother a scrap of paper he's just finished writing on, all the townspeople are actors I can cast in this inner drama, summoning them from the woodwork whenever I choose. But it's dangerous, because they're trying to cast me at the same time, so I have to find a way to overpower them, to render their inner worlds moot as compared with mine. To make them slaves to my vision, and glad to be slaves. It's either that, he thinks, as his mother tells him to hop off the bed and get ready to go, or vice versa. There's no middle ground.

He thinks again of the Tyson Meat Truck, this time picturing himself hanging on a hook in back, en route to a massive freezer in the heart of the country. Again, he thinks, as déjà vu descends like a morning fog over the truck, it's them or me. There are many hooks in back, but only one driver's seat in front.

As the doctor tells him to get plenty of rest and listen to his mother, Jakob bares his teeth and feels a surge of malevolence such as he's never felt before. Though he knows the doctor's done nothing wrong, and is most likely a decent man, weary after a lifetime of meeting the ordinary needs of the people of this town, he wants to obliterate him. To reduce him to a state where he has no option other than to play an extremely minor part in Jakob's waking dream, a figure under glass in a diorama. Witness the magnitude of my Genius, he wants to shout, and bow down before it!

I will ensure that this happens, he pledges, as he settles back into the car and nods when his mother says they have to go to the pharmacy to pick up medicine. In time, I will do all this and more.

The Father
Says the Final
Vision is Near

When Jakob and his mother return with the medicine just after dawn, his father's lying on a pile of comforters on the couch. He looks at the pharmacy bag that Jakob's mother holds and says, his voice weak and phlegmy, "Bring me those," and Jakob's mother does. He sucks down a handful of pills with the glass of milk he'd been nursing, then motions for Jakob and his mother to take their seats on either side of where he lies.

After a long silence, he begins, "I feel the dream brewing hot in my innermost mental chamber. The image of the New Jerusalem is growing stronger, even as my body weakens. Soon it will become fully clear to me. All the maps," he gestures at the spread of string, butcher paper, and hand-drawn topographies that covers the floors, walls, and ceilings of the kitchen, living room, and playroom, "will coalesce into one, and it will be a map of the town we are meant to return to, the one in which we will, at last, be safe. The town of my youth, in which my forgotten mother and father raised me to be the prophet who appears before you now, whether they meant to or not. The cruel irony is that I feel my body weakening at the very same rate at which the vision grows more vivid, such that I am riven by the fear that the moment of my greatest insight will coincide with the moment of my death. The stress of what I have put myself through for your sakes is beyond what can be expressed in words, so let me say, simply, that you must both be ever-ready to leave here at a moment's notice. All these years, I've traveled through the Desert on my own, in dreams, exploring, inching my way toward the revelation that's been so slow to come. But now I truly believe it is close at hand. The house we are in now is making me sick, as you can see, and the degraded *volk* of this town are trying to kill me, but my sickness and my suffering are the ultimate stage, beyond which fruition surely lies. The world is growing ever more chaotic, and the future thus ever harder to discern, but I do believe I will succeed in snatching the decisive glimpse before it is too late. The day when we will finally move, in body as well as spirit, out of this Egypt and into the New Jerusalem, is closer than it's ever been. This is a happy occasion, though it is also a solemn one."

Jakob feels himself riveted into the kind of semi-human state he always enters when his father begins an extended sermon, and yet something inside him remains unsoothed. Part of him remains alert, and therefore angry. Words are welling up in his throat in a way they never have before. The notion of leaving this town now, when the strings are just beginning to connect, the woodwork just beginning to release its actors, is intolerable. If they try to get me to eat the rice pudding tonight, he thinks, I'll throw it so hard at the wall it'll end up outside the house.

"Jakob?" his father asks. "This meeting cannot be adjourned until you've pledged your readiness. The Days of Wonder are nearly upon us, the Great Season is nearly here, so any lacunae in the family structure now would be fatal. The preparation to move, the prospect of leaving one's childhood home of course isn't…"

"I'm not leaving!" Jakob shouts, shocking himself as much as his parents. To interrupt his father's speech so near its conclusion is uncharted territory. Jakob feels his chest fill with hot liquid, so that his words pour like steam from his mouth. "This is the town! This is it, dad. This is where your father's been all this time. I found him, in the woods! I know he's up there, and he's already built the New Jerusalem for us."

A mad hope passes through Jakob's head as he hears himself speak, a possibility that he knows will cease to be a possibility as soon as he expresses it. Still, he can't keep it to himself. "We could all go there right now," he says. "Right this minute, we could walk out of this house and go up to the woods and meet Wilhelm Wieland as a family. The place we've been seeking all these years?" Jakob can't believe he's still talking. His father and mother are both stunned, staring at him like they're about to pounce, but neither's moving yet. "The place we've been seeking all these years is right here. We've been steadily moving toward it, and now we've arrived, and I'll never leave again!" He shouts, his voice low and angry, but also swollen with hope. His throat feels like a lizard's, puffed up nearly to the breaking point. "I'm going to the woods. If you'd like to come with me, get your shoes on. He'll take us in if we go right now."

The thrill of giving this order, in his father's voice, is profound but short-lived. He's halfway to the back door when a hand clamps his left arm and then, a moment later, his right. His mother and father are on either side of him, looming above, quavering. He freezes, watching his spirit drift out of his body and then turn to regard the three of them standing there like Giacometti sculptures, posed, ready for an action they have not yet decided upon.

I'm ready to heed the call to battle, his spirit thinks.

"Now!!" he hears his mouth shout, summoning his spirit back into his body and wrenching it out of his parents' hands. Then he's running, faster than he ever has before, over the threshold of the house and into the town, past the neighbors socked into their houses by tremendous snowdrifts and through the Tick-singing Meadow, across the river and into the woods, flying over the sharp pine needles and into the heady, cold fog, arms outstretched for Wieland's cabin, desperate to make it inside before the twin giants of his mother and father catch up with him. He feels as though the pressure that built up in the basement over the long months of confinement has now boiled over, so the fact that he's running, rather than flying, is true only in the most banal sense. In reality, he knows, in the real reality that actually matters, I'm soaring on a furious gust of steam, flying high above the town like an angel in a Chagall, never to return as myself.

PART II

In the Wilderness

"If there are sprits that inhabit empty houses, why wouldn't they also inhabit the bodies of dolls?"—Felisberto Hernández, "The Daisy Dolls"

Marrow Stew

As he flies, Jakob looks back once, unable to resist the urge to check if his parents have followed, either still as giants or back in their human forms, but all he sees is the town sealing itself off beneath him, a curtain of beaded ice zipping shut.

Tears come to his eyes and freeze there so that, by the time he turns his back on the sealed-off town for the last time, he's wearing a mask of glistening ice, like a celebrant approaching a private Carnival deep in the woods.

It gets so dark so quickly that Jakob decides today must be the solstice. This brings no comfort, but it does bring considerable aesthetic pleasure, insofar as it perfectly underscores the gravity of his decision to leave home, which he can now see that he's done, as the neon of his mother's gravestones glows under the snow in the clearing that separates what he now thinks of as the Near Woods, fringing the path that leads back to town, from the Far Woods, fringing Wieland's cabin. "All the parameters of the next phase of my life are defining themselves here in the dark, like a stage set being assembled behind a curtain," he explains, as if he were leading a group of art students on a tour of this classic cusp scene.

Then he begins the lonely trek across the clearing, determined not to look down and read the epitaph on the grave that's been reserved for him.

"No, the time for that's still a long way off, although there's no question that this is where I'll end up eventually. It's always easier to move through life," he continues, as he crosses the last stretch of the clearing and enters the Far Woods, where the dark is doubled because the night sky is occluded by a seamless roof of evergreens, "when you are moving in a straight line toward a predetermined destination, because then all you have to do is keep moving!"

The simplicity of this warms him as he crosses beneath the metal spiders and trudges over the gnomes and other fetishes buried underfoot, dragging his soaked sneakers toward the dim light of Wieland's door.

As he draws near and the smell of gamey meat washes over him, both sickening and heartening, he relishes the final seconds before it will be time to knock. I could still turn back, he thinks, though he knows it isn't true. I could still turn around, retrace my steps, and be back in my bed in my father's house before dawn, thereby ensuring that no major change in my life occurs.

He smiles, toying with this thought the way a kitten toys with a ball of yarn. There's nothing wrong with playing around a little, he thinks. Life can't be all grim duty.

But, after a minute, the grimness of the cold and the night and the way the fantasy yearns to keep him out in it cuts through his pajamas and his wet shoes begin to grow icicles that drill into his ankles and so, accepting that the point of no return has arrived, he knocks, stands back, and knocks again.

It takes three knocks, each harder and longer than the last, to summon the old man. When he finally appears, in his slippers and bathrobe, the stew reek makes Jakob wretch.

Wieland grins. "Thick with marrow, slick with fat."

This utterance hangs in the frosty air between them, not quite an invitation, though also by no means a refusal of entry. Jakob peers past the old man's bulk into the dim, cluttered cabin, and thinks, The whole place is so thick with marrow and slick with fat that the stew, if that's where the smell's coming from, is just the densest part. The boiling center of whatever my new life is going to be. The beating heart. Suppressing a second gag, he says, "I'm here for my mouthful of heart. Let me in."

Wieland stands aside, letting Jakob pass into the

warm, yellow steam of the interior, which carries with it the uncanny sense of merging memory with perception, so that, by the time he sits down at the table, he half-expects Wieland to serve him a glass of rotten chocolate milk and for it still to be autumn outside, his business in the town below still unfinished. And would I prefer that? he wonders, as he accepts a steaming bowl and a dirty spoon, then watches the old man decant half a glass of liquor from a cloudy, unlabeled bottle.

"Baby needs its top-up," Wieland smiles, handing Jakob the glass and keeping the bottle for himself. "Milk of Mother Night says hi."

He swigs down a throat-bulging mouthful and chuckles, his eyes roaming around the kitchen, passing over Jakob as if he were just one of the many objects strewn on the counters, bursting from the cupboards, and piled on the other chairs, either haphazardly or according to some highly precise internal scheme known only to Wieland himself, or perhaps, Jakob thinks, to Greta as well, if what the Boys' Boys say about the two of them is true.

Have I joined a bustling family housed in this cabin, he wonders, or am I its first guest in decades? He knocks on his stew with his spoon, trying to postpone the moment of tasting it as long as possible.

"Never mind the stew," Wieland mutters, lips on the rim of the bottle. "Drink what's in your glass. What're you, about fifteen or so? A little old to hesitate at the threshold of a stiff drink, wouldn't you say?" Wieland tries to laugh but ends up belching instead. He sits down as the belch blows his robe open, revealing his glistening, pocked stomach. Jakob can tell that if he were to peek under the table, he'd find himself eye to eye with the man's purple penis, bunched up in a nest of ragged hair. He sits there considering it until Wieland says, "Go ahead, what are you afraid of?" For a moment, Jakob's certain the man's read his mind, and a fresh wave of déjà vu hits him. He hears himself think, Somehow, my whole life has been leading up to this moment, me alone in the woods in the middle of winter in the middle of the night, about to crawl under a strange table to make eye contact with a strange penis, possibly the one that called my father into being, who in turn called me. He's about to crawl off his chair and face what's waiting under the table when Wieland pulls his robe closed and repeats, "I said, what are you waiting for? Are you going to drink, or aren't you? Cuz if there's one thing I don't like around here, it's finks that can't stomach their portion."

The déjà vu lifts as quickly as it descended, and Jakob picks up his glass and slugs its contents down, thanking the Boys' Boys for having trained him. Then, before the numbness in his mouth wears off, he swallows a few spoonfuls of stew.

Wieland looks satisfied when the liquor's gone and the stew's been reduced to a brownish-red smear on the bottom and the sides of the bowl. "Well," he says, belching again and taking a last swig from the bottle, "it's been great talkin' to ya. Tomorrow it's back to work, yes?"

Before Jakob can answer, Wieland stands up, robe wide open, revealing his gnarled penis and low-hanging testicles, utterly banal now, devoid of whatever mythic potency they might have had a moment ago, and says, "There's a couch in the sitting room you can sleep on, if you feel like sleeping. And leave the dishes on the table. Tobin'll be by in the morning, assuming he can find a suitable pig."

His eyes glint in a way that sends a chill through Jakob's body, freezing out the warmth of the alcohol, and then he's gone, tramping down to the basement to sleep in some cramped nest among the mannequins and paint cans, or to else work in a drunken fever through the night.

Jakob sits at the table and listens to his stomach churn, trying to process the stew as if it were mere food rather than a haunted substrate, cousin to the rice pudding that induces the Desert Dream.

When this grows unbearable, he takes his dishes to the sink, though he knows that Wieland told him not to. The face he made when he said that Tobin was coming in the morning was so unsettling that, now, Jakob finds himself desperate to put it out of mind. Maybe if I wash the dishes, he thinks, I can also wash that name away.

As soon as he gets to the window, a flashing neon light attracts his attention, and he finds himself looking past the wicker fetishes and the spiders to the center of the clearing where, among the glowing gravestones, his mother is rooting around in the snow, forlorn and shivering in her white nightgown under a puffy jacket, trying to unearth something that Jakob very much does not wish to see. The longer he looks, the more certain he becomes that, before long, she'll feel his attention and turn to meet it, and their eye contact will be more than enough to pull him down to the old house below, or into one of the graves she's digging, which may, in some sense just beyond his comprehending, amount to the same thing. I'll run blubbering into her arms if she so much as glances at me, he knows, as Wieland's exhortation to leave the dishes on the table starts to replay in the back of his head, like a reprise of a show for a lone audience member who refused to leave the theater. The prospect of being carried back to town is so frightening that he drops his smeared bowl into the sink and turns his back on the window, thinking, Never again will I question one single thing that Wieland ever says.

A Few Restive

Hours

Vibrating with the full-body sense that nowhere is safe, Jakob retreats into the sitting room and curls up on the sagging cushions of the couch, adjusting his arms and legs so the exposed springs don't puncture them. Lying in this pose, like an articulated dummy on a display table, he pulls his palm up to his teeth and nuzzles it, longing to summon the Blood Clot. If only she were here with me now, he thinks, I wouldn't be stranded on the absolute outermost edge of the earth, completely alone except for a muttering madman. He sinks his teeth into the soft flesh where his thumb meets his wrist, and is about to draw blood when he stops and decides, No, this is for me to suffer alone. Only a coward would bring her into this. Wouldn't a brave man protect his sister, rather than force her to suffer alongside him?

Jakob retracts his teeth and wipes his spit-slick hand on the sweaty cushion under his head, while he uses the other to play with one of the loose springs, pushing it in and out of the couch's frame, his eyes dimly aware of the bust of a devil on an ottoman halfway across the room.

Lulled by the drone of the spring's recoil, he drifts off along with this devil, the two of them slipping out of the cabin and into a shadowland adjacent to sleep, a neighboring country restrained from waging war by an old, tenuous treaty. It's a wide, drafty space that resembles the clearing just outside the cabin, a proving ground as thick with menace as the clearing in the trailer park where the fishermen beget Boys' Boys unto eternity, though, up here, the nature of the menace is less terrestrial. "As below, so above," Jakob informs the devil. "All things from down there are copied up here, though never exactly. Never quite..."

"Don't dillydally!" a voice in his head shouts. "Tobin's coming!"

As soon as he hears this, a surge of adrenaline cuts through him and he begins to run, though he can't tell where to. All directions look the same; the murk is ubiquitous, punctuated at random intervals by his mother's neon graves and by dolls made to look just like himself, his mother, and his father, some of them emerging from the dusk, others being sucked back into it.

Injecting this all with actual danger, and thus daring Jakob to try to make it across the shadowland and into whatever paradise might lie on the far side, is Tobin himself, who could be coming from any direction, or all directions at once, firming up out of the dusk until he stands in the foreground as the dusk's physical embodiment, drenched in blood, grinning with blackened, empty gums, holding a cleaver in one hand and a leaking bag of trash in the other.

"Good morning, little fink," he slobbers, his voice like that of a pig who's been trained by some lonely pervert farmer to speak.

Tobin

Back in his body in the cabin, Jakob tries to block out the wet thunk, but as soon as he realizes that this is what he's doing, he knows it's too late. The sound is overwhelming, all pervasive, stuffing itself into the folds of his brain until his only recourse is to stand up and go toward it, in the semi-absurd hope that by seeing where it's coming from, it'll shed its awful power.

He stumbles onto the front steps in his pajamas to join Wieland standing in his robe with a mug of coffee, watching the pig-man stab a pig in the snow ten or fifteen feet away. He stabs it over and over and over again, limited only by his breath, which gives out every five or six stabs, forcing him to lean against the carcass and heave for a moment before resuming.

Then, revived, the pig-man tightens his grip on the knife and goes back to work.

Wieland looks rapt, his grin so wide that coffee leaks down his chin every time he takes a sip. When he finally notices Jakob standing beside him, he looks down and says, "Meet Tobin. This is him on a good day." He takes a dribble of coffee, then adds, "Anytime he can find a pig means he'll manage to be almost human for a couple hours. Helps him get the crazy out, I guess. Though of course it always comes back!" His grin grows wider still.

As Tobin goes on stabbing the pig, befouling the snow until its whiteness is a distant memory, Jakob can't suppress the feeling that the monster from his dream has been conjured, in exact detail, here in the shared reality of morning.

Either that, he thinks, or I simply had a premonition of what was coming. Either I glimpsed a reality that exists outside of me but to which I alone have early access, or else I've created this man out of the malleable clay of the universe, which is now under my control. He tries to decide which possibility to embrace, but the spectacle of Tobin sawing the pig's head off and howling with lust monopolizes his attention.

"Alright then," Wieland says, once Tobin's dropped the head and made eye contact with him for the first time, "shall we all traipse indoors and see what you have for us today?"

Sitting around the kitchen table with mugs of coffee and cups of clear liquor, Tobin, who does indeed seem slightly less insane, pulls out a series of objects from a dripping trash bag he's dragged through the pig blood and into the cabin. He pulls out a plastic army man whose gun has been smashed to a nub, a thimble clotted with fur, and a lump of wax with a face on each side, one of them pinched and sneering, the other fat and jolly.

"You see," Wieland explains, pouring his liquor into his coffee before refilling his glass from the bottle, "Tobin brings me things from Ragtown. Rare things, strange things, things too deeply buried for anyone else to find. Only he's crazy enough to dig all the way down there. I'd go myself, like I used to, but I am, you see, much too famous to be seen in public anymore!"

He laughs, and looks disappointed when Jakob doesn't join in, but then he shrugs and says, "Ah well, you have plenty of time to learn the fuckeries of fame. For the time being, why don't I take these toys down to the basement and you help Tobin feed his dearly departed friend into the smoker out back before he turns savage again?"

Jakob stands in the snow in his soaked-through sneakers as he watches Tobin hack apart the remaining gristly strands of pig and stuff them, one by one, into the roaring smoker. The pieces are irregular hocks, some with bones protruding, others half-covered in skin; Jakob gags with his mouth closed at the prospect of eating them at Wieland's table tonight, though anything is better than more stew.

Tobin works without paying Jakob much mind,

though, when he occasionally looks up and notices the boy standing behind him, he grins in a way that erases all distinction between person and pig. He'd be just as happy to throw me in there, Jakob realizes, watching the last few pig pieces vanish in the smoke, even though he's the pig-man, not me. Never forget, Jakob imagines telling Tobin, that I conjured you last night. And I could un-conjure you just as easily. So watch yourself.

He wishes he could be sure this was true. But, for now, he flinches and pees a little when Tobin shoves the smoker shut, picks up his cleaver and trash bag, and stands towering in the bloody snow. "You live here now?" he grunts, leaning forward to let a long yellow string of mucus trail out of his mouth. I'd like to yank that string and see what happens, Jakob thinks.

"I asked you a question," Tobin grunts again, after the string has fallen from his mouth.

Jakob can't remember what it was, and somehow doubts that Tobin can either, so he just nods, then looks away at the metal spiders.

"Those little boys eat you," Tobin says. "They yum-yum splats like you in a jiffy. Just like me," he laughs, though his eyes look sad.

Jakob wonders if he lives in the trailer park down below, with the Boys' Boys and their fisherman fathers, or if he's too far gone for them. Perhaps, he thinks, forgetting the idea that he conjured the pig-man in his dream last night, Tobin used to live there but then got too crazy and was banished to the woods by some masked midnight tribunal, warned never to return.

"You live in there?" Jakob asks, pointing at the woods when Tobin leans in too close, his breath hot with decay.

Tobin leans back, pondering Jakob's question. Eventually, he nods. "In the deepest, darkest hollow," he stammers, less confident now that he's answering a question rather than asking one. "Where the ants turns to flies and the water snakes grow wings." He pauses, grumbling, trying to drag more words from wherever inside him they reside. "Where the moss is wet with rabbit-dew, and the mushrooms stink like girl-screw!"

He laughs, at first slowly, then faster, with more volume, his lips creeping up his face until they're winged way out to the sides, revealing the hot, dank pit of his mouth and throat, full of trembling white canker sores. He heaves back and forth, his breasts bouncing under his apron as spittle flies from his lips.

Unsure what else to do, Jakob starts laughing along with him, embarking on his own journey from mild amusement to unhinged mania, until, soon enough, they're both howling under the winter sun, making the wicker fetishes clank, in a paroxysm of fearful hilarity punctuated only by a gunshot that tunnels through the thick air and bores into a tree with the sharp *thunk* of a woodpecker.

Jakob stops first, wiping his eyes and lips to regard Wieland outside the cabin, holding a rifle, a smile on his face. "Seems you two are getting on like a couple of gimp brothers on shore leave in Bangkok!" He lowers the gun and coughs. "So I hate to break up the party, but Tobin here's got maybe fifteen minutes before he reverts, so I'd suggest getting inside before that less than pleasant spectacle takes place out here."

Jakob stands still and waits for Wieland to continue, but he doesn't.

A moment later, Wieland sucks the smile off his lips and bellows, "Inside! Now! Did I not just say that? Don't tell me I'm losing my memory that bad. I did just say it, didn't I?"

Jakob nods and backs away from Tobin, unable to suppress his curiosity at the reversion that's supposedly about to occur, but well aware that Wieland is not a man who enjoys repeating himself, especially not when he has his rifle out.

Back inside the cabin, he watches through the window as Wieland hands Tobin a wad of money. Then he watches Tobin scamper away, his movements growing more porcine with each step.

When he's gone, Jakob sits on the couch and asks himself, So what is there to do up here now? This question, in its aching wintry emptiness, strikes him as far more frightening than any fate he might have suffered with Tobin outside.

Pig Dinner

All the light goes out of the cabin when the sun sets in the early afternoon, and Wieland turns none of the lamps on. Though he doesn't forbid Jakob from turning them on himself, the atmosphere is solemn and dank, as cold as the bloodied snow, and this seems fitting for the mood Jakob finds himself in. He sits on the couch he tried to sleep on last night, and imagines trying to sleep on it again. Then he imagines summoning the Blood Clot and, though the notion of sparing her the desolation of seeing where he's ended up still brings him some pride, he knows his resistance won't last much longer. He starts looking around the room, trying to decide where to do it, which corner will draw the least attention, while, in another part of his mind, he tries to decide which part of his body to let her out through, whether it ought to be his toe or another place, his inner arm perhaps, or a virgin spring like the back of his calf, if he can get a good enough grip with his teeth.

The permutations of these possibilities occupy him until the smell of meat smoke fills the room and Wieland shouts, "Grub!"

Jakob traipses into the kitchen to find the old man sucking bones and tearing flesh, standing over the sink where the pig meat is piled, leaning back from the dripping juice the way his mother used to eat ripe peaches. Though he invited Jakob to share the grub a moment ago, Wieland now looks angry and protective, like one of the Ragtown dogs snarling at a squirrel that's come too close. So Jakob hangs back until Wieland takes a last bite from the hock he's holding and leans against the counter with grease hardening his whiskers.

Peering into the sink to see what's left, Jakob picks up the hock that Wieland had been chewing and tears into it, aware that a ritual connecting his blood to Wieland's is now underway. With each bite, he thinks, I'm swallowing not just the flesh of this pig, but also that of the master, drawing his essence into mine, swallowing what he's swallowed, mixing what makes him him with what makes me me, until we're both some third thing.

Heredity is not, he thinks, merely a matter of what transpires in the moments leading up to one's conception. It is, like all things, an ongoing process, subject to constant renewal and revision, fraught with constant danger and opportunity.

"So that was Tobin," Wieland says. At first, Jakob thinks he means the meat, which sets him to wondering what he'd do if it were. Probably nothing, he decides. He takes another bite, momentarily unsure what, or who, he's eating.

"And you know Greta already, so there's no one else for you to meet. Except me, of course." He grins and swigs from his bottle. "But for that, you'll have to wait."

Jakob digs into the sinew around the innermost part of the bone and tries to grasp what the old man's saying. At some point, he knows, I'll have to find out what I'm doing up here, why I came and why he's letting me stay, but not tonight, and maybe not for many nights to come. As he finishes what's on the bone and drops it back in the sink with a pleasing clack, he tries to decide whether, if given the choice, he'd choose to find out right now. Am I eager to get on with it, so as to move past the boredom I'll otherwise have to endure, or would I rather put it off as long as possible?

It all depends on what it is, he answers, and then he looks up to see Wieland staring at him so intently that he's certain the old man just read his thoughts.

If you know the answer, tell me, he urges in Wieland's direction, but the old man just keeps staring, grease beginning to drip from his chin onto his collar, mingling with his chest hair as a fresh snow falls just outside the window.

Jakob Sees His Mother

Late that night, Jakob curls on the couch with his toe in his mouth, about to summon the Blood Clot even though she's probably asleep, when a light through the window diverts his attention. He knows what it is, and yet something compels him to go over and investigate anyway. His body feels outside of his control, like he's elsewhere in the room, watching a frail boy-body obey the sophisticated impulses of a hidden master. Perhaps I'm sleepwalking again, he thinks, as his feet slide into his shoes and his shoes lead the rest of him through the door and into the fresh snow, black in the foreground, neon green and yellow and orange further back.

Beyond the spiders, which quiver as he walks between their legs, he sees his mother fretting over the generator that powers the neon gravestones. With trembling fingers, she pulls out the dead batteries, stuffs them in her bag, and removes fresh ones from a plastic case, stuffing them into the same hole the dead ones emerged from. The neon flickers off and on as she works, different quadrants of the cemetery coming in and out of view depending on which batteries are living. Sometimes the lights of a particular quadrant come on to reveal a gathering of ghostly figures on the peripheries, other mourners, wrapped in dark garments, unless, Jakob considers, they're actually the dead people that are being mourned... but then who's come to mourn them? The math doesn't quite work out.

That quadrant goes dark before he can consider the question any further, leaving him alone and unable to remember which direction his own grave lies in, let alone those of his mother and father. Beginning to panic, he runs toward the only light he can see, that of his mother's nightgown, emanating its own inner glow.

When he reaches it, he buries his head in her soft belly as her arms rise up to envelop him in a cold but firm embrace, and there they remain, as still as the gravestones, for as long as Jakob can resist speaking.

A mini-lifetime passes. Jakob imagines his mother and himself as two battery-powered sentries guarding the cemetery, watching the comings and goings of the corpses and the mourners, who, little by little, grow indistinguishable, until they too freeze in place.

When this vision grows too bleak to bear, he pulls

his lips off the skin around her belly button and asks, "How's dad?"

Of all the things he might have asked, it shocks him to hear that this is what he chose, but it's too late to retract it now. The words are already out there, crystallizing in the frosty air.

His mother steps back and looks down, still not quite seeing him, but she registers the question and responds in a voice that sounds just enough like hers to convince Jakob that it must be, and just enough like someone or something else's to make him doubt this same conviction.

"Your father is still sick," she says. "He is still lying on the couches and cushions of the house, surrounded by his maps and charts, desperate for the crowning vision that will not come. He knows better than to rush the Demiurge, yet it would be clear to anyone who could see him, were he willing to be seen by anyone but me, that he is not well. His patience is closer to its end than I've ever seen it before."

She stops abruptly. Jakob considers stopping too and backing away from her until he's reached the door of Wieland's cabin, but the loneliness of the instant after that—the instant of opening the door and letting himself back into the cold room where he cannot sleep—is so overpowering that he sniffles, wipes his nose on his wrist, and asks, "And what about me? Does he miss me?"

She takes a step back and looks at him more closely, a glint of unguarded recognition playing across her face. "Does he miss you? Jakob, he doesn't even register that you're gone. He's replaced you with the doll he made in the garage, which he insists is the real you, while the doll that used to be in the garage was, as he puts it, 'lost in an unfortunate mishap in the night.'"

She pauses again, but then continues without prompting. "I am to educate this doll every morning, and feed it every evening. That it eats little is cause for some but not, in the grand scheme of things, very much concern. Aside from this, all is as normal. And there are times, I'll admit, when I too am no longer certain which Jakob is which. Who's to say I'm not talking to the replacement boy now, with my real son safe in his bed in the town below? If you insist I'm wrong, I'll know you're lying."

She looks past him, addressing the flickering graves rather than the boy still clutching her waist. "Perhaps, I find myself thinking these days, what my husband says is correct, as it has so often proven to be in the past. He may be cruel, but his gift is genuine. The things that only he can see are real. So if he says that the boy at our dinner table is our beloved son, and the boy who's vanished is nothing but a garage-made doll, then who am I to argue?"

She may well have continued speaking after this, but Jakob breaks away, peeling her arms off his torso like they've become two thorny vines. He runs across the neon expanse toward the spiders, desperate to reenter their embrace, aware now that the world contains many things worse than this.

When he passes back through the door that only a moment ago he'd dreaded returning to, he sits down on the couch, nestled among springs that tickle his anus. He's so shaken that he tries to summon the Blood Clot again, but finds his toe frozen solid. He bites as hard as he can, but only his teeth suffer.

Thus commence many long hours of waiting, the dawn seeming to toy with him, always about to come and yet always still just over the horizon, in the sky behind the sky, rising in all its glory over the New Jerusalem.

Jakob's First Dream of His Other Life

As these stubborn pre-dawn hours hover in place, Jakob ruminates on the question of whether the woman he saw in the cemetery really was his mother. If she was, he decides, then she's turned against me, trying to sell me a lie because my father can't accept that I'm gone. He twists on the couch, licking his aching teeth and swallowing the spit. And if she isn't, then an even weirder game is afoot, because she looked and sounded close enough to convince me.

The near-circularity of this logic makes him laugh, but it's a short-lived laugh, since his next thought is, What if all my uncertainty is the uncertainty of a doll-boy, built to resemble the Jakob it only thinks it is?

This becomes impossible to discount as soon as it occurs to him. It disturbs his rest even more, though he tries to reify it into an image of a sculpture he could set about making now, rather than continuing to think in a circle which, he knows, will never end up anywhere other than where it began. He writhes, wedged between waking and dreaming, his head full of thoughts that may or may not be human. Thoughts of shocking animus toward his mother, in which she's become the Bad Witch, drifting upward from the town to poison the pristine garden in which he might otherwise have spent the rest of his life, intertwine with thoughts of the paradise he abandoned in his family home below, until he finds himself swimming through a thick, hot murk, away from Wieland's cabin and down toward the glimmering beacon of the town, the only place where, he now believes, it is still possible to be a real boy.

"I must, at all costs, escape the Wilderness," he tells himself, unable to discern whether he's dreaming, "and reenter the life in which I was a son to two parents in a house on a street in a town, the life I heedlessly tried to abandon because..."

But he can no longer remember why he tried to abandon it. There's nothing to do but swim, down, down, down, through the murk, which seems to be both time and space at once, such that he's swimming through the physical embodiment of his own lifespan, moving across the border between old man and little boy, fighting to take his place at the breakfast table before his lungs give out.

He feels his chest vibrate as the pressure of the murk increases and he pushes past floating houses, animals, cars, and even the aged faces of the Boys' Boys, using up all the force his system can muster to break through the roof of his house and fight his way down from the kitchen ceiling and into his seat, empty for all these weeks or months, or, worse, occupied by an imposter.

Jakob sits behind his bowl of Wheaties and Training Mug of coffee now, panting like he's been reborn. The snake in the wall slithers by, encircling the kitchen, suspicious at this apparent setback in Jakob's progress toward the Art World.

His mother and father gleam at him. They both look well rested and ready to take on the day. A mood of peace and prosperity hangs over the table in the orange morning light, and, for the time being, Jakob is content simply to breathe, after his long, frightening descent.

The memory of the cabin recedes the way even the worst dreams recede in the morning, and he looks into his parents' faces with nothing but gratitude for the existence they've granted him.

"Today," his father says, with a genuine good cheer that Jakob's never seen before, "I will finish what I have been laboring over so long, and then, in honor of the Sabbath, I will unveil it to the family, so that we might all be unified in our appreciation of the sublime fruition that I alone have wrought."

His mother takes a sip of coffee, then adds, her voice overflowing with pride, "Which means, Jakob, that today your studies will conclude. Today you graduate. Congratulations! You have worked long and hard to assimilate the perspective that is now second nature to you, and which will enable you to occupy this town, and, by extension, the world, as a knowing subject, rather than a dweller of the fog, as the vast majority of all people are, and will always be. You are now old enough to see the eternal mythic structure inside all ephemera, the bones and muscle that are hidden, in this temporal world, by so much fat and skin."

Jakob tries to smile and feel as good as he knows he ought to on this momentous occasion, but as soon as the words *fat* and *skin* come out of her mouth, the smell of Tobin's pig begins to fill the kitchen. He looks over and sees that the window has flown open, and he starts to shake as it occurs him that the smell must have forced it upward. He looks back at his parents and sees their smiles straining higher and higher up their faces, the edges of their lips almost touching their eyes, until the skin starts to pucker and peel, and the gnashing gears behind slice through.

Gagging, Jakob tries to suck shallow breaths of the porky air through his mouth as he looks away from the two parent-things and toward the walls, which are now shaking like an earthquake's about to hit. At first he thinks it must be the snake getting riled up from the commotion, but then the wall directly across from him buckles and leans almost horizontally outward.

It hovers like this for a moment, like a still photograph.

Then it cracks and sends up an angelic puff of plaster, out of which walks Wieland, three or four times his normal size, so tall his head is squashed flat against the kitchen ceiling. He looks down at Jakob, winks, and picks up the three bowls of Wheaties, stacking them in the sink. Then all the mirth leaves his face as he picks up the two parent-things, crushes them together, and stuffs them in the kitchen trash, their gears biting through the plastic bag.

When this is completed, he tears down the kitchen's other walls and then, out of the pile of sheetrock, wood, and wiring, hastily assembles a new room.

As the plaster dust settles and the cold and dimness filter back in, Jakob yawns, rubs his eyes, and recognizes the new space as Wieland's cabin where, for a moment, he feels he's arrived for the very first time.

"**Hello**? Anybody home?" Wieland, human-sized again in his open bathrobe, snaps the fingers of one hand in Jakob's face. With the other, he gnaws on a hock of pig, biting off more before swallowing what's in his mouth. "Up here," he mutters around the meat, "we don't usually go in for what the tax-man calls *breakfast*. We tend to eat what's around." He gestures with his bone toward the kitchen.

Jakob nods. Though he has no intention of eating any of Tobin's pig just now, he gets off the sweat-damp couch and shuffles to the kitchen, his mind filled with a vision of the entire town beneath a thick, hot murk. As he pees in the cold bathroom beside the open door to the basement, he recognizes, with a mixture of gratitude and trepidation, that a glimmer of his next project has just been revealed.

The Sunken
Town

Later that day, once Jakob's accepted that the basement is now open to him—Wieland seems to have smashed this boundary along with the walls in last night's dream—the question of getting back to work can no longer be postponed.

Determined to face it, he walks down the stairs, back into the forest of mannequins that so frightened him on his first visit, and clears a space on one of the disused workbenches. Wieland, hunched over a diorama on the other side of the basement, his bottle of clear liquor beside him, neither condones nor forbids the intrusion as Jakob gathers knives, pens, rulers, putty, cellophane, and other materials whose names he doesn't know, and assembles them on his workbench where, for the first few days, he simply sits and thinks.

He thinks about time passing, how it seems to be speeding up, as it always does once the initial phase of adjustment to a new house has worn off, and that house has become folded into his ever-evolving definition of the word *house* itself. Now, he accepts, slumped over the workbench and staring at the materials arrayed before him, my presence here is as well established as my presence anywhere. There's no denying that it's where I happen to be, and thus where I belong.

Still, the dream of his return to the house below lingers, and Jakob starts to picture time's accelerated pace as a form of ice melting, the winter at last giving way to spring.

He almost never goes outside, for fear of meeting his mother in the cemetery again, but he stands on the porch in the early mornings before descending to what is now his day's work in the basement, and he listens to the snow melt and pictures it rushing across the clearing and off the mountain, first in trickles, then in streams, then in an overwhelming torrent, flooding the entire town below.

Or, no, he decides, back at the workbench, not just flooding the town, but making a flooded town... birthing *The Sunken Town* out of nothing.

A town built by the very same forces that flooded it.

Suddenly giddy, he begins to stuff blue plastic into a terrarium he found beneath a pile of gamey turtle shells at the back of the basement. A town that is sealed off from the rest of the world, he explains while he works, so that everyone who lives in it lives forever, but has no access to anyone but the same five or ten other people. A town where those five or ten people play every possible role, from kings and queens to rapists and lunatics. Sometimes they play many roles at once, because there are never enough people to divide the roles among, and because there's no one to decide how many roles a person can play.

He grins and sweats as the days in the basement pile up, each bleeding into the next, exhaustion and exhilaration combining under his skin to egg him on as he hammers *The Sunken Town* into being. At night, he lolls on the couch and drifts back to the photographs of a town at the bottom of a reservoir from a book his mother showed him when he was little, and he tries to imagine the loneliness of living there. Half-asleep, he pictures the residents of the sunken town with gills and fishy puckering mouths, and then he pictures himself and his mother and father in this state, as he swims back through memory to the breakfast table, again with his Wheaties and Training Mug of coffee, but now struggling to stay grounded on the floor, fighting against the water, which has filled the kitchen that Wieland destroyed, and wants to push him and his mother and father up against the ceiling, like dead goldfish in a tank.

He carves fish-people from blocks of soap that he took from under the bathroom sink, and he sews clumps of his own hair into their slick white heads. He chisels out their teeth with the sharp point of an Xacto knife, which he also uses to cut their gills straight and deep, covering their mouths and looking away as he makes the incision. Then he cuts his pinky and, tuning out the screams of the Blood Clot, smears the gills with blood to prove the fish-people are still alive.

When he's finished five of them, he places three around a table made of wires and tinfoil, and the other two just outside, peering in through the windows, like extras in the wings, waiting to be called onstage. He fills the remainder of the terrarium with other, empty houses made of more wire and foil, arranged along winding streets of glued-down toothpicks that intersect at odd angles, all of it under a mix of blue cellophane and actual water, which he brings down from the bathroom sink in a red bucket. Then he brings the entire *Sunken Town* upstairs and places it behind the sink in the kitchen, hoping his mother will see it in the window when she comes up to the cemetery, like a menorah in the deep gloom of a Polish winter night.

Stepping back to regard his work at the end of the long but fast period during which he was consumed by it, Jakob hears his father's voice rumbling to life in his head. "The memory of the life we once lived," the voice begins, slipping easily into the old sermon cadence, "is coterminous with the life we dream of one day living. The New Jerusalem is thus, at one and the same time, always both the unremembered town of our birth, and the as-yet-un-glimpsed town to which we must return if we hope ever to be delivered from exile."

This is all to be expected, but what happens next is not, even if it should have been: his father's voice modulates into his own, even more precisely than it did at Traitor Joe's. "And the artwork known as *The Sunken Town*," that voice continues, "is my so-far greatest approximation of how the New Jerusalem, if it could take on physical form outside its place of privilege in my heart, would look. If the simultaneous yearning to return to the deep past and to discover the far future could be rendered using physical materials, then I have just now rendered it as well as I possibly can, given the limited capacity of the human form I currently occupy."

Returning from a vision of the dinner table at which his father is still lecturing, Jakob looks up to see Wieland sitting across from him at another version of that table, grinding the heel of his spoon into the edge of a plate that houses a greying pile of Tobin's pork. "Look alive, Bub," he says. "Time to clean this sty up. Greta's coming tomorrow morning and let's just say, if she knew how we really lived up here, we'd never see her again!"

Greta's Visit

The atmosphere in the cabin as they clean is both solemn and celebratory. Wieland scrapes the pig grease off the walls and the ceiling, collecting it on a tray where, he gloats, "I'll put it to good use later on."

Jakob trails behind him, collecting crumbs and stray hairs and heavy pieces of dust, all of which he too gathers in a bag for later use. There's something very pleasurable about the feeling of making the cabin appear emptier and less lived in while, in reality, preserving all of its shameful secrets, making sure nothing goes to waste. Like the Demiurge sweeping through Ragtown, Jakob muses, as he helps Wieland pull plates of congealed bones from the fridge and stuff them into a scented trashbag, we're repackaging the detritus of the universe without creating or destroying a single atom.

Though Wieland never stops working, and never

speaks other than to bark, "Scour the drying tray," Jakob starts to feel a rare camaraderie growing between them, like they're each equally invested in Greta's visit, two bachelor brothers preparing for the return of their long-lost sister. When Wieland turns on a radio that leaks rhythmic static into the room, Jakob feels like dancing.

This dynamic develops throughout the night, which is shorter and milder than the nights have been until now, confirming Jakob's suspicion that spring is nearly here.

He drags bag after bag of gathered material to the yard, stacking them against the smoker, which has been cold since Tobin's last visit.

Tobin's last visit?

Now that he thinks about it, it occurs to him that Tobin has come more than once, and thus his image of Tobin stabbing the pig while he and Wieland watch from the porch is actually a composite. Vivid though it is, Jakob realizes, forcing his eyes to remain on the smoker lest they wander toward the clearing where, no doubt, his mother is fussing over her graves, Tobin with his flying cleaver isn't a single image at all. It's a film I've blended together to give myself the sense of continuity when, in reality, time has been chopped and spliced in ways beyond my comprehending.

As soon as he thinks this, the night itself begins to fracture; images of the cabin peel off from one another and disperse through the woods, like the Demiurge is toying with him, providing a literal example of the very phenomenon he'd been musing on theoretically. Either that, he thinks, or I just dozed off against the smoker again. Maybe it's a longstanding habit of mine. He shivers, wipes his eyes, and lets the projector sputter to a halt as he makes his way, back inside a single image now, around the cabin to the front door, where he sees a white-clad woman limping toward him.

Everything except his heart freezes as he watches her come closer, carrying a picnic basket in one hand and a bottle of wine in the other. His terror at his mother's invasion of his sanctum here with Wieland is so absolute that Greta has to say, "Why, hello, Jakob, nice to see you again," twice, verbatim, before he realizes that it isn't her.

Soon, he's sitting at the breakfast table with Wieland and Greta, coffee in a French press between them, a basket of fresh pastries and jam beside it, and his lips are pulsating with the effort to keep from laughing at how similar this all feels to his breakfasts in the sunken town below. He wants to laugh because it's funny, but also for another reason, one he can't quite name. He looks from the old man to the old woman to himself, imagining he can see all three from an objective distance, and tries to determine what's tainting the obvious levity of the overlap. He watches the old people's mouths move as Greta shares gossip about the townspeople, referring to everyone by first names like "Kate" and "Scott," so there's no possibility of Jakob guessing who she means, while Wieland, his voice smoother and dryer than before, says, "Things are coming along quite nicely up here. Day by day, I'm nearing the finish line. Whenever I get a moment to think," he flashes a glance at Jakob here, not quite accusatory but not quite amicable either, "I make the most of it, as you know I always do."

All this time, *The Sunken Town* sits on the windowsill where Jakob placed it last night. The more he studies it, the more he comes to understand the source of the dark hilarity hanging over the old people: their mouths and eyes and ears, posed as they are up here, around a simulacrum of the breakfast table from the house below, make them look like drowned people who've swum up to the surface, soft and bloated, so that age and swimming-distance are one and the same phenomenon. Taking a warm croissant from the basket and slathering it with apricot jam, he thinks, They look awful, as must I, as must this whole house, which could well be—why not extend the thought to its ultimate conclusion?—a waterlogged version of my house below, turned drafty and weird after floating so long in the murk.

He looks at his sculpture, then back at Greta and Wieland, who've gone silent behind cups of dreggy coffee and piles of pastry flakes. This silence starts amicably, but soon it starts to weigh. As the two of them rub their hands over each other's wrists and forearms, looking eagerly at one another and a little resentfully at Jakob, he gets the hint that it's time for him to leave.

Fearful of being on his own while the two of them are off together, he looks down into his coffee and does all he can to pretend he hasn't received the message they're trying to send.

Another, increasingly testy silence ensues.

It expands until Greta clears her throat and says, very gently, "Look, Jakob, could you, well…"

"Beat it!" Wieland interrupts, his accent thickening. "Go away for a while, you hear?"

Greta blushes, but she doesn't chide him, nor does she try to finish what she'd started saying before. She simply gets up from the table with a smile, holding Wieland's right hand in both of hers. They go behind the kitchen and into Wieland's bedroom, where Jakob's never been, leaving him alone in the midmorning quiet.

He pours more coffee, declaring his training regimen complete, and sits alone at the table, trying not to breathe, as if some predatory force were waiting to pounce at the first sign of life. But when Greta moans loudly from the closed room, he moans too and jumps up from the table, knocking his chair over in his haste to get onto his belly on the couch and summon the Blood Clot from his big toe.

He bites as hard as he can into the skin, harder than necessary, and comes away with a mouthful of scabby flesh as the blood leaks out into a glass of water he must've brought with him from the kitchen. He watches her take form as the liquid goes cloudy, then comes to a pale orange equilibrium.

Another moan issues from the back room as Jakob leans over the glass and whispers, "Hello, sister. I'm sorry it's been so long since we..."

"Shh," she says. "I know why you summoned me this time. Let's not put it off with chitchat. We'll both lose our nerve if we do."

Jakob tries to stall, but, as soon as she says it, he knows she's right. She always is.

"C'mon, help me onto the couch," she whispers from her glass, and, though his hands are shaking, he does. He pulls her up to his level and dumps her onto the cushion, where she spreads out luxuriously, not at all shy.

"Are you..." Jakob can't quite fathom the word.

"Naked?" She laughs. "Yes. Now you get naked too."

Jakob complies, wincing as he pulls his skinned toe through his pants. He shivers, though he knows it's springtime now, and huddles up beside her, hoping she'll tell him what to do. He feels frantic with how long he's waited for this, frightened by his own ability to deny himself what he needs, even though, at the same time, he wishes he could deny it a little longer.

"Close your eyes," she whispers.

When he does, she grabs his hand and guides it roughly down his front, stopping right on top of the thirteen hairs that have recently sprouted an inch below his belly-button. "You're going to feel a little squeeze," she says, her voice like a nurse's in his head, and he doesn't protest as she wraps her fingers around his penis.

A moan fills the room, and Jakob loses several seconds trying to tell whether it was his sister's, Greta's, or his own. By the time he's allowed this question to end in a stalemate, a series of quickening sensations are passing through him that he's never felt before, though they feel so instinctually familiar he can't be sure this is true. He lets them continue and compound, the Blood Clot guiding him into her body now, which squeezes his penis even more tightly and warmly than his hand had a moment ago.

Now both he and she moan, and he feels something pulling on the skin in a way that almost hurts, though not quite, and then he feels something rumbling inside him, like vomit but lower down, closer to pee, something she's coaxing up, perhaps even summoning for the first time, a liquid self within him, drawing energy inward from the stars, and then he finds he's unable to think of anything except a glass milk bottle that's been dropped onto a hardwood floor.

As it shatters and releases its contents, he passes out, determined to lie where he is for as long as he can.

He awakens to Wieland sniggering while Greta stands silently beside him.

"Looks like you're playing both parts," Wieland says, pointing to the mixed red and white puddle that Jakob has left on the cushion.

Greta elbows the old man and says, "Are you alright, Jakob? You're bleeding."

Jakob looks down at his toe, but he senses that this isn't where she means. Instead of checking anyplace else on his body, or his sister's, he nods, though he can feel that something is indeed broken. "I always knew this would happen one day," he mutters.

When no one responds, he seizes the opportunity to move the conversation forward, skipping over what he'd feared was going to be a long, rocky middle. "I made something," he announces. "It's in the kitchen. My next piece. Will you…"

He can't finish the sentence. The hubris of asking Greta to take it all the way down the mountain and put it in the Town Museum, in place of Wieland's work, though perfectly justified in his head, sticks in his throat.

Fortunately, she doesn't make him say it. She smiles, nods, and pulls a fresh ten-dollar bill from her purse. "Wilhelm has already shown it to me. We're both very impressed, Jakob. It's rare that a young person in this world shows promise, and rarer still that such a young person turns up in our little town."

She stops, though she'd looked like she was going to say more. She hands Jakob his payment, smiles again, and walks into the kitchen. Returning with *The Sunken Town* wobbling in her arms, she leaves through the front door, saying only, "I'll tell you how it's received next time I'm up here. I don't suppose you're coming down anytime soon?"

Jakob looks to Wieland before answering with an emphatic shake of his head. No, he thinks, as Greta leaves, much as I might wish to return home, I'm not yet sufficiently changed to make such a thing possible.

The Night Crusher Returns

That night Jakob and Wieland sit at the dinner table, barely speaking, as the cabin falls back into disorder. The leftover meat is nearly gone, which means that Tobin must be riding a new pig up the mountain, spurring it on with the knife he will use to gut it. This too would make a great sculpture. He pictures it with a revolving motor in its base, bringing Tobin up the mountain on his pig just as Greta walks down with *The Sunken Town* in her arms, and vice versa, in endless repetition. *The Two Poles of Wieland's Life* he names it, as if it already existed, which perhaps, given that he can picture it so clearly, it does. In some realm just beyond the physical, it's already there. Maybe that's all that art is, Jakob thinks. The brute dragging of heavy objects from the world in which they already exist into the world in which strangers, ignorant of their origins, can admire them in comfort.

Wieland cuts through a particularly tough bone and scrapes his plate, bringing Jakob back to the scene in front of him.

"Sorry," he mutters, though he's not quite sure what for.

Wieland eyes him. "Big day today. You look like a changed man." His smile pools in a valley between kindness and cruelty.

Jakob shivers and pushes the leavings on his plate into the center of the table.

"It's officially spring now," Wieland continues, leaving his smile on his face. "I can see your shell starting to crack and a new birdlike part of you emerging. That's good. Summer up here gets heady. You up for it?"

Jakob considers and rejects several responses. He looks at the pile of meat leavings in the center of the table and pictures it as a one-eighteenth scale model of the pile of unspoken things that has grown between him and Wieland. And what are these things? he wonders. Why are you letting me stay here? What are you working on? What do you want from me? Do you believe in my work? If not, am I free to go?

He opens his mouth, curious to see if these questions will pour out unbidden, but, for now, they stay wadded in his throat.

A moment later, Wieland gets up, wiping his fingers on the edge of the table, and walks away from his bones and muscle scraps, taking pride in the mess now that Greta's visit has been accomplished. He goes to the windowsill and retrieves the clear liquor, pouring some into a glass, which he then brings back to Jakob, keeping the bottle, as usual, for himself.

"Seeing as now you're a man," he gloats, "drink a full one with me. Cheers." He clinks the bottle against Jakob's glass and takes a long swig, motioning for Jakob to do likewise.

As the burning sour grain falls down into him, Jakob thinks back on the conversation he had with his father on the rock behind their house, when they'd discussed puberty. He said we'd both go through it together, he remembers, and then he wonders if this moment, here with Wieland, both of them sweaty for almost the same reason, is proof that his father's pronouncement was true. But if Wieland's my father, Jakob thinks, already giddy with what he's swallowed, then that means I'm my father too, because he's my father's father, my grandfather, so the generations have moved a click back in time, which means that...

Here his thinking blurs and falls into incoherence, taking his body with it. He slams to the floor and happily fades out.

When he comes to, it's deep in the night, though the kitchen lights are still on. His head is squashed sideways against the floor and no amount of wishing allows him to move it.

"That's right," the Night Crusher says. "I'm back. You didn't think I was gone for good, did you?"

Jakob makes no effort to nod in either assent or dissent, knowing it'll be impossible either way. He doesn't even try to answer the question in his head. All he thinks is, The Night Crusher was gone for awhile, probably still crushing the version of me that stayed below, in the old bed, and now he's up here, leaving that other me alone for the time being. Jakob envies the version of himself down there, going through the motions of school and dinner and bed and breakfast and school again, probably still wandering through Ragtown as a ghost, passing right through the Boys' Boys' frightened gaze. He envies that boy, but he also pities him, knowing full well that the real work is getting done up here.

The Night Crusher pushes Jakob's head harder into the kitchen floor, nearly drilling it through to the basement, where he can see his workbench, until recently occupied by *The Sunken Town*, and now conspicuously empty. He enjoins the Night Crusher to push him harder still, to force his vision to merge with that of the world below. The Night Crusher obliges, proving something that Jakob had only just begun to suspect: that the tables have turned and now he directs the monster's behavior, not vice versa.

After all, he thinks, I had sex today. Everything's different now.

Emboldened, he orders the Night Crusher to position him at the workbench and then, once this order has likewise been carried out, to crush the two houses together so as to alleviate the pain of living stretched between them.

The Night Crusher groans but nevertheless obliges, reaching his furry arms out all the way across the clearing and down to the town below, scooping up the old house and crushing it into the cabin, until the two spaces become one and Jakob finds himself behind a workbench that is now most definitely his, neither Wieland's nor his father's any longer.

"Thank you," he says to the Night Crusher, who now stands behind him in the obedient pose of a studio assistant. He feels his body aging as he leans over the bench, his belly thickening with decades' worth of fries and milkshakes, the skin on his forehead pulling tight and spackling with liver spots, the skin around his throat sagging and folding in on itself. The Night Crusher, still behind him after all these years, is older and grayer too, and perhaps a little weaker, though still more than able to break up blocks of brass, cement, and plaster whenever an old sculpture needs to be revised.

Jakob wanders the house as this version of himself, reminiscing on his first days here, back when his father was still convinced the New Jerusalem was within reach, and his mother taught him every day at the breakfast table that only the Visionary Jews stood a chance of living lives free of self-deception and bad faith.

He walks those same halls now, haunted by the feeling that he too has ended up in exile, far from home, even though he hasn't gone anywhere, hasn't once left town. He feels like a prisoner, either of the house or his dream of the house, he's no longer sure which, and even though he can tell that his prison sentence is self-imposed—that he could have left long ago and never come back, had he chosen to; he could've gone to New York and lived like Andy Warhol, had he chosen to—this does little to ease the painful boredom of having been cooped up here so long, though he knows it was the only way to flesh out the magnificent and unholy body of work he will now leave behind. Like a monk to Christ, this was the commitment I had to make to save my soul, he thinks.

His neck starts to hurt as he wavers between states, part of him crushed on the floor of Wieland's cabin, part of him wandering what used to be his parents' house, and he wants to tell the Night Crusher to let him up, that enough's enough, but he can't summon the will to do so.

"So then let me ask you," the Night Crusher whispers, breath hot and foul with blood he must've drunk on his way up here, "who's really controlling whom? If you want me to let you up, just give the order and I will."

Nothing happens. Jakob tries to picture himself

getting up, cutting his tether to the house below and his glimpse of his future self, letting the doll-boy take his place, or vice versa, but he can't summon the will to force this picture into reality. He can't be sure he wants to. So he just lies there, lips spread out on the floorboards, watching himself putter as an old man while the Night Crusher sits on his back and says, "That's what I thought, little fink."

Just let me black out a while longer, Jakob finally manages to wish and, satisfied that he's made his point, the Night Crusher obliges.

Wieland
Shows Jakob
The
Wilderness

"**Alright** princess, time for our stroll. It's a tradition here on the first day of spring, and who knows, at this point, how many more sweet first days I got left in my little candy-holster before the sour jellybean at the bottom turns up."

Wieland, wearing an overlarge windbreaker on top of his robe, makes a yanking gesture like he's pulling Jakob up on a string. Jakob half-jokingly responds by jolting to his feet and hitting his head on the side of the kitchen table.

In a daze, he accepts a mug of coffee and a stale

croissant, smashes his feet into his sneakers, and follows Wieland into the bright, mild spring morning. They skirt the blood from the last pig that Tobin slaughtered, creep under the spiders whose mandibles are dripping dew, and begin to cross the clearing, navigating around Jakob's mother's graves, their neon barely perceptible in the daylight.

Wieland regards them but says nothing, so Jakob doesn't either, though he can feel them emitting a charge, a headiness of recent or impending relevance. Soon, he can see, these graves are going to force me to reckon with them. He succeeds in shaking off the feeling that either he or Wieland is going to end up buried there, but the feeling remains, wasp-like, in the air near his head.

"Okay," Wieland says, once they've crossed the clearing and entered the woods on the far side, a zone that Jakob's never penetrated before, as if, until right now, it'd been a solid green wall. "Here begins of the Wilderness of Resurrected Myth." Waving his coffee mug violently enough to spill half of what's left in it, Wieland gestures at a bank of trees that, upon closer inspection, reveals itself to be half-natural and half-sculpted. The sculpted trees are not really trees, Jakob notices, but wooden totems of the same width and height as the trees beside them. As soon as he leans in to study the faces and phrases carved into their trunks, absentmindedly nibbling his croissant, Wieland interrupts by asking, "Do you want me to lead on as creator or discoverer? Because I can do either, but not both."

Jakob turns. "You made all these?" The answer is obvious, but the question still feels important to ask. We seem to be moving, he thinks, out of the Days of Assumption and into the Days of Explanation. He can tell that now would be a good time to start paying closer attention than he has so far, as if all of his schooling down below were dedicated to preparing him for exactly this.

He resolves to try. "Creator," he says, remembering that Wieland asked him a question.

Wieland nods. "Okay. Well, these totems you see here are the pillars of the New Jerusalem 2. I had to rebuild the universe from the ground up after some bad luck came to the first New Jerusalem, back in the 60s. Before your time, I'm guessing?" He laughs. "Anyway, my early work sparked something in people that I wasn't ready to take on, though I did a good job of pretending to be. So I tore down everything I'd built, except the spiders, which remain as reminders of the desperate, bloodthirsty thing that hunkers down low in people, just waiting for the chance to rear up. Never forget that, Jakob. People will die, and die gladly, to pursue even the slightest glimmer of a doorway out of this world," he gestures to the trees and the totems and the slices of sky filtering between them, "and into the world within. People—most people, anyway—know they live in bad faith. They know the things they sweat and fight and fret for aren't real, or if they are, then they're real only in the most trivial way possible. They know all this, but they force themselves to forget that they do. They shove the knowledge down as deep as it'll go, all the way to the bottom of their guts, where it festers and turns to the cancer that will eventually, mercifully, kill them. So when they get a glimmer, no matter how faint, of a way out of that world and into the one they know exists deep inside it, even if that glimpse is considerably narrower than a doorway—just a crack or a seam, a hairline fracture—it's enough to send them into a murderous frenzy, like refugees at a sweltering African port trampling one another to board the last boat to Gibraltar. This is what happened in the first New Jerusalem, so I built another. In time, if you can bear the calling, you'll build a third."

Wieland coughs and wheezes, leaning against one of his totems, which creaks in sympathy. One of its simian faces leers down at Jakob, like it knows something he never will, but he leers back confidently, trying to mask how unsure he feels about the threshold he now seems to be approaching.

But the threshold to what?

He decides to let this question simmer, and hurries to catch up with Wieland, who's now deeper in the forest, surrounded by more totems, as well as human and animal figures in various poses of combat and conversation.

"The Wilderness," he continues, once Jakob's caught up with him, "is a crucial location in the life of an artist. Never forget this, nor allow yourself to doubt that it's true. All artists, including the very greatest, like me, spend years in the Wilderness. Unsure of the way forward, doubting the ground they've covered already, roiling in the wasteland between private vision and public renown. The Wilderness is at once a state of mind and a very real location."

Here Wieland waves his coffee mug in a wide circle, encompassing everything they can see. His voice grows clearer and faster, like these words have been stored up all winter and are now, finally, flowing free. "Never worry about how long you've spent in the Wilderness, nor hesitate to return when you feel the need. And one more thing, which is the most important: if you refuse to visit the Wilderness, it will visit you. It will take up residence in your heart and colonize your house and then you will be in it everywhere, for all time. It will sleep in your bed with you, and in time it will sleep in your bed *as* you. You will find that everything you thought of as yourself is gone. By refusing to come here when the need arises, you will have succeeded only in inviting it to come to you. And the *it*, the need, is a thing, Jakob. It's a living entity, a monster."

Jakob thinks of the Night Crusher, but says nothing, remembering that he's resolved to pay closer attention to the scene unfolding outside his head. Picturing the spiral of self-consciousness as a whirlpool on the forest floor, he steps gingerly around it to keep pace with Wieland.

"So, at the first sign of the Wilderness'

approach—and you'll know it's coming when you feel your vision of art's transcendent purpose begin to waver like a TV set losing its signal—come here without delay. Right here. Spend as long as you need to. Here, in the heart of the Wilderness, is a cabin where I've often sequestered myself when the need arose to spend some time alone, cementing myself back into the heart of the cosmos, the seat of power from which I conjured the New Jerusalem and its sequel into being, and etched my name for all time into the book of world history."

They come to a cabin that looks precisely like the one they left behind. An exact replica. Jakob swallows, determined not to let his fear shine through, though he can smell it in his sweat as Wieland shoulders the door open to reveal the same couch he lost his virginity on yesterday afternoon.

"This piece is called *The Fraught Homecoming*. The return that is not a return. Sorry I didn't make a replica of you," Wieland says, laughing as he leads the way into the kitchen, where a wooden man in a bathrobe slumps over the table, his wooden fingers wrapped around a bottle of clear liquor. "I didn't exactly, heh-heh, expect company!"

He laughs again, but it devolves into a coughing fit as confusion spreads across his face. For a moment, he looks as dizzy and disoriented as Jakob feels, and the distance between them, the certainty that they're two people and not one, collapses. Jakob wavers in the replica kitchen, uncertain now whether they've gone anywhere at all.

He grabs one of the seats and falls awkwardly into it, taking his place at the table across from the wooden Wieland, and feels himself—the transition is almost a cliché by now, he thinks, it's happened so often lately—becoming a wooden boy across from a wooden man, posed in the woods for curious visitors to discover centuries from now, as they pass by looking for a good place to picnic.

The reverie hovers here until Wieland's sharp fingers dig into Jakob's shoulders from behind, and he feels himself being pulled back to his feet. "It's bad to linger too long," Wieland says, leading the way through the back of the cabin and into the yard.

"I built this place as a counterpoint to the life I've led," he explains, as they wander through waist-high weeds, past male, female, and hermaphroditic sculptures in various stages of decay. It's unclear how much of the decay was part of the sculptures' original concept and how much is simply the effect of nature acting on exposed wood, though surely, Jakob thinks, that confusion *is* the concept. They leer back at him with horrible eaten-away grins, their mouths and nasal cavities and eye sockets full of moss, mushrooms, and, in the case of one particularly desiccated old woman, small blue eggs.

Wieland leans against one, his shoulders sinking into the rotten wood of its chest, and says, his breath still short, "These are all versions of what I would've become if I hadn't become famous. That's all it amounts to, Jakob. Do all you can to ensconce yourself in the Art World. Whatever it takes. Because without the Art World, we're nothing but lonely lunatics, wandering the edge of Creation with no one at all to care if we fall off. And believe me, I've spent my fair share of years wandering that edge. No one will ever know what I've suffered, the length and breadth of the valley of the shadow of death that I've walked through. There were many, many times when it seemed endless, when I believed I'd been abandoned for all time. There were even times—and I'm talking about decades here, not days or weeks—when I believed that any hope I'd ever had of finding my way into the Art World was nothing but the sadistic work of the devil, toying with me for sport. What I wouldn't have given to rip that devil out of my head and drown him in a sink full of bleach. But I couldn't. He kept whispering to me, egging me on, pushing me forward, saying, "Wilhelm, the New Jerusalem will only ever enter this world through you, you are its conduit, without you it will..." He trails off, eyes clouding over as a bubble of spit crests his lower lip.

Jakob stares at him, mesmerized.

"Now, where was I?" Wieland looks at the top of Jakob's head, as if afraid to make eye contact lest he fail to recognize the person he's addressing.

"Wandering the edge," Jakob says.

Wieland nods, clicking back into the mode he was

in before, though at a diminished pitch. "Right. The edge. Make no mistake, Jakob, everyone who wanders there without digging their heels into the fundament of serious work eventually falls off. And not because they fall, but because they jump."

As if to prove his point, Wieland wheezes and collapses, taking a rotten wooden version of himself down with him.

Jakob sits on a mossy, partially collapsed bench and regards the two-body pile, trying to decide how to feel about it. He knows enough about human beings to expect some emotional response to sooner or later emerge unbidden from his heart, but, for now, his system is overwhelmed by Wieland's invocation of the Art World. Is he actually famous? Jakob wonders. And if so, how should that make me feel about him as opposed to my father?

He sits and pulls up bunches of moss and squishes them in his fists as he tries to come to some inner consensus. But all he feels is split in half. He closes his eyes and pictures himself going about his business in the sunken town, living with his parents underwater, enduring his father's sermons and his mother's lessons, quietly making his drawings in his room as the family waits for the final prophetic dream to reveal the town they're meant to live in. The ultimate end of exile. At the same time, he pictures Greta installing *The Sunken Town* in the Town Museum and the hordes of stunned townspeople pouring in like maggots on a Bellmer. He remembers how he felt hiding in the back office during the opening of his *Burned Alive* show, and imagines that feeling multiplied by a thousand, or a hundred thousand. My true entrée into the Art World, he thinks, the snake's voice hissing in his head as if his skull were the walls of the house in the sunken town, and his brain the snake's now-aqueous habitat. New York, London, Tokyo, Parisssss. He pictures the old issues of *Frieze* and *Artforum* that he found under his parents' bed when he was ten, the forbidden images of Art Basel and Art Miami and the Hauser + Wirth Gallery in Los Angeles, the thrill he'd felt in his chest and his groin upon considering that perhaps the world represented in those magazines was real. And not just real, but accessible. Graven images pointing toward a higher transcendence than dreaming ever could. Fame as the soul's only reward for leaving the family, the town, all of it behind… and yet a reward worth trading it all for, if only he could be certain it were within reach.

Then he remembers his father's hands on the back of his neck, he remembers watching his own feet leave the carpeted floor like he was levitating on the power of the images alone, he remembers falling down the stairs onto his left arm, which bent outward like it'd grown a second elbow, and he remembers his mother holding him, sobbing in her arms, saying, "Shh, shh, shh, you're okay baby. You're okay. We'll fix this, just please stop crying. You don't want the bad people to hear you and come inside and take you away, now do you?"

He's back there now, in her arms, looking up at her trembling chin, accepting her reassurance because he's too scared not to, while, at the same time, aware that suspicion is taking root deep in his system. Suspicion that something isn't right, that the truth isn't being told. That her reassurance is nothing but a doubling-down on the primal lie whose unseating will come to be his life's work.

He's there, in her arms, and also here, in the Wilderness, studying that scene, considering how best to sculpt it, how best to dredge up and express the suffering he experienced so as to fashion it into a battering ram he can use to force his way into the Art World. Maybe it's all backward, he thinks, ruminating on Wieland's body with one eye while picturing his father with the other, maybe the Art World isn't hell but is rather the New Jerusalem itself. The only version of reality in which a person can be more than a block of rotting wood. The only container strong enough to hold the Genius that makes me who I am and not let it slop away like the stuff you flush the toilet to get rid of.

He shivers harder than before, ambition coursing through him, making him febrile. "If I saw the other version of myself right now, the one who fears the Art World and wishes at all costs to keep his hands from ever yielding a finished product," he declares, getting to his feet because he can no longer sit still, "I'd kill him with my bare hands, stuff his body with moss, and sell it to the Met."

He paces the yard, driven by these thoughts,

wondering if Wieland's dead. And if he is, he thinks, each time he passes the body, what then? Bury him, and return to the cabin myself? Carry him back down the mountain and present him to Greta as my next piece, his beard full of twigs and spiders?

This last thought sparks the possibility that Wieland is indeed his invention. Perhaps he was never alive, Jakob considers, peering at the body on the ground. Perhaps I sculpted him out of clay and wax and some vegetal skin-like material I synthesized at my workbench. As these thoughts gain speed and traction, he runs faster and faster around the yard, the snake's voice slithering up his spine, whispering, "What if you invented the whole town? The mountain, the cabin, your parents, your house, all of it? What if none of it is real outside of you? What if you've been the Demiurge all along? How are you going to take ownership of that and get the credit you deserve?"

"Stop it!" Jakob finally manages to shout, diving onto the moss and wriggling to free himself from the snake. He forces it off him, then lies on his back nestled beside Wieland, panting and watching the clouds drift until something like sleep comes over his exhausted body.

When the sun starts to set and a spring evening chill comes over the yard, Jakob stirs and gets to his feet before he's fully awake. As soon as he does, Wieland sits up, pulling wood pulp from his face like he's just clawed his way out of a soft coffin. Spitting, he holds out his hands. Jakob hesitates, afraid that he's about to be pulled down into the land of the dead, but when Wieland reaches out even further and groans, "C'mon, help me up," Jakob complies.

"Okay, hope you had a good time. Now let's get back to the real cabin before it's too dark to tell which is which," he says, setting out into the eerie twilight without checking if Jakob's behind him. "You play around with this stuff, you better not get mixed up."

They walk in silence through the groves of totems until they come to a clearing like the one that houses his mother's cemetery, but smaller, more enclosed. Or perhaps it's just as big, only much more crowded. On all sides, figures as tall as he is are posed in battle. It's too dark to make out their faces, but some appear to be dwarves, while others are children, naked from the waist down, their genitals elaborate bouquets of growths and depressions. They wield battle-axes and spears made of wood and irregular pieces of metal, like tin plates, while others defend themselves with strips of leather and even, in a few cases, the stems of long-rotten flowers.

Wieland caresses the lace frock of a female warrior near where he's standing. "*The Battle for the Soul of the New Jerusalem*," he sighs. "One of the bloodiest battles in history. A narrow victory for the forces of good," he leans in and kisses the girl's head, "but a victory nonetheless. Originally, my audience believed that I was commemorating the battle, as if it had already happened, in another time and place." He laughs. "Only slowly did they come to understand that this *is* the battle. It's happening right now, for all time, all around us. That, Jakob, is the secret of art."

He pauses, like he's about to say something else, but seems lost. He teeters, looks around, and leans hard on the warrior he'd been caressing a moment ago. Fearing that he's about to fall over again and strand them in the midst of this battle for the rest of the night, Jakob grabs his hand and says, "Let's go. You know the way?"

"Maybe we should've started the tour here," Wieland replies. "Maybe everything would've been different if I'd shown you this first. I'm sorry if, years from now, you come to believe that this mistake has doomed us both."

The Cemetery
in the Shadow
of Death

The way back is straight but not short. Jakob can't
believe they've walked so far. It seems so improbable
that he starts to wonder if some spatial break or loop
occurred, such that they're no longer traveling along
the same path they traveled this morning. Otherwise,
he thinks, though he wishes he didn't have to, we're
approaching the wrong cabin. Who knows how many
there are in the Wilderness?

He holds Wieland's hand and feels it tremble as they
process down the long aisle of the forest, in search of
home. At least an hour passes like this, totems and
trees growing interchangeable in the darkness, the air

overhead filling with bats and newly hatched insects, the night turning cold and windy.

Finally, a light begins to glimmer at the end of the long green-black aisle. As they approach, it glimmers red, orange, and yellow, shades of neon that Jakob can't help but recognize.

They're halfway across the clearing before it becomes apparent that not only is Jakob's mother present, but she isn't alone. Jakob has an instinct to hide, as if his mother and the people around her were dangerous, but Wieland is already skirting the back of the crowd, so Jakob has no choice but to follow.

He scurries along beside Wieland until they're interspersed among the ten or twelve people standing and listening to his mother, dressed in dark sweatshirts and spring jackets, some in boots, some in sneakers, all of them wavering nervously as their eyes flick from the glowing gravestones to his mother who is, as ever, clad only in her white nightgown. They look like reenactors of *The Battle for the Soul of the New Jerusalem*, just about to begin the main event.

"And so," she says, looking off into the distance, her hands resting on one of the gravestones, squeezing it so the neon flows away from her fingers, "here lie the futures that could've been. The lives we might have lived, had the wages of fate not intervened. Had certain other visions not come between us and those futures, the people now symbolically buried here would still be living and we," she gestures at the crowd, "would be buried in their place. We are all, in this sense, zombies, living out futures we never chose, going through the motions of lives that were, for various reasons, foisted upon us."

She falls silent, surveying the crowd. Her eyes stop for a moment on Jakob and Wieland in the background, but they don't linger. Though he knows it's possible that she didn't see them, Jakob can't help fearing that the truth is much darker. That she did see, but didn't recognize me. That she's no longer my mother, and perhaps never was. That we've peeled off from one another, into different worlds that just happen to share the same space, the way two different plays can share the same stage.

And if that's true, he thinks, then where did I come from? Who birthed me?

"But the good news," she continues, raising her voice over his confusion, "is that the bodies symbolically buried in these graves are not lost forever. The very same contingencies of fate that have kept us from these futures could one day reunite us with them. The dead can always rise again if the conditions are right. Perhaps one day," she tears up, "I will encounter the version of myself who's had a long and successful career as a postmodern sculptor at the highest levels of the Art World, the modern urban woman with pieces at LACMA and the Broad and the Whitney, and then the version of myself who stands before you tonight will be the buried one, and justice will at last be served."

She raises her arms and encourages the crowd to cheer along with her, honoring the possibility that they might all be reunited with their Lost Futures one day. "Together," the crowd begins to chant, "we are ready to exit this dishwater world and enter paradise on earth, born again as the selves we know we could still be, but who have been cruelly withheld from us for far too long!"

Jakob's mother, if that's who she is, nods and squeezes her graves harder, chanting along with the crowd until their words break down and turn to noise.

The mourners keen and moan and grab at the graves until Wieland breaks away from Jakob and walks into their midst. They go from hysterics to stunned silence when he appears in the yellow and orange glow. Jakob can only see their backs and, in some cases, the sides of their heads, but it's enough to tell that Wieland inspires a rare form of awe.

He remembers the Boys' Boys' story of the parents who brought their children to be sacrificed here in the 60s, and he wonders if these adults know about that too. Perhaps, he thinks, Wieland is a figure of death for them, a reaper they'd hoped never to cross paths with again. Most likely, they were children too back then. Perhaps it was their friends who were sacrificed.

With all the townspeople's eyes upon him, Wieland falls to his knees and begins to dig at the ground in front of one of the graves. He pulls up wet fistfuls of earth, throwing them at the crowd, until the glowing grave behind him tips over and he holds up a shrouded form about the size of a baby.

"It's only symbolic, it's only symbolic! It represents the new people we all hope to be reborn as!" Jakob's mother shrieks, but her voice strikes such a note of panic that Jakob doubts it's true. And even if the cemetery is symbolic, he thinks, what if Wieland brings it to life now, showing these poor people the living babies they allowed to be buried for the sake of their own possible rebirth? Maybe he really is a satanic magician, just like the Boys' Boys said. Maybe everything I've ever heard is true.

Before the scene resolves one way or the other, Jakob turns and runs across the rest of the clearing, past the spiders and Tobin's pig blood, and shoves his way into the cabin, swallowing, as best he can, the rising yet already redundant fear that this isn't the same one they left this morning.

He shoves the door shut and leans against it, trying to catch his breath, but the fear won't go back down. Perhaps you can never return to the same place you departed from, he considers. Like a game of Russian Roulette, the true cabin is lost among five blanks, spinning and spinning and spinning.

Or perhaps it only feels lost because it's the first time I've been here alone. The first time I've felt what it is to be in Wieland's cabin without Wieland. The first time—he stalks through the kitchen in search of the clear liquor—when I've felt the possibility that it's my cabin now, the setting for my adult life.

When he finds the bottle, he heads down to the

basement, keeping the lights off until he arrives at his workbench, where he turns on a single lamp, just enough to see his fingers by. The atmosphere surrounding the bench, as he takes a swig and tries to focus on the project at hand, feels suffused with death: either the death visited upon the world by Wieland—and might he be killing the people out at the cemetery right now, burying them in their own pretend graves?—or that of Wieland himself.

Either way, Jakob feels nothing but relief to discover the Night Crusher standing in the shadows behind him, solemn and alert and ready to get down to work.

The Adoration of
the Sunken Town

Jakob burrows deep into the basement, deeper than when he made the dummy that burned in Ragtown. As deep as a creature that was born down there and wants nothing more than to live out its life in the same humid darkness it emerged from. He burrows this deep in, and then he burrows deeper, hunching over the workbench with the Night Crusher behind him, pressing him downward, so far down it feels like he's falling through the mountain and back to the sunken town, through a chute inside the mountain itself.

Down here, as he begins to coax inner life out of plastic, cloth, and hair, he has a vision of the entire town as his head, all of its people crammed together like early Christians in a cave outside of Rome, worshipping *The Sunken Town*, which—he reminds himself, as if he might've forgotten already—Greta promised to set up in the Town Museum. He reaches into his pocket and fingers the money she gave him as proof that this wasn't a dream.

Once he's reassured himself, he returns to work. Reading the plaque on the wall in the Town Museum, he learns that his new piece is called *The Adoration of the Sunken Town*. In it, all the townspeople, reduced to five or six for the sake of the model, are gathered in a hollow space inside Jakob's skull, meaning, he realizes now, that he'll have to make another effigy of himself, this time partly decapitated.

After he promises the vision that he's willing to do this, the next facet of the work is revealed. He sees that all these shrunken people are clinging to the model town for dear life because without it there'd be nothing at all. There'd be only abyss, the black hole that Wieland seemed to open when he crossed the cemetery. A Wilderness without return. Only *The Sunken Town* stands between them and this fate. It's not the same as the search for the New Jerusalem, he thinks, as he roams the basement in search of a dummy, but it's a version of the same phenomenon displaced into time rather than space. Rather than roaming the country in search of the lost town, the people in the model are roaming the past in search of their own town as it used to be, or as they used to believe it would one day become, clinging to that possibility as it sinks into the wastes of time.

He smiles.

That's it! he thinks, simply and clearly. He's tempted to explain the idea to the Night Crusher and ask if it's any good, but he stops himself. No, he decides. I'm the master, he's the slave, and that's all there is to it.

This exploratory phase opens onto a longer period during which Jakob never once leaves the basement. He pisses and shits in a bucket in one corner, and subsists on the clear liquor even though he can tell it's making him crazy.

He senses that to come up now would be to admit defeat. So he carves open the head of one of the dummies he found in a pile in the back by the turpentine, choking down the déjà vu as his work on the first effigy comes back to him, its smoke almost palpable in the still basement air. This, he thinks, carefully sawing off the rest of the top of the dummy's cranium, is a version of that, but deeper, darker, closer to the bone. Either that, or newer, later, more evolved... if the first was me in the Old Testament, this is me in the New.

Moses, meet Jesus.

Taking a deep breath, he leans over the exposed cranium and spits a hot mouthful of déjà vu into its rubbery crevices. Then he massages this into the rough edges where he sawed the top off, pokes out its rubbery eyes, pulls its plastic teeth, and chisels its earholes wider, so that the spectacle inside is visible from any angle.

"**And** what is that spectacle?" the Night Crusher asks, a night or two later.

"See for yourself," Jakob replies, stepping aside in hopes that the work he thinks is finished actually is.

He leans in close to the Night Crusher, trying to see what he sees. Inside, they see the model townspeople, made of wax and soap, clinging to a miniature replica of *The Sunken Town*, stapled in three places to the dummy's spine. The townspeople, on the other hand, are pulled by wires that attach to the upper rim of the dummy's cranium. Seeing it through the Night Crusher's eyes, Jakob understands this pull to represent the force of forgetting, the buoyant, future-seeking energy that separates people from the paradise of their youth. Like the water pushing my parents and me up toward the ceiling of the sunken house, he recalls.

He can feel himself wavering from exhaustion, his eyes watery, his hearing dull, but just before he collapses, he catches a final, transformative glimpse: deep in the spinal column, hidden behind the staples like a saint in the wall of a church, is Wieland's body, dead but not forgotten, his bones merging with my bones, such that he and I, in the guise of this dummy, are finally one.

Jakob comes to much later, feverish, sweaty, covered in ants.

It wouldn't have taken much to convince him that he was dead and that the ants were feasting on his body, but, rolling onto his side, he sees a bowl of oatmeal even more covered in the wriggling black lines than he is, and then the Night Crusher says, "I brought you that, but you collapsed before I could get any down your throat."

Jakob tries to grunt thanks, but finds his lips sealed shut with a gummy film.

"Here," the Night Crusher says, "I brought you water too."

Jakob swivels his head in the other direction and glimpses the glass, half full of water, half full of dust. After mustering as many of his dispersed inner resources as he can, he manages to drink several mouthfuls of this cocktail and then, once it's lined his belly, to choke down several spoonfuls of antsy oatmeal.

When he's restored enough to get back on his feet, he returns to the workbench and tries to pick up where he left off. He can dimly recall a thought of tremendous importance occurring to him in his last conscious instant, but it's not until he sticks his head into the dummy's head to examine his work up close that he remembers. Beneath the miniaturized version of *The Sunken Town*, and far beneath the townspeople anchored to it, is Wieland himself, the anchor of all anchors, the root of the entire system.

Though he knows that no one looking at this piece will ever see what's hidden there, he carefully removes his model of *The Sunken Town* and all the people clinging to it, and gets to work fashioning a tiny Wieland.

This model, he decides, will have to be perfect. It will require a level of care and craftsmanship that he's never mustered before. In order to move on with my life, he thinks, panting in the basement, which he's just now realized is as hot as the earth's core, I have to pass this test, even if I'm the only one who will ever know that I did. It's my first and only shot at the big time: the gate that is open for me now will not open again.

After finishing the rest of the oatmeal, he takes his shirt off, stretches it over the waste bucket to dampen the smell, and gets to work. He takes another of the soap figures he carved earlier and sets it up beside the dummy, his fingers shaking as they hold the scalpel and begin to carve Wieland's face into the creamy off-white flesh.

He squints when the vision wavers, flashing back to the children nailed to the walls, kept alive with spoonfuls of mayonnaise. After coughing to clear this image, he drags the scalpel along the edges of the soap figure, tracing Wieland's withered jawline. Then he collects a pile of curled soap-shavings and glues them back onto the face to form its whiskers. Regarding the figure once it's properly stubbled, he feels it shudder in his hands, vibrating with endangered life, a transmission from the world within the world. A tremor passes through the ant thoraxes he's inserted into the figure's eye sockets, rendering them potent enough to lock onto his own eyes, and for a moment he and Wieland commune, so intensely that he can't help flashing back to his study of Martin Buber's all-important *I and Thou.*

Now he knows what the final step will be. He laughs, and the figure laughs with him. Then he gets serious again. Gripping the scalpel between his left thumb and forefinger, he closes his eyes and tries to remember how he'd imagined Wieland's penis on his first night in this cabin, before he'd ever seen it, before it was claimed forever by the banal. Opening his eyes, he begins to carve into his right pinky, whimpering as the skin peels off and lies curled on the table. When this is done, he licks up the blood, hoping to spare the Blood Clot the sight of what comes next.

Luckily, he manages to lick enough off the table to keep her at bay, peeking out of him without quite coming into her own. He shoves his pinky into his mouth and rolls up the removed skin with his other hand, creating a flesh cylinder he attaches to the figure's groin, consecrating it for all time as the ur-image of the Father's generative organ, the font from which he, like the universe itself, emerged after the Big Bang.

Then, grinning again, he thinks, Okay Wilhelm, time to bury you inside me.

"If you bury me in there," the figure says, primping its new appendage, "I will die in one sense and live forever in another. If you impact me in your brainstem now, don't expect to get me out later."

Jakob looks for the Night Crusher, desperate for a second opinion, but there's no sign of him. "It's just I and Thou," the figure says. "You and me. Savor the last instant of our separateness, then do what needs to be done."

Powerless to refuse, Jakob sits there with his shirt off, smelling the dust and the sweat and the distant reek of his waste in its bucket. The figure waits, its ant-eyes wriggling.

"Okay," Jakob says, when he knows that the time has come and any further postponement will only brand him a coward. He pulls his pinky from his mouth, clears his throat, wipes his eyes with his forearms, and picks the figure up, walking it delicately across the workbench and over to the dummy that had been lying on its side, its head stuffed with gauze to keep the dust out.

He removes the gauze with one hand and inserts the figure with the other, twisting it hard into his brainstem. He feels the pain inside his own head. It makes him dizzy and fills the room with spots, but he persists, panting, grunting, even screaming a little, until Wieland has been drilled in as deep as he'll go.

Then he spits onto the concrete floor and attaches the miniature *Sunken Town* with its desperate hangers-on to Wieland's buried body, thus successfully reifying a vision that feels like it's been percolating inside him all his life.

He takes a step back to regard his work and knows,

with a lump in his throat and a hot ball of pride in his chest, that *The Adoration of the Sunken Town* is complete, and Wilhelm Wieland is dead.

Burying the
Wieland-thing

Having killed him in his mind, all that remains is for Jakob to retrieve Wieland's body. He lingers in the basement another day, licking up the last sweet flakes of oatmeal clinging to the edges of the bowl. When all that remains is ants, he closes his eyes, forces all the versions of himself that have dispersed throughout his mind to cohere again inside his body, and lumbers over to the workbench, still shirtless. He bows his head and, extending his arms in a gesture that is both genuinely ceremonial and self-consciously performative, picks up *The Adoration of The Sunken Town* as if he too were one of its devotees.

Leaving his oatmeal bowl and waste bucket down here as a record of the crucial period during which he occupied this space—a crumb for my future biographer, he gloats—he carries the sculpture up the stairs, savoring the creak of each step, aware that, on the one hand, he'll never come down here again, while, on the other, every future basement he'll ever occupy will be identical to this one.

Upstairs, he places the sculpture on the window sill, in the exact place where *The Sunken Town* resided before Greta carried it down the mountain, and he gathers his thoughts, his eyes on a glass of milk on the table. He knows he'll have to drink it in order to be released from this house, and that, once he's vomited as a result, the final transformation will be complete. He stares at it and conjures the boy he was the first time he came up here, following his mother into the dead of night. He can see that boy sitting at the table now, drinking the first cup of spoiled milk as he met Wieland for the first time. "Tonight I could do milk," he whispers, practicing the German accent, trying to perfect it. "But tonight I won't do milk. Tonight I'll..."

Tears fill his eyes as he watches the scene play out, the boy bringing the cup to his lips and back to the table and back to his lips again, while his mind fragments into one part that wishes to simply stand here and cry, and one part that wishes to log the image in his growing bank of Raw Material and formulate a plan for how to build it into a shape that can then be displayed in public with his name beneath it, and a price tag beneath that.

Just before his own body becomes incorporated into

the reverie, he shakes it off and sits down at the table, replacing the boy he used to be with the man he hopes he's become. He wipes his eyes, licks his lips, and pours the foul milk down his throat.

Before the sickness becomes paralyzing, he gets up and elbows his way into Wieland's bedroom, the one sanctum he's never violated. An initial survey of the interior reveals walls so densely covered with art that nothing solid is visible behind it. From in here, he thinks, it would seem that the cabin is literally made of mobiles, dreamcatchers, collages, and tattered prints, held together by nothing except the overlaps within and among one man's manifold vision of the universe, his endless, doomed ploy to supplant God in his own imagination. Over the walls, the floor, and the ceiling are maps of connections between the river, the Ticksinging Meadow, the few streets of downtown, and the mountain. Throughout, entrances to the New Jerusalem 2 are marked with closely printed instructions for earning access, and warnings about the danger of even the tiniest mistake. In some cases, elaborate anatomical illustrations of the demons guarding these entrances, and depictions of the torments suffered by those unfortunate enough to have been captured sneaking through, overwhelm the map so thoroughly that it comes to resemble Bosch's illustrations of the Art World, depicting an anal rape so climactically violent that he can smell the blood and shit and demon seed intermingled.

Jakob swoons from this smell mixed with bad milk

and something deeper, which, after the swoon has evened out, he understands to be a kind of unholy identification with the work adorning the room. As soon as this thought occurs to him, he's lost in it, spotting the fish he electrocuted, the sketches he made of the fishermen on the bridge and the snake choking them down taped to the walls of a wicker model of the Ragtown shack where the Boys' Boys forced him to run a gamut of scarecrows. There's even a dollhouse whose front is cut away to reveal a neat row of Boys' Boys hanging from dental-floss nooses.

"Be glad it's not your skinny wieners," he whispers, afraid to speak too loud but unable to keep the sentiment to himself. They tilt and knock together in response.

His certainty that he created everything in this room grows so extreme that, by the time his eyes settle on Wieland's body on the bed, there's no question about its origin. "My mummy," he says, louder now. "The mummy I made of the man I used to be, before I was reborn to live my life again, buying another six or seven decades to push my work that much closer to fruition, even if there is still no end in sight."

The force of this thought hitting home sends him sprawling forward, onto the bed beside Wieland's body, his eyes locked onto its eyes. He regards the body as an *it*, a thing, though a thing with inner life, the same as all puppets and dolls, or perhaps a little more so.

A thing I made that also made me.

The clarity of this thought, even as it collapses into mystery, pleases Jakob. That's the truth as best I can state it, he thinks, looking to Wieland for approval.

When he's lain there long enough to take in the full impact of the room, which he's come to believe contains both the records of all his past work and the seeds of his whole future, he gets up, the bad milk sloshing audibly in his stomach, and drags the Wieland-thing off the bed.

He drags it by the feet out of the room, whipping the dreamcatchers and mobiles into a fit of clanking. Then he drags it across the kitchen, through the front door, down the steps, across the yard through the shadows of the spiders, and into the clearing, all the way to his mother's cemetery.

Dropping the body in front of the plastic stone marked WILHELM WIELAND, Jakob tries to imagine what happened here after he ran inside the night his mother was found with her adherents. Wieland must have rearranged the graves, he thinks. Maybe, after casting the Shadow of Death and scaring all the townspeople away, he and my mother worked together to dig up all the plastic babies those people had buried and replace them with the skeletons of the children Wieland sacrificed in the 60s, and kept in one of his other cabins, the cabin in which he lived the life of a murderer rather than that of a Genius.

Jakob is floored by this revelation. He lies back in the

soft dirt and lets this new story sink into his expanding mythos, itself an open grave in his mind.

Once it feels like part of the canon—it's self-evident, now, that Wieland lived many lives, one in each of his cabins, and in one of these he was a murderer of children, and maybe not only children—Jakob sits up and returns to the task at hand.

He digs Wieland's grave on his hands and knees, spraying dirt between his legs. Though he can feel the dead listening, he doesn't let their attention distract him. If they speak, I'll reply, he decides, and if they don't, then they're of no concern to me.

When the grave's deep enough, he catches his breath, swoons, and vomits up the bad milk, lining the dirt bottom with stomach acid like it, too, is a stomach. Into this stomach he tips the Wieland-thing, watching and then hearing it slop into the brine.

Regarding the body in its milky hole, he's feels himself splitting into the boy who wants to cry at the loss of his grandfather, and the artist who wants to admire his newest work as a masterpiece of the grotesque.

Both hear Wieland's voice, as loud and clear as the father's at the height of his sermonizing. The corpse opens its mouth, licks milk from its lips, and says, "What's happening here is the exact opposite of what you probably believe. You probably believe that Jakob is burying Wieland and preparing to live on as himself. In reality, Wieland is burying Jakob. The thing you used to be, before you came up here? That thing is gone forever. Now I'm in you. I *am* you in every regard except the bodily, and even that will converge in time. Take a good look at me, because I am what you will end up as. Now, say goodbye to yourself as Jakob with no last name and walk down the mountain as Wilhelm Wieland. You screwed me into your brainstem, now go find out what that means."

When the corpse closes its lips, the boy in the cemetery tries to think of himself as Jakob and finds that he can't. In a daze, he kicks the dirt back over the hole he dug and twists the plastic stone in deep enough to keep it steady. Then he turns back toward the cabin to retrieve his sculpture.

Wieland's

Return to the

Sunken Town

Arms outstretched to cradle *The Adoration of the Sunken Town*, Wieland turns his back on the cabin for what he imagines will be the last time. As he walks away, looking through the model head of the boy he used to be, he catches sight of Tobin riding a pig and stabbing it beneath him as the creature lurches and buckles. Wieland thinks of announcing the burial, but fears interrupting the pig-man at work, just as he used to fear waking his mother when she was sleepwalking. Either he'll find out on his own, he thinks, leaving Tobin to his own devices, or he doesn't need to know.

Beyond the cemetery, he presses into the woods, panting in the heat. It's blazing summer now, everything in full, obscene bloom. The hot, wet air coats his bare back until he feels feral, like something born in these woods, about to emerge for the first time.

This, he decides, will be my story, even if there's no one to tell it to. It'll be the mode I proceed within. He feels it click into place inside and all around him. "I was born here, came of age here," he practices, "and now, my arms full with my first mature work, I am ready to take my stand in the sunken town below."

Once the ink on this story has dried, the rest of the journey passes without incident. He retraces the steps he took the last time he trekked up here, though that time the snow was so high his feet came nowhere near the soft ground he's now ankle-deep in, tracking mud, brambles, and small insects as tokens of the Wilderness that forged him. As soon as I reach the Town Museum—he pictures Greta opening the front door in awe—I'll take off my shoes and donate them to the growing archive of my work, symbols of my lost period, the time I spent away, becoming the man I was destined to become.

The man, he thinks, crossing the river on the bridge that always seems to appear when he needs it, who made *The Adoration of the Sunken Town.* Halfway across the river, the feeling of return is so heavy that he has to put the sculpture down and lean on the bridge, thinking, The townspeople will once again witness the manifestation of Wieland in the flesh, a moment they'd prematurely relegated to the netherworld of local myth.

Buzzing with a jagged mixture of elation and melancholy, he picks his sculpture back up. Carrying it now like a pilgrim bearing a plank from Noah's Ark down from Mount Ararat, he proceeds toward the Sunken Town, assuming that every stray dog and pigeon along the road has come out to beg for a place in his soon-to-be-legendary body of work.

PART III

The Future Museum

"Yet my father's egoism was really only a part of his *Weltanschauung*, his pantheism. His egoism knew no bounds. In his paneogoism, everything was subordinated, everything was meant to be subordinated to him, as in the characters of the Old Testament usurpers. And so, while the powers and energies of springtime were bringing nature to bloom, my father felt still more intensely the weight of the injustice inflicted on him by God and man alike. His metaphysical revolt, this belated monstrous offshoot of his lost youth, blossomed in spring with greater force, rose up volcanically, like an abscess."—Danilo Kiš, *Garden, Ashes*

Wieland Brings His New Piece to the Town Museum

Wieland continues down the road he's often imagined Jakob's family driving when they first arrived in the new house. Arms aching from having carried *The Adoration of the Sunken Town* all this way, he can't help but feel that this moment is the sequel to that one. Once again, he thinks, Jakob is coming to town, but this time—he looks at the model in his arms—he's being carried by his grandfather in the real summer heat, not by his father in a Desert Dream!

"That's right," he adds, for anyone who might be listening, "I really am Wieland now. Jakob's grandfather. An eternal cycle has clicked two steps back, giving me that much more time to become who I really am." Even though he knows he's older than he was the first time he took this road into town, it feels much earlier, much closer to the obscured or botched beginning of things.

His sweat beads up as a breeze whips across the field he's now passing, and a trio of crows flies from the telephone wires overhead. Looking up, he follows their flight across the field and over to the trailers further along the road, before which the Boys' Boys are clustered in absolute stasis. Wieland laughs at the Demiurge's obviousness. Come on, he thinks, squinting at the sun, are you really too lazy to be any subtler than that?

He keeps laughing as he approaches the Boys' Boys, some of them shirtless, the rest in tank tops. They stand at the edge of the field and watch, open-mouthed as the boy they once knew as Jakob passes by, back from the dead. Tom stands at the front of the group holding a motionless dog on a leash. Posed like that, they look like a Bellmer, boy and dog conjoined with stitching that only shows on the inside.

Just like I made you, Wieland thinks. If I wished to revise your proportions now, I easily could. Tom, I could remove your face and swap it with that dog's, and there'd be nothing you could do to stop me.

"And I would do it," he shouts, in Tom's direction,

"if I had the time, but I'm a busy man now. The days of listening to you talk are long gone." He puffs up his chest and dandles the model boy in front of him like a sacrificial offering. To formally mark my return to town, which is also my first genuine entrée into it, I will entrust this model to the Town Museum, in perpetuity. Whatever value my subsequent works attain, he explains to the Boys' Boys in his mind, this piece will remain there for the rest of time. Those who truly wish to see it will have to travel here to do so.

With the Boys' Boys posed behind him like a roadside sample of the artwork to be found in the Town Museum, a cheap reproduction to entice the casual tourists whose patronage even Great Artists sometimes require, Wieland proceeds past Wing Hut, Giant Chinese, and Mama's Pizza. He crosses the Museum's weedy lot and walks up to the CLOSED FOR REORDERING sign hanging on loose chains across the front gate, where he stops to rearrange the sculpture in his arms. Then he heaves his way up the steps, taking care not to spill the remaining inches of water from the miniature *Sunken Town* embedded inside the skull of the... but who am I explaining my work to? Surely Greta will understand it with a single silent glance.

Surely, he adds, still addressing this imaginary interlocutor, she'll understand it better than I ever could!

Heartened at how true this rings, he catches his

breath and leans forward to bang on the front door with his forehead.

Like he just inserted a quarter into a nickelodeon, the interior of the Museum comes to life with wheezing, scratching, coughing, and, after a long overture, shuffling. He listens as this shuffling grows louder and nearer, only remembering that he summoned a living being he'll now have to interact with when Greta opens the door a crack and regards him with a mixture of surprise and relief.

"Oh!" she says, once she's checked that no one's behind him. "Come in, I didn't expect to see you down here, but I, well... come in, come in."

She hobbles aside—the crutches are gone, but a brace still supports her ankle—and motions to the back office, from which a faint stream of classical music issues through buzzy speakers.

"Put that thing down and let's talk in there," she mutters, setting off in the direction of the office and trusting that he'll follow.

After placing *The Adoration of the Sunken Town* on his old chair behind the desk at the gift shop, he follows her through a disorder of boxes and crates and into the back office where he received his first ten-dollar commission, for the sale of his Bellmer, back in the Old Testament. His eyes fill with tears for reasons he doesn't quite understand, but he knows that, in time, in one basement or another, he will. In time, he thinks, sitting down in a rickety armchair while Greta bends over a mini-fridge and pulls out two cans of Coke, I'll understand it so well I will have gone beyond the real reason and into a lush, spidery mythos of sub-reasons that will form a nearly infinite piece of work, modeling, as it will have to, the larger mythos of the town, which is ever fertile... ever fecund... always hungry for new shavings of the lives being lived upon its cracked surface, such that the psychological subterranean realm of myth, and the physical subterranean realm of basements are in some sense...

"Hello?" Greta shouts. "I asked if you wanted a Coke."

She holds one out and he takes it. As he cracks it open, her expression softens and she cracks hers as well.

The combined fizz fills the room.

They both sip and Greta, swallowing, says, "So *The Sunken Town* was a hit. Your biggest yet, by some margin." Her eyes narrow, something sad creeping across them and disappearing off to the left. "People ate it up. I think it resonated with something a lot of them have been feeling these past few years. The sinking of everything real and true down to a murky, unreachable bottom, and the resulting sense that we're all floating in some airless upper ether, some place without substance or purchase, where time's barely passing, where the things we say barely register..." The thing creeps across her eyes again, and she stops talking until it passes. Then she adds, "Anyway, I can understand why so many of us wanted to visit *The Sunken Town*. Needed to visit."

Wieland smiles, though something about the dimness of the back office and the buzzy classical music and the now-flat Coke in his hands dampens what he knows ought to be a moment of celebration. The look on Greta's face, when next he checks in with it, only exacerbates this dampening. Something, he can tell, is bittersweet about all this.

"I have a new piece," he blurts, "as you saw. Sitting in the chair out there. It's, well, you'll see. I was thinking it could be displayed directly across from *The Sunken Town*, as a sort of carnival-mirror-image of it, which could, in a way..." He can't decide whether he sounds to her like a child or an adult, nor, quite, which he'd prefer.

"I'm sorry," Greta interrupts, reaching into the desk drawer in front of her and pulling out a wad of cash. "*The Sunken Town* sold. Some couple from another town. I don't know who they were, but they wanted it badly. That's $500." She flicks the wad toward Wieland, but it's so heavy it only gets partway across the desk. "Why don't you take that, and I'll go out and look at your new piece in a little while. I need to get my bearings. I didn't expect to sell the other piece, but they insisted." She shudders, and Wieland pictures a moment of freak violence at the opening of *The Sunken Town*. Something erupting from the hearts of the couple from another town akin to whatever compelled those parents to impale their children on Wieland's—*my*, he corrects—spiders all the way back in the 60s.

Now he doesn't want to take the money, but he knows Greta will insist, so he spares her the indignity. Scooping it up like a wad of dead, wet leaves, he shoves it into his pocket and gets to his feet. Then, scratching his chest, he remembers that he's still shirtless and asks if she has anything he could wear.

A few minutes later, he's on the Museum's porch in the summer dusk in an olive-green ladies' raincoat, trying to stall so he can listen to Greta's first impressions of his new piece. He hears her lift it out of the gift shop chair and he sees her turn one of the main lights on, but then the sky cracks with lightning and thunder rumbles in the distance, and he has a premonition of himself stuck on this porch for hours and hours of heavy rain, so, clutching his money, he sets off running toward the diner before that future arrives.

Back at the
Diner, Flush
with Cash

He makes it inside just as the first heavy drops splatter down. The second he closes the door, an enveloping wall of water seals him and the few other patrons off from the world, lending the diner's interior the feeling he remembers from going through the carwash with his mother back in the Old Testament. He shivers and zips his raincoat all the way up to his chin, taking a sip of pleasure from the thought that everyone else in here surely assumes he's wearing a shirt underneath.

He pulls his wad from his pocket and places it on his napkin, staring at it suspiciously as the man behind the counter comes over and likewise stares at it, though he says nothing.

"A basket of fries and a chocolate shake, please," Wieland says, without looking up. A moment later, he listens to the oil scald its frozen prey and stares at the wad again, imagining it transfigured into a new piece, reverting from the product of art back into a component of its ongoing process. The grinding of the milkshake machine soon joins the scalding of the fries and both together soundtrack his ruminations on the *Transfiguration of Money*. He feels on the verge of a breakthrough, of making the all-important leap from concept to protocol, but the counter-man plunks his food and drink in front of him before he can stick the landing.

Beginning to nibble and sip, he finds that the only remnant of the thought-world he'd recently inhabited is a hovering fear of the couple from another town. He feels them haunting him, or hunting him, embodied by the money but by no means limited to it. How much more is there where that came from? he wonders, pouring ketchup onto his plate and dragging four fries through it, one for each non-thumb finger. He closes his eyes and sucks down the hot, sweet, greasy mass while at the same time picturing himself in a gated mansion on the edge of town, surrounded by a moat and a field in which roam... well, why not... tigers.

He smiles and, switching to his milkshake, gulps down as much as his throat can handle while allowing his consciousness to drift upward, across the moat, over the backs of the tigers and up through the third-floor windows, into the studio where he sits in regal contemplation, surrounded by no fewer than ten workbenches, each one laid out with its own materials, ranging from diamond-studded files to heirloom oil paints, from 3D printers to spindle-bore lathes, each guarded by its own assistant, all of them versions of the Night Crusher, but more human, more convincingly real.

When he feels his plate being slid out from under his greasy fingers, he opens his eyes and looks up at the counter-man, who's attempting to clear it away. Wieland, however, isn't ready to leave, so he drains the rest of his milkshake and calls for seconds on both. A little incredulously, the counter-man complies, and Wieland listens for the familiar sounds of the fryer and the milkshake machine, hoping to be lulled back into his mansion. But, like a dreamer awoken just before the climax of his dream, he finds that the world he yearns to return to is no longer a world at all.

Try as he might to overcome it, reality has intervened, stranding the mansion on a mental island he can no longer reach. He laughs at the thought that now only the moat is real, and he's nothing but one more desperate townsperson trying in vain to storm the Big House. Alone in the diner with the rain pounding outside, he flips through his cash and again thinks about the couple from another town, who may well, he thinks, be in here now. He looks around the room, past the four single men in booths against the far wall and the two further down the counter from him, to the three couples in booths near the window, lined up like they were posed that way for his inspection. Were they here a moment ago? he wonders. In the first booth is an elderly couple supping from bowls of chicken soup; in the second is a middle-aged couple gnawing on tough steaks and drinking from green bottles of beer; and in the last is a young couple, both slightly overweight, drinking coffee and sharing a sundae. If any of them can tell they're being watched, none let on. They continue to eat and talk quietly, muffled by the rain, presenting themselves without complaint for Wieland's inspection.

Mashing up his second plate of fries and beginning to stuff it down his throat, thus passing the point of satiety and approaching that of sickness, he wonders whether it's up to him to choose which couple it is. How strict are the rules, in the town in general, and in this diner in particular? If I want the couple from another town, the one who bought my work—and thus who bought the meal I'm eating now, and may well buy all the meals I'll eat from now on—to be the older couple, or the younger one, can I simply choose that and have it be the case?

Watching these couples eat while continuing to eat his own food soon mesmerizes him. He puts fries in his mouth at the same rate as the older couple sips soup, then sips his milkshake at the same rate as the middle-aged couple gnaws steak, and thereby tastes what they're tasting, trying to inhabit their bodies so as to see himself as they see him and thus determine whether, in their eyes, he too is a piece of meat.

More broadly, or more deeply, he wonders if they can see him at all. Am I here with them just as they're here with me, or is it a one-way street now, all of them present in my world but not vice versa? This possibility both terrifies and thrills him. Perhaps I've fallen through a fold, he thinks, a crack that opened in the woods, the same crack that consumed both the boy-Jakob and the man-Wieland, fusing us into the... what, the young man I am now?

He tries to decide how old he is and finds that he cannot. No stable account of how much time passed in the Wilderness is within reach. It could've been a year, he thinks, meaning that now I'm thirteen, or a decade, meaning that now I'm twenty-two.

He giggles at the possibility that something so fundamental is nevertheless impossible to determine. Now the couple sharing the sundae turns to regard him, but, though he keeps giggling, they soon turn their attention away, back toward their melting ice cream, which they finish and then go to the counter to pay for.

Wieland waits until the other couples and all the single men are gone. Then it's just him and the counter-man, and perhaps a cook hidden away in the kitchen. Now that the rain has stopped, the windows are slowly unfogging, and he knows that, just beyond them, lies the town, wet and fresh and waiting to be reentered. It's waiting for me to take the side streets that lead to Main Street, and then to follow that up all the way to the other side street that leads to my house, or the house that used to be mine.

There's every reason to put this journey off as long as possible, but he knows that soon the counter-man will say, "Okay, closing up sir," and then he'll be forced to gather his cash and stuff it back in his pocket and walk through the dinging door, back into the hot, wet night and toward the confrontation that will, in no small measure, mark the completion of his return.

Overfull like a tick that's gorged on the rich blood of a child, he waits for this moment to come and then, when it does, he complies without protest, so that now, before he's fully gathered his thoughts, he's outside again, heading toward the dead center of town, his raincoat unzipped over his bare chest as he makes his way past the bridge where the fishermen surely had to cut their session short at the first crack of lightning. The buildings grow sparse again as he approaches the street on which lies the house where he used to believe his father, mother, and the boy-Jakob, despite everything, lived in something resembling harmony.

The Lone

Lecher

Wieland roams among the houses on the street, pretending to be unsure which one used to be his. He entertains himself for half an hour this way, passing one freshly-soaked lawn after another, the air redolent of soil and pollen and a thousand other rain-borne scents. He peers into the lighted windows as he sinks into the persona of the Lone Lecher, which he's often inhabited in dreams of being a derelict in a giant City, down and out in New York or Los Angeles, haunting bleak rows of private galleries, waiting for his ship to come in. "The Lone Lecher," he recites, as if auditioning for the role, "is the man for whom the door of no decent house will ever open in welcome."

He passes one house after another on the street, falling more and more into this mode, dredging up all the fear and desperation he's ever felt at the prospect of stepping off a bus at the Port Authority with his portfolio under his arm and a note from Greta in his back pocket, entering the thrum of Times Square with no more than this to show for himself. He strides back and forth and back and forth, no longer sure if he's having fun or putting off that which he should have found the courage to confront long ago. *The man for whom the door of no decent house will ever open in welcome.* He repeats this to himself as he walks back and forth over the lawns, unsure now whether it's a line he's just thought of, or one that dates back to some classic work of the macabre his mother read to him when he was tiny.

Pushing himself even further, he starts to wonder whether there's a difference. Perhaps I'm the author of every story that's ever existed, he lets himself imagine. Both the Demiurge and its lone reader, writing stories for myself forever and ever and ever, in a permanent, perfect, sealed-off loop. Unable to die, unable to affect the living. Unable to be certain whether I exist at all.

And if that's the case, then it's up to me to force the end. To bring down the Apocalypse and find out, for certain, what becomes of me in its aftermath.

He starts to shiver in what he senses is both an imitation and a genuine inhabitation of the Lone Lecher. The Lone Lecher would shiver just like this, he thinks. Then he thinks, Of course I would!

He shivers more, aware of how close he just came to wishing that his life was over, and then he starts laughing, pawing at one of the lawns, digging up its rain-softened dirt. "The man for whom the door of no decent house will ever open in welcome." Still laughing, he repeats the line yet again, this time putting the question of its origin aside in order to seize upon its central phrase. *No decent house...*

He passes the houses, eying them, wondering, given that no decent house will admit him, which the least decent one might be. Where do the sad sacks live? The shut-ins, the dust collectors, the other Lone Lechers like me?

When he's stalked the whole street ten or eleven times, up and down and up and down, pushing himself deeper into the persona, until every other aspect of his being has been filed away in a storage cabin, he marches up the driveway of the house he's decided is the least decent and pounds on its back door, the one through which he remembers himself having come and gone and come and gone as a boy. The valve that titrated his presence between basement, bedroom, and town, the three nerve centers, at the very heart of which was the kitchen table, over which the father presided like a...

His ability to imagine the father is abruptly truncated by the appearance in the doorway of a man who looks just like him. The combination of shock and expectation—this is, after all, exactly what I came here for, part of him knows, while the other part feels, or feigns, shock at this particular Indecent House producing such a convincing replica of the man—sets him to blubbering.

"I... I... I..." he blubbers, knowing full well that, *I'm back, after all these years in the Wilderness*, is the phrase he's looking for.

The father, draped in his white robe and skullcap, his features more chiseled than before, his jawline sharper and his black eyes blacker, bears down on the Lone Lecher in the doorway. Then he turns and gazes into the kitchen where his wife, who looks just like the woman that used to come almost every night to the neon graveyard outside my cabin, Wieland thinks, sits at the kitchen table with a boy who looks exactly like the one that came up to visit me.

Jakob. He forces himself to admit that he remembers the name. Jakob—he cranes around the thin but imposing mass of the father to see as far into the kitchen as he'll be allowed—is that really you?

The boy is off to one side of the table, partially hidden by the doorframe, which the father has made clear he isn't about to vacate, so Wieland can't be sure if the boy is real and, even if he is, whether he's the same boy or another one. After all, there's no shortage of boys in this world. They're not, when you come right down to it, such a special form of life, now are they?

He can feel a belly laugh coming on. His lips quiver and his eyes water and his knees buckle. If the father had asked him what he wanted right then, he would've answered, "To come into your house just long enough to make it mine, as it used to be," but of course the father asks no such thing.

As soon as the Lone Lecher releases the laugh that can no longer be contained, the father puffs up his chest, narrows his eyes, and grunts, "Alright, whoever you are, time to go."

Just before he slams the door, the woman in the kitchen, pretending for the sake of all involved that she hasn't just seen, asks, "Who was that, my love?"

The father grips the doorknob like a neck he plans to wring and grunts, "A raccoon." Then he slams it in Wieland's face.

Feeling as raccoon-like as he ever has, Wieland scuttles across the yard, past the Talking Rock, and down the hill toward the low-lying neighbors' houses, without a plan or destination in mind until, like he's reached the edge of the known world and been bounced back by a forcefield, he finds himself running up the hill the way he just came, straight toward the garage, where the padlock on the side door has been left open. He catches his breath as he pries it off the latch and lets himself in, immediately calmed by the scents of dried paint and wet fur.

Unzipping his raincoat, he beds down on the mattress he knew would be there, the one on which the father surely napped away many of the afternoons he claimed to have spent working. After he's closed his eyes but before he's fallen asleep, Wieland feels a hairy paw brush his face and knows that the Night Crusher has been waiting for him, wondering, in whatever brutish way he's able to wonder, how long it would take his master to find his way home.

Back in the

Garage

With his raincoat open and his face full of fur, Wieland falls through a chute and lands in a dream so deep that no deception is possible because no space between appearance and reality can survive the tremendous pressure. Down here, all dualities are crushed together into precious stone. This notion pleases him. It is good. He smiles and walks with it, drawing his open raincoat closed over his bare chest, proceeding through the rank dark of what has either revealed itself to be or has just now become a teeming City.

And I have come to this City, he can clearly see, in order to hammer my name into history. If only—he laughs—I could remember what that name was supposed to be! He wanders down an alley full of passed out, sometimes dead, sometimes disemboweled

316

and decapitated people, toward a gaslight shining in the fog. Drawn to it like a moth, the Lone Lecher steps over the dead and the dying as his arms fill with a tightly wrapped mass. Something heavy, he gleans, and unknown, even to me. Dimly, like a storm brewing in the distance, he begins to sense that it contains his next work, whatever comes after *The Adoration of the Sunken Town* has heaved his career up to the next level. His arms ache and he has the sense that he's been carrying this new work all the way from the town of his origin to the City where his legend will, at long last, take root.

But I'm not newly arrived, he starts to realize, his stomach filling with gas, much as I might like to wish I were. No, I've been here for years already, bedding down in flophouses, slurping bowls of soup from scuffed lunch counters and squirreling the rolls away in my pockets for dinner, supplemented with peanuts or whole milk when possible, which, these days, it rarely is. His voice ages in his head until it becomes that of a middle-aged man, his window of opportunity closing, the gaslight at the end of the alley beginning to dim.

As he staggers toward it, the bundle in his arms grows heavier without revealing any clue as to its nature, and it becomes clear that the gaslight belongs to a gallery, the central art depot of the entire City, which, by a logic of absolute and unquestionable association, here resolves into the Art World itself.

So the name of this City is *The Art World*, he thinks, and that gallery is my only hope, the only place on earth where what's real and true and crucial inside me stands a chance of being tendered as currency by those who exist outside.

"Strangers, Jakob," a gruff voice up ahead barks. "Nothing but strangers. A filthy million-headed mass of strangerflesh."

Knowing, with a sense of non-negotiable fate, that he'll have to respond to this voice in a moment, he tries one last time to determine what the bundle in his arms consists of. He knows that, if he can just do this, he'll be able to take whatever he gleans back up to the surface with him, into the waking world of lies and smokescreens, and rebuild up there what already exists down here. The instructions for my next piece will be revealed if I can simply unwrap what's in my arms... and yet every time he inches his fingers toward the string holding it shut, the bundle nearly falls to the ground. He tries to balance it on his bent knee, but it wobbles and slips, forcing him to crouch and grab it with both hands just before it cracks open on the wet Art World pavement. His guts fill with hot adrenaline as he tries to stabilize it, listening to its fragile inner components clack, quieting to an uneasy equilibrium only once he's promised never to try opening it again.

"You can keep it intact but never know what's inside," the gruff older voice warns, "or you can find out what's in there, but you'll end up breaking it in the process. Kind of like with souls, don't you think? Speaking of which, come with me, Jakob. The place our bodies are in misses us."

Powerless to resist, he follows the man out of the queue and down another grim alley, past more bodies, all pilgrims crushed on the road to the gallery, their souls sliced open by forces far too abstract to care what they used to consist of.

He follows past the flophouse where he's been staying, past the diner where he eats his soup standing at the counter when he can afford it, and up a street he's never seen before. The landscape quickly turns rural, the skyscrapers shrinking down to one- and two-story homes as the slick pavement gives way to cracked country roads and then hard-packed dirt.

An interval of pitch black follows, punctuated only by the white moonlit faces of possums, until a new light begins to shine in the distance. The man speeds up now that he's certain where they're going, leading the way past a darkened house and a garage, the source of what was, a moment ago, that distant light.

Inside, the man sits at a desk against one wall, as Wieland lies on the bare mattress that, he begins to remember, he's been lying on all this time. "I'm back! Did you miss me?" He imagines his soul asking his body.

In place of any answer, his body rolls over to watch his father, or the man he used to believe was his father, tinker with a model City under the glare of a banker's lamp, muttering, "Jakob, Jakob, I know you're there, Jakob."

Jakob. Wieland considers the name again, aware of

its familiarity without yet pinning it to a face, or a body. The boy I saw at the dinner table inside the house last night, the automaton... that boy was Jakob, but not the only one.

Not the real one.

He watches the father tinker with his model cityscape—an exact facsimile, he sees now, of the part of the Art World where we met last night—and he wonders whether the father is about to make contact with him. Does he know I'm here, he wonders, or is he still too deep in the dream to notice anything at all?

"Jakob," the father goes on muttering, as he dips a brush into a pot of ink to paint the City's streets a darker shade of grey, "where are you? Show yourself before it's too late..."

Wieland lets these mutterings, even though he can sense they're directed at him, serve as background noise while he tries to fall back asleep. In time, he succeeds, though he can tell there will be no return to the dream. Whatever was in that box in my arms, he accepts, mournfully, will remain concealed for now.

A few hours later, dawn strikes the garage's eastern window and Wieland stirs. He yawns and feels everything that just happened wash away in a heavy undertow. Before sadness paralyzes him there on the damp mattress, in the now-empty garage, he heaves to his feet and lets himself out through the side door. After peeing against a hedge and rubbing his eyes with his inner forearm, he grips his cash roll in his pocket and decides to head downtown for breakfast.

Breakfast at
the Diner

At the diner, he orders pancakes and coffee, revising his order for the first time. When both have arrived, he finds that he's fallen back into the Art World in his mind. *My years of struggle... the decades I spent away from this town, fighting the million-headed stranger, before I'd made enough of a case for myself to come back here and stake out my own territory. Before I was someone critics would travel hours to interview.* He sips his coffee and considers this, letting the relief of being back in town wash over him. *I fought a bloody battle out there,* he recalls, staring at the diner's foggy windows and inwardly thanking Hopper for inventing not only the space but the entire atmosphere he's now soaking up. *I fought a battle to hammer my name into the world, and now that I have, my reward is the* freedom to return here, back to the place that my work has always been about.

He strips the top off a packet of faux syrup and dumps it over his pancakes, stuffing his mouth while he chews over the idea that this memory could be real. What difference does it actually make, he wonders, if I did my time in the Art World out there—he looks at the shadows moving on the far side of the foggy Hopper windows—or in here—he looks around the diner as if it were a model of the contents of his own mind, mapping the snarled network of cities, galleries, and Museums onto the folds and peaks of his brain. Couldn't the two very well be the same, making me... the Demiurge?

Laughing as he mushes the rest of his top pancake with his fork, he slugs down half of what's left in his coffee cup and thrills at the power he's just given himself, or just realized he has.

He laughs harder as he thinks of the father searching the endless interior of the nation for the New Jerusalem, one town after another after another, unable to part with the foolish belief that it exists somewhere outside of himself. As if the New Jerusalem were readymade! He wants to shout this phrase derisively to the few other people eating breakfast in the diner, but something inside him, a lingering ember of decency or shame, won't allow it. So he closes his mouth around more pancake mash and sits chewing, feeling his guts tremble with the mounting urge to speak.

When the urge grows unbearable, he excuses

himself to the bathroom, through a door at the back and then along a narrow, unlit hallway, fringed on both sides by boxes and cans and bottles and bags. In the bathroom, though there are two stalls and a urinal, he shoves the trash can in front of the door, then plugs the drain and runs the sink as hot as it'll go.

Watching the sink fill with steaming water, he presses the side of his thumb against his teeth and bites into it as hard as he can, willing himself to forget that it's anything other than a piece of warm flesh, a morsel leftover from breakfast.

As his blood spews into the sink, he licks his teeth and closes his eyes, absorbing all the pain he'd momentarily succeeded in postponing. Repaid in full, he thinks, tears running down his cheeks even though his eyes are still closed. Thanks, whoever you are, for lending me a moment of courage.

When he reopens his eyes, the Blood Clot has taken form in the sink. She's swimming peacefully back and forth, splashing around, looking up at him with affection. "Long time no see, little brother," she says, once he's made it clear that he's not going to start the conversation on his own.

Wieland nods. He tries to remember the last time they spoke. "I was afraid you wouldn't recognize me," he manages to say. "I... I've changed."

The Blood Clot smiles. "Not to me, you haven't. I've always known who you really were."

He waits, hoping that perhaps she'll tell him who that is, but she doesn't, and he can't summon the confidence, or the humility, to ask. Instead, he says, "Look, I was in the diner just now, thinking back on my—I mean, our—years of struggle in the Art World. All the ups and downs we suffered, that fleabag hotel we lived in, that first gallery show that got written up in *The New Yorker*, the, um..." He trails off, once again hoping she'll intuit the kind of relief he's looking for, and find a way to give it to him.

She takes a lap around the sink and says, "It feels good to be back in town, doesn't it?"

He nods. Then, just as he's about to say something else, a fist pounds on the door. A moment later, a voice shouts, "Hey! Anyone in there? I gotta get in."

Wieland shudders and grabs onto the sink, loosening it from the wall.

"Open the goddam door!" the voice shouts, pounding harder and trying to shove its way in. "I've been going to this diner all my life, and I know damn well the john's not a one-seater!"

Aware that there's nothing he can do to prevent the invasion, Wieland scrapes together whatever courage he can find and asks her, "Look, do you remember living in the City? If not, will you agree to remember it? Can that be our story now?"

The Blood Clot gazes up at him compassionately and seems like she's about to speak when the door bursts open and the trash can flies across the tiled floor and overturns against the far wall. A heaving middle-aged man looks at the sink full of blood and says, "Oh, fuck this!" and barrels past Wieland into a stall, leaving him to open the drain and run out, past more boxes and shrink-wrapped cases of tomato sauce and sunflower oil, on his way toward the employee exit.

Back to

Ragtown

In the alley behind the diner, he runs past two cooks on their cigarette break and stops to catch his breath behind a dumpster where the Boys' Boys are braining a dog with a chunk of concrete.

The Boys' Boys, the blood on his teeth, the dead dog staring up at him... the déjà vu grows so strong that Wieland swoons. He can tell that, if his head hits the ground, he'll fall unconscious and wake up many years ago, newly arrived in this town, as yet unsure what his future might hold, determined only to show these boys that the line between life and death is much more ragged than they'd like to believe.

Though this possibility holds an undeniable allure, he manages to grab the green metal edge of the dumpster just before it takes over. He leans there, licking the remnants of the Blood Clot from his teeth while staring the Boys' Boys down. Are they the originals? he wonders, unchanged after all these years, or does the term *Boys' Boys* refers to a type rather than a set of specific entities, like a species that self-replicates the way all species do in the wild, "Except those that go extinct?"

"Yes, I am talking to myself," he barks. "Which one of you's Tom? Is there a Tom still?"

The Boys' Boys don't respond. The biggest among them kicks the dog one last time, as if to prove that he's still in charge, then says, "C'mon guys, let's leave this pedo in the dust."

Just as they're about to leave, Wieland reaches into the dumpster and retrieves a jar of Hellman's mayonnaise, which he's certain has been planted there for this reason. He unscrews the top, dips his left hand into the warm goo, and pulls it out, shouting, "One second, please."

They watch him approach, frozen in place. "If I remember correctly," he says, smearing mayonnaise across the nearest boy's lips, "this is what you said I do to boys who venture up to see me in the woods." He smears the rest of the jar across the remaining boys' lips, pressing it deep into their mouths and across their teeth and gums, making sure to use all that he can extract from the jar. "Tonight, I could do mayo," he intones. "And so tonight I think I will."

Then he steps back to regard the tableau, and smiles, satisfied with his work. "A kind of justice for the boy

I used to be," he says, before throwing the empty jar on top of the dog. "Move as soon as you dare," he tells them.

Then he turns and heads toward Ragtown.

He walks down Pleasant St. until it intersects Main and leads him to the strip, past Wing Hut, Giant Chinese, and Mama's Pizza, with the Tyson Meat Truck idling outside. In front of the Town Museum, he stops to peer in the windows at Greta vacuuming while listening to music, and he considers asking how the setup of *The Adoration of the Sunken Town* is coming along. This thought leads him to imagine going back to the alley and getting the dog and presenting it to her as his latest piece, and tears come again to his eyes as he pictures how she'd refuse to accept it. "No," she'd say, "no, you're past that kind of thing now. I won't stand here and watch you regress."

He shivers and wipes his eyes and nose and nods, thinking, You're right, you're right. I'm sorry. I just wish I could start over again. Just one more time. But what would you do differently if you could? He shrugs. I don't know, I guess I'd have to try it to find out. Even in fantasy, he resists articulating what he fears may be the truth: *if I had it to do over again, I would never have sold my Bellmer when I was twelve.*

The air turns chilly and he knows that if Greta sees him through the window, she'll open the door and then he'll have to interact for real, so he shakes off his growing hesitation and hurries toward Ragtown, thinking, Maybe I'll unearth the first few components of my next piece under a rusted fender or in the grill of a dented A/C unit.

Enlivened by this prospect, he ducks through the hole in the fence and into the same clearing he sat in all those years ago. He sits for a moment on the throne that used to belong to Tom, and perhaps still does, feeling its springs scratch his testicles. Then, getting to his feet, he leaves the realm of the Boys' Boys behind and skirts the tremendous trash pile around the cabin, which he now understands is a profane model of the one he will inhabit once his existence as Wieland has been fully sanctified, and the current transitional period reaches its inevitable finale.

He makes a circuit of the cabin, letting his memories of training for his first journey up the mountain fade as he replaces them with anticipation of his second. I haven't been up there yet, he thinks, not really. Not as myself. After his first circuit, he pauses to ruminate on the problem of rebuilding the spiders out front, or building them for the first time, if, as he now suspects, his memories of having been in the cabin before are in fact nothing but premonitions. He stops and looks out at the trash piles, beginning to see the jagged chunks of metal and snarls of wire in a new way, each suggesting its place in the bodies of the spiders that will, in time, guard the cabin of an artist whose singularity will come close to justifying the entire American experiment.

His muscles surge as he imagines the cabin designed

exactly to his specifications, the spiders built by him and therefore entirely under his control. This feeling lasts until a wall of dark shapes moves in on the pile, forcing him to remember that Ragtown belongs to the Rat People. As they begin to forage for scraps, slicing open trash bags and pouring out their contents, he feels their gaze moving through the dusk toward him. He leans against the rickety wooden wall of the cabin and returns their gaze, trying to send the message that he's here but not one of them, that he's better than they are, smarter, sharper, more vested with purpose, but the light's too dim to get this across. They root through partly empty cans and gnaw chicken bones and eye him with dull malice, not approaching but making it clear that they'll show him no special respect if he gets in their way.

For now, he backs down, unsure whether there's any active conflict between himself and the Rat People that will in time have to be worked out. His zips his raincoat up to his neck and circles the cabin again, pulling his eyes off the trash pile. When he makes it back to the cabin's far side, imagining that the distant fences and buildings are the walls of forest that surround the cabin on the mountain, he senses something missing. For a few moments, he can't tell what it is. Then he thinks, The smoker!

As soon as this thought enters his mind, Tobin comes hurtling in behind it. He spends two or three seconds remembering Tobin stabbing a pig and then jamming its hocks into the smoker; then he spends two or three more remembering how, as soon as he'd dreamed of Tobin up on the mountain, the man himself appeared. Then, like the punchline of an old-fashioned skit, Tobin appears again out of the dusk, staggering toward him in his apron, butcher knife dangling by his side.

"Hello, little fink," he whispers, spittle running in dual streams from the corners of his mouth. "Nice to see your peach fuzz again." He stumbles toward the cabin, tripping on the trash-strewn ground, making no effort to look where he's going.

Swatting flies with the flat side of his knife, he leans in and says, "Well, what did you call me for?"

Wieland blanches, unsure how to respond. Though he knows he may be inviting a chop between the shoulder blades, he elbows open the cabin's back door and slams it shut behind him. After pushing the kitchen table against it, he lies down on the dirt floor and listens to Tobin circle outside.

As the heavy, uneven footsteps become mesmerizing, and the fear and the unreality of the moment compound one another, Wieland feels himself losing consciousness. He pulls his knees up under his chin in the hot dark and closes his eyes, willing his innermost self to sink.

Once he's sunk back into the town within the town, Tobin's footsteps drift into irrelevance overhead and he sees his own earlier incarnation, back when he was Jakob, enter the cabin with him. Though he can't touch this version of himself, and it can't touch him, each can watch the other and, together, they become aware that those early days belong now to a mythic age. A sanctified time. Not exactly a paradisiacal one, but one in which the groundwork for the greatness I am now approaching was being laid, the dream asserts. An Age of Revelation, when the Demiurge was entirely unconcealed, reworking the matter of the whole town and all its inhabitants, and thereby all of its spirit as well, because spirit, while distinct from matter, must reside within it.

As he writhes, huddled there on a floor that is really just ground, he prays to be allowed to remember these thoughts next time he's awake enough to implement them. Because if I do, he thinks, then I'll know what my next piece must be.

"Yes," whispers the snake threading itself back through the walls. "Yes, time to start your next piece. And then time to meet your patrons. The couple from another town. Never forget: $500 is nothing to them. Seek them out, and you'll be wealthy beyond your wildest dreams. Remember the mansion with the moat, the tigers, the diamond-studded files. It is all within reach, Jakob, but only if you act soon."

The Couple
From Another
Town

After this initial round of vivid dreams, Wieland bobs back up, disturbed by Tobin's lurch. He listens with half his mind while the other half ideates on chutes and elevators, passageways up the mountain and up mountains beyond that, higher highs, more vivid enchantments, Anything, he prays, to keep my bildungs-years underway, to prevent this, here, from being my final form. To prevent any final decision from having to be made.

Any hope that this cabin could be his sanctum, his center of power and the one place in the universe where he might feel safe, now seems at best a bout of wishful thinking. He groans and shivers through the night, frightened and alone, aware that, without the spiders' protection, all manner of flies are likely to feast on his body.

When dawn locates him under the table against the door, it reveals a cramped, sweaty man with a scabbed-over thumb and circles under his eyes. He tries to yawn and ends up whimpering. Whimpering more as he gets to his feet, he stretches and goes outside, willing himself not to think about Tobin, lest he summon him again.

He walks over to what looks like a pile of cat skulls and pees on it, aiming at the eye sockets. The gruesome delicacy of this task clears his mind, which makes it receptive to an unexamined memory from last night. The Town Museum, he thinks, the snake's tongue tickling his left ear. Time to pay my patrons a visit.

First he retraces his steps, down the alley and up to the employees' entrance of the diner as the summer morning heats up. Passing the dead dog by the dumpster, which a family of flies has already begun to dismantle, he stops and reflects once again, though he knows it's redundant, on the image of himself presenting its carcass to Greta. He leans against the dumpster, eyes half-closed, and watches himself drag its leaking body up the street, drawing a molasses-colored line past the Tyson Meat Truck and up the steps of the Town Museum. He pictures himself knocking on the door and Greta hobbling over to open it. Then he pictures her initial disapproval at his lack of evolution, same as the last time he pictured it, but this time he pictures himself insisting, "No, the Bellmer is a staple of my production, now just as then. A classic. Some things need never change. Either accept this or let me go. I'll find another gallerist whose tastes better reflect my own."

Some Things Need Never Change. He closes his eyes more tightly and pictures this sign across the door of the Town Museum as the title of his next show, which, he now sees, consists of a dozen Bellmers lined up side by side, each in its own bed or alcove, each slightly different in specific composition but, in terms of general concept, exactly the same. A litter of Bellmers, every generation identical, proud in its refusal to evolve. "What the show represents," he imagines telling a massed crowd of wine-sipping strangers, "is my desire to remain permanently inside the mindset I inhabited when I made my very first piece, rather than consenting to, as so many artists feel they must, perform an evolution merely for the sake of proving true the theory that artists, like sharks, must keep moving in order to remain alive. Sometimes our best selves are our first selves. Why can't this be alright?"

Applause!

He swallows a lump as his eyes reopen onto the desolate alley, the dog still dead at his feet, a busboy smoking on the stoop behind him. When the lump's fallen into his stomach, he bends over, aware that the busboy's watching him, and heaves the dead dog, destined never to be a Bellmer, onto his shoulders and then into the dumpster, where it nestles among wet rice and melon rinds, bringing its flies down with it. Then he bends over again to pick up the empty jar of mayonnaise, and tosses this atop the animal, muttering, "Tonight, I could do mayo, but I won't, because I don't have any left."

This image likewise tempts Wieland to reify it, but he forces himself to override the temptation. Nevertheless, perhaps the fraught allure of going backwards can itself be the theme of my next work, he thinks, sneaking in through the employees' entrance after the busboy, but this is very different from actually going backwards. One shows perspective, maturity, the acceptance of loss, while the other...

He lets this question dangle as he returns to the bathroom he was forced out of yesterday and, once again, shoves the trash can under the door. The remnants of the Blood Clot remain on the edges of the sink, dried and peeling, but he doesn't try to reconstitute her now. A conversation with a partial Blood Clot, one whom he barely recognizes and who barely recognizes him, would be little more than a second stillbirth... and it's not like I need any help barely recognizing myself these days, he thinks, looking at the weary man in the rusted mirror. "Hello Stranger," he quips, winking at his reflection and imagining this phrase as an alternate title for his next exhibition. He studies the man's face in the mirror and tries to remember how Wieland appeared to him back when he was Jakob, back in the Old Testament, or *My First Life*, which he decides now is yet another possible title.

As he stares deeper into the mirror, trying to conjure that original face, from the long dark winter or string of winters in the Wilderness, a grizzled, suspicious old man appears behind him, blooming out of the rough metal.

He pauses, unsure how to respond, until that man's voice says, accompanied by his mouth's moving reflection, "You washing up or what?"

Still dazed, Wieland steps aside and inhales, only now realizing, thanks to the smell of shit in the air, that the man must've been in one of the stalls all this time. He smiles and pushes the trash can aside and, just before he bursts out laughing, manages to say, "It's all yours, sir!"

Shaken from this failed attempt to center himself, Wieland runs through the main part of the diner and out the front door, then up Main Street and the strip, past Wing Hut, Giant Chinese, and Mama's Pizza, the Tyson Meat Truck idling, as ever, in the parking lot, and up to the front lawn of the Town Museum, where he finally stops to catch his breath. He leans forward with his open palms on his thighs and counts his inhales, trying to stop his heart from racing before he goes in.

But as he's standing there in an inadvertent pose of obeisance, like a penitent about to enter the temple where he will beg the high priest for forgiveness, two dark forms materialize on the lawn behind him and say, in unison, "Going in?"

He has no choice but to nod.

"Well then, after you," they say, and, again, he has no choice but to begin the climb up the front steps and onto the porch.

Soon, he's knocking on the front door and soon after that Greta is answering, her face a complicated mixture of warm and dubious welcome.

"Come in," she says, her gaze encompassing both Wieland and the twin dark forms behind him, whose faces he still hasn't seen and which, he senses, he may never fully see.

After a brief confusion of bodies, he finds himself seated on a folding chair in the center of the main gallery, across from Greta and beside the couple from another town, who have just introduced themselves as such.

They're both wearing suits of all black, hers tailored in such a way as to lightly hint at the feminine, while his hints just as lightly at the masculine. The difference, as far as Wieland can tell without staring, is so subtle it's almost invisible, but all the more powerful for that. Whatever it is, he thinks, it's all-important, such that if they traded suits, they would either have to trade identities as well, or else look like two divas in drag.

All four of them have Cokes in their laps, as the man describes their national circuit. "Every summer," he says, his gaze swiveling around the gallery, "my wife and I drive around this whole country—we like to say that we visit every single town—in search of new talent. New diamonds in the rough, like you," he says, in a tone that sounds like he thinks he's speaking either to a child or an imbecile.

His wife nods, closing her mouth exactly in unison with her husband's so that, a moment later, Wieland can't be sure which one was speaking.

Looking at Wieland, Greta says, "I take it you've deduced that this is the couple who purchased *The Sunken Town*. Shall I show them the new piece as well? Something tells me it may interest them just as much, if not even more."

He knows he should acquiesce, and that soon he will, but first he takes a moment to marvel at the change in Greta's tone. He wonders if she, too, in the final reckoning, is a mere automaton, like the Jakob he glimpsed in the kitchen of what used to be his home. Is the couple controlling her just as they hope to control me?

He smiles. "Sure. Why not?"

Greta smiles too and goes into the back room, leaving him alone with them.

"This is a nice town," the woman says.

A moment later, Greta returns, carrying the package under a cloth. She places it on the gift shop table, which she then laboriously pushes toward the couple from another town. Nobody offers to help. Panting, she wipes her brow with her forearm and pulls off the cloth with a slightly self-conscious flourish.

Wieland, who realizes that he hasn't seen the piece since he dropped it off, is as impressed as the couple is. A true masterpiece, he thinks, the culmination of everything I'd become up to the point when I made it. He blushes at the thought of the miniature Wieland hidden in its brainstem, a detail he now renews his vow never to reveal.

He shivers with pride.

"Yes, yes, brilliant," the man says. "I can see a clear progression from the last piece that we purchased. This one is... hmm, richer and stranger somehow. In the same lineage, aesthetically, of course, but a step further along. It would make a handsome addition to the show we're mounting this fall. At the American Folk Art Museum near Lincoln Center?" He looks at Wieland, his eyes boiling. "I don't suppose we've mentioned this yet, have we?" Now he looks to his wife, who takes over speaking in an incrementally higher version of the same voice. The uniformity of their affect, which gives the impression of a single consciousness alternating between two mouths, makes it impossible to imagine them both speaking at once.

"No, I don't suppose we have. But let's not talk business here in the Museum. Is there someplace we could go? Someplace celebratory?"

She turns to look at Greta, whose attention is still on the piece.

"Excuse me," she repeats, her voice gaining an edge. "Is there someplace celebratory we could go?"

Greta still doesn't reply. She looks deep in thought, perhaps seeking refuge in a distant memory.

The woman from the couple turns to Wieland and says, "Excuse me, what's her name?"

Wieland also finds himself deep in a memory, that of receiving his first $10 after burying the Bellmer in the backyard, and buying himself a milkshake and a plate of fries at the diner. He hears the woman's voice summoning him out of this memory, and he hears the snake slithering faster and faster around his head, urging him to respond, but he tries to resist a little longer, to remain inside that lost moment between himself and Greta. He has the sense that, as soon as he returns to the present, his connection with Greta will die, and that, in short order, she will too.

"Excuse me!" the woman shouts, and this time he responds involuntarily, making direct eye contact with her.

"What's her name?" she asks again.

"Greta," Wieland replies, certain that he's just sacrificed his first patron upon the altar of his second.

The woman smiles. "Greta, is there someplace nice we could go to celebrate?"

"Celebrate?" Greta rises reluctantly out of the past.

"A fancy restaurant." The man takes his turn. "All the towns we visit have one. Never two, but always one."

Greta looks at the left wall, as if she could see through it to scan the street for someplace suitable.

Without breaking that gaze, she murmurs, "Chez Pierre."

The man smiles, appeased. "Chez Pierre. Sounds nice."

"It is," Greta replies, looking at Wieland with tears beginning to moisten the bridge of her nose. "It's where we went on our wedding night, years and years ago. Before the beginning. The only time we could afford it. Don't you remember?"

Wieland unfocuses his eyes, committing all of his attention to tuning out the couple and regarding Greta, and only Greta, one last time. The squint begins to hurt, but he holds it, fading out the Museum to envision him and her together at a table with a white tablecloth, a candle, and a bottle of deep red wine, on the night they would go home and make the man who would, in time, make Jakob. This and only this, he thinks. This is where I am until I can stay there no longer.

When he feels blood running from his eyes, he knows he has to let go. He blinks them open, wipes his face with his sleeve, and says, reestablishing focus on Greta for the last time, "Of course I remember."

"Can you direct us?" the woman interrupts, and Greta nods with a heavy sigh.

At Chez Pierre

After Greta has given directions to the restaurant, her voice quavering with the effort of conjuring it from an adjacent dimension, and after the man has made it clear that she isn't invited, Wieland allows the couple from another town to guide him down a series of side streets he's never seen before—one of which looks exactly like the alley he dreamed of haunting in the Art World—and across a cloistered parking lot, toward a burgundy awning that reads, in gold cursive, *Chez Pierre: Fine French Dining & Wine.*

The couple strides in with such familiarity that Wieland imagines they eat at this exact restaurant in every town they visit. He knows he'll never manage to find it again and so, like it does for Greta, it will for the rest of his life exist in memory as the setting of a onetime event.

Or, in my case, a two-time event, he thinks,

shuddering on the threshold as a shadow looms up behind him. He turns to regard the Tyson Meat Truck pulling into the lot and men in full-body white suits unloading sealed packages from the back. A moment later, a chef in a more refined version of the same white suit bustles out of the kitchen to greet the driver and sign a stack of papers on a clipboard.

"Coming?" the man asks, forcing Wieland to break off his gaze and follow the black-suited couple into the dim, velvet-upholstered interior.

As soon as they're seated in their deep booth, the couple on one side, Wieland on the other, it might as well be nighttime. The windows are frosted a deep amber and the décor suggests some combination of Parisian bistro and Tyrolean hunting lodge, if Wieland's memory of Nerval and Walser is to be trusted.

"Cocktails while we choose our wine?" the woman asks. She orders three dry martinis as soon as the black-vested elderly waiter drifts into earshot.

"Cheers," she says, after waiting in silence for them to arrive. "To the newest member of our fall collection."

"Well, not yet, my love, we haven't formally asked him," her husband cautions, weakly.

"Cheers," she repeats, clinking Wieland's glass and draining half her martini.

When the waiter returns, she speaks to him in French.

"I'm sorry ma'am, I..." he mutters.

Scowling, she says, "A bottle of your 2013 White

Burgundy, a large raw oyster platter, steak tartare, lobster polenta, and the rabbit au poivre, please. Yes?" She looks to Wieland and her husband, before repeating, "Yes," and handing the waiter all three menus.

"So," she says, once the oysters have arrived and Wieland has begun mimicking the couple's process of dressing them, "as my husband mentioned, we are putting together a group show at the American Folk Art Museum in New York City. *Americans on the Edge: Dreamscapes, Private Worlds, and Secret Obsessions.* There are, so far, eleven other outsider artists signed up, eight of them still living, and the estates of the other three. It will be the first show for all of them. You would make twelve."

I would make twelve? Wieland thinks, the father scowling in his head. Twelve what? Twelve tribes? My work is all there is. It's a vision of the entire cosmos, of the town within the town within the town, all the way to the bottom of everything. Beneath that there is nothing at all.

The couple slurps down the rest of the oysters, finishes the bottle of wine, and calls for another while dishing out the creamy lobster polenta. Wieland feels his stomach soften as it lands on his plate, as if he'd already swallowed it.

When the next bottle arrives, the man says, "We are experts, Wieland, at bringing in artists from the fringes and finding them homes in the most prestigious collections in the world. The American Folk Art Museum is just a jumping-off point. Think Tate, think Whitney, think MoMA. Seriously. And even this is only the tip of an iceberg which extends downward into an echelon of private collectors whose names must never be uttered aloud. What we do is find artists with sharp, jangly edges like you, artists who, no offense, are playing with a few cards less than a full deck, and we sand you down just enough. We make it so you're city-edgy, not," he gestures at the empty French restaurant, "town-edgy. Get it?"

Yes, yes, yes, the snake whispers in Wieland's head, straining to gain control of his tongue. These people will make you rich and famous, Jakob. He flinches at the invocation of that old name, which brings with it the thundering voice of his father, who shouts, No, no, no! Remember Bosch: the hell he painted was the hell he lived in. Remember Bacon: picture the rending of flesh and the twisting of sinew that his poor figures suffered on the racks and wheels of the Art World. Resist any temptation to forget this. We are prophets, Jakob, Jewish prophets descended without dilution from the Age of Revelation. Never let anyone pervert the reality of what we do for their own short-term gain. That is the road to Nazism.

What *we* do? Me and you both? He's astonished to hear his father say this. He begins to think he should get up and leave, but the snake won't let him. He feels it wrapping itself around his central nervous system, tighter with every inhalation, while the wine spins him in circles.

"We give you a context," the woman says, nibbling raw steak off an overlong fork. "You outsider artists, you all think the universe revolves around you, like you're the only ones out there making anything, like you invented the fucking concept of art, but that simply isn't true. We put you in a show with your peers and make it so that the right class of people in New York and London and Los Angeles can pay you a visit on a Saturday or a Sunday afternoon, after a nice lunch or brunch with their friends. That's what people pay for, Wilhelm. They pay to touch the weird without fearing that the weird will touch them back."

He drains his fifth or sixth glass of wine, sweating while the oysters squirm in his stomach, still living, and the Blood Clot squirms in his veins. What would she want me to do? he wonders. Would she be proud to see *The Adoration of the Sunken Town* in a group show in New York City? Or would she hate me forever?

"Is there... dessert?" he finally manages to ask, pushing his slimy plate of raw steak into the shadows on the far side of the table, where his view is slightly less obscene. The couple from another town smiles and snaps their fingers, and a terrine of chocolate mousse and a plate of madeleines and a pot of hot chocolate appear in unison on the table.

"Look," the woman says, growing exasperated, while Wieland thinks, Surely all the other artists, except the dead ones, said yes during the oyster course, making the rest of the meal a celebration. "Look, we already own *The Sunken Town*, so we'll do as we wish with that. The only question now is whether you want to be a one-off, a curio relegated to the hallway of the exhibit, which people will pass on their way to the restroom, or whether you want to be at the center of the main hall, perhaps even on the cover of the brochure. Both are possible, but after tonight, only one will remain so."

He chokes down mousse and tries to silence his father in his head so the snake can speak. "Yes, yes!" the snake shouts, "we want to be in the main hall. We want, more than anything, to be on the cover of the brochure!"

"Jakob," his father booms, "the Demiurge moves through you. You are reworking the foundational matter of the universe. Do you have any idea how few people are granted the power to do this? And you'd be so crude as to imprison it on a pedestal in some drafty room in New York City that strangers have to pay to enter, and that they'll only ever stroll through on their way to the gift shop and then a restaurant like the one you're eating in now?

"If you acquiesce to that, you'll prove for all time that the Demiurge was wrong to believe in you. Wrong to believe in the Jews at all. Let me be very clear when I say that there's a special hell reserved for real Jewish prophets who turn false. Picture that hell; then accept that it has a name. And what is that name?"

Wieland tries to resist, but "The Art World" forces its way out of his mouth.

The couple from another town beams. "That's right, Wilhelm. We are here to usher you into the Art World. We are the bridge. All you have to do is walk across."

"Can I go to the bathroom?" he asks, heaving up from the table before they respond.

In the bathroom, which has hammered tin walls and ceiling tiles and little rolled up cloth towels in a brass rack beside the marble sink, Wieland shoves his thumb into his mouth and readies himself to summon the Blood Clot. He closes his eyes and orders his nerves to postpone the pain, just as they did in the diner bathroom, but the oysters and the wine and the mousse in his stomach seem to have rendered his nerves unresponsive.

You're on your own, they tell him, as he jams his thumb deeper into his mouth and, instinctively, begins to suck on it. His teeth feel slick and dull, while his tongue caresses the stubby cylinder and he rocks back and forth, trying to reason with himself. But his reasoning now seems dusty and bloodless, lacking any fresh angle. The longer he stands there, the dustier his entire body comes to feel, until it seems that he can't summon the Blood Clot because his veins are too dry to host her.

He sucks his thumb harder and feels the emptiness of his body correlate with the emptiness of his mind, both of them admitting a stalemate on the question he came in here to consider.

And what was that question?

Even this, he finds, is more than he can recall. Yawning, he splashes warm water on his face, dries it with one of the rolled up, rose-scented towels, and dabs cream from the dispenser by the sink onto his nose and cheeks.

Then he flushes the toilet, though he knows he hasn't used it, and resolves to return to the table.

"Ah, we were wondering if we'd see you again," says the man from another town. "Everything shipshape in the bowel department? We took the liberty of ordering you an Armagnac. A little nightcap, even if it's not quite night yet. It will be soon enough, is what we always say, don't we?"

Once Wieland has taken his seat and molded his hands around the fluted glass, the man continues, "So, tell us, are you working on anything new?"

Wieland has a delirious desire to once again bring up the dead dog in the alley, insisting, now that Greta's out of the picture, that this is his latest piece, but he restrains himself by fixating on the cabin in Ragtown, to which he now desperately needs to return. When the woman echoes her husband by asking a second time, his thoughts spill over into speech. He hears himself say, "As a matter of fact, I am. An installation piece. A cabin in the middle of Ragtown, which is what I call the town dump. It represents the home I will one day live in, once I've grown back into the old man that I also, in a sense, used to be. This story will be part of the piece, too. It will be, um, written on the walls in red marker.

The timelines of my life will loop and crisscross and contradict in all directions. The many lives I've lived, all over the walls. Each jealous of the others, making its case for being the original. Your customers will have never seen anything like it."

The man grins while his wife pays the check and hands it to the waiter without looking at him. "That sounds intriguing. Museumgoers love interactive art. They love to take their shoes off, leave them on a wicker mat, and wander in their socks through a bumpy, mysterious built landscape with mood music playing softly overhead." He smiles and closes his eyes. "I don't imagine that the dump is a place for my wife and me at this time of the evening, assuming it is evening by now, but would you show it to us in the morning? If you tell us where it is, we'll meet you there at seven o'clock sharp, on our way out of town."

The Tyson
Meat Truck

Belly full of oysters, Wieland stumbles out of Chez Pierre at dusk with the couple from another town, grumbling noncommittally when they remind him that they'll be at Ragtown tomorrow morning at seven. Then the Tyson Meat Truck pulls back into the lot and he swoons again, his vision wavering as they disappear into its foggy cab. By the time he's gotten ahold of himself, only the truck remains. Please don't follow me home, he prays in its direction, as he zips himself back inside the shell of the Lone Lecher and tiptoes around the restaurant, already half vanished in the fog, toward what he hopes will turn out to be Main Street.

After a few false starts, including a turn down an alley that reveals the Boys' Boys sitting on skateboards and huffing from paper bags, the Lone Lecher finds himself down at one end of Main, in the direction that leads to what used to be Jakob's house. Forcing himself to reverse course, which takes more effort than he'd like to admit, he sets out for Ragtown and, before long, finds himself crawling through the hole in the fence, dragging his feet past the still-foraging Rat People, and making his way into the cabin.

Inside, he grabs the back of a wicker chair and leans over and retches, anticipating both shame and relief. Neither arrives. The mousse and oysters merely churn and resettle. Running his fingers through his slick hair, he lies down on the dirt floor and resolves to sleep in this cabin one last time while it's still his home, before the couple arrives in the morning and forces him to recast it in terms that will allow it to be assessed, sold, and carted off in sections.

Eyes closed and head on the ground, he spends a few seconds in a welcome, warm blackness. Then the Tyson Meat Truck pulls into view, the words "New York City" glowing in red neon at the top of its windshield. He tries to get out of the way, but finds that he can't. His muscles are frozen. Whatever I ate at dinner, he hears himself think, whatever they fed me, must have shut down my system and deposited me in the road like a dummy. The bloodlessness I felt in the bathroom? That was just the early onset.

He lies there now, arms pinned to his waist in the middle of the road, and watches as the truck pulls toward him. The doors of the cab open in slow motion and the couple from another town, dressed in butchering smocks like the one Tobin wears, step down and smile.

"We're so glad you decided to come with us," they leer, their voices conjoined as they lift him off the road. Either he's weightless, or they've developed superhuman strength. Perhaps, he thinks, whatever it was in the meal that paralyzed me had the opposite effect on them. They lift him onto their shoulders and open the back of the truck and climb inside, where eleven bloodless hocks dangle on meathooks.

Tobin sits on a wooden crate beneath them, licking his butcher knife. He rises to his feet when the couple deposits the Wieland-bundle and says, still in unison, "Alright, here's number twelve. Hook him up and let's get out of here. If we hit the road now, we might still beat the morning traffic in the Lincoln Tunnel."

They climb out as Tobin lurches over, his footsteps clanking on the truck's metal bottom. He grabs the bundle, salivating as he whispers, "Hello again, little fink. Ready for our little field trip?"

He carries the bundle over to the twelfth hook and lifts it high, about to slot it into place, when Wieland manages to fight his way through the paralysis just enough to whisper, "Tobin... Tobin, I want to go back to the cabin. The real one. The one where you and I were friends. With the snow and the smoker. Remember? I'm sorry I ignored you in Ragtown... but if you let me go now, I'll meet you up there. We'll have many happy years together if you just throw me onto the road and..."

Tobin pauses and seems to think. He picks up his butcher knife and scratches his leg with it, drawing blood.

"It's our paradise," Wieland continues, "the place where we were happy. You must remember. Before all this. Before we were exiled. Let me go, and I'll find a way to get us back there."

"Promise?" Tobin asks, his voice startlingly gentle, almost babyish at the mention of paradise.

Wieland tries to nod, but finds he can't move his neck. He barely manages to gasp, "Promise."

Tobin sighs. "If you don't," he says, "remember my pigs? You'll wish that was you."

"I would welcome such a fate," Wieland gasps, trying hard not to picture it.

A minute later, he finds himself facedown on the road, bones aching, as the Tyson Meat Truck pulls away with its back doors still open, rattling in the wind. Still unable to move, he closes his eyes and focuses everything he has left on summoning the Night Crusher, who, in due time, lumbers out of the scrub brush by the side of the road and says, yawning, "Yes?"

"I need you to carry me home," Wieland manages to whisper, too spent to sigh with relief as two giant hands reach out and scoop him up.

Wieland

Returns Home

Wieland rides through the town at dawn held against the Night Crusher's chest. He passes the bridge where the fishermen are unpacking their bait and opening their first cans of Schlitz, then he passes the diner where the counter man is swabbing the greasy windows, polishing the Hopper he inhabits from within. Then he and the Night Crusher make their way up the part of Main Street that leaves downtown and threads through the neighborhoods. Wieland closes his eyes and sinks into a mini-dream of Jakob's arrival in this town, his body drugged and blanketed in the back seat, the station wagon bridging the miles between the old house and the new, each a replica of the other and thus both approximations of some Platonic ur-house lodged deep in his father's prophetic imagination.

"Keep going straight?" the Night Crusher whispers.

"Yes, all the way home," Wieland responds, determined to repeat the ritual one last time. And it will indeed be the last time, he knows, sinking back into the dream of arrival. But now the dream's been bifurcated, like the old legend of men and gods occupying separate chambers of the bicameral mind, such that one chamber contains the belief that the journey he's reenacting now was a real one—that my family really did roam from town to town according to my father's dreams, seeking the lost paradise of his youth, which required the commission of a great number of identical houses—while the other chamber is busy taking credit for having dredged this story up from the stagnation of a small-town childhood, the formless American boredom from which epochal Geniuses sometimes emerge. This chamber is now busy determining the best means of aestheticizing and reifying that account... a comic strip, perhaps? A series of mobiles accompanied by audio recordings, with a young boy playing me as a child, reading off notecards that I've written for him?

Wieland squirms like a baby in the Night Crusher's arms as the two scenarios rub up against one another and send chills down his spine.

"**Okay**, we're here," his mother says, waking up the sleeping Jakob in the back seat and pulling his blanket off. "Back home, after a nice little drive."

"We are?" he asks, looking up in search of her familiar, consoling face.

"Just where you told me to take you," the Night Crusher replies, putting him down on the back steps and lumbering into the back yard.

Wieland stands alone now, the sun a few degrees off the horizon, the garage door behind him, the back door of the house in front. He adjusts his raincoat's zipper until it's comfortably poised between his chest and his chin, and, without knocking, grips the doorknob and feels it turn.

As soon as the door opens, the interior of the house emits a whoosh, like he's popped a bubble or released a pressure valve. The atmosphere sighs past him, carrying ancient odors of Wheaties and coffee. He takes his shoes off and runs his hands through his hair, just as Jakob used to when coming down to breakfast for the first time in the new house. Then, as ready as he'll ever be, he approaches the kitchen, where the family is arrayed around the table.

He makes eye contact first with the doll Jakob, then with the mother, then with the father. He forces himself to sideline the Lone Lecher so as to feel, as much as humanly possible, like a legitimate son of parents who have worked hard over the years to find a way to love him.

Standing there with his mouth open, he realizes that he has nothing planned to say, and nothing is coming out on its own. All he wants, he can now see, is to take his place at the table behind his Wheaties and his

Training Mug of coffee and prepare to face the day's
lesson, in which he will learn, yet again, about the
all-important distinction between the Dogmatic and
the Visionary Jews. As he imagines himself sitting at
this table, in place of his replacement, he feels
simultaneously several feet and several lifetimes away.
I could throw that doll in the trash and sit down there
right now, he knows, but nothing would ever be the
same. I could pretend that the couple from another
town didn't exist, I could pretend that the couple sitting
here were still the parents they used to be, but, though
I might convince myself, none of those things would
become other than they are.

Reality feels like an invisible but impermeable wall
between where he stands, at the edge of the kitchen,
and where the doll-Jakob sits, beside his mother and
across from his father, his bowl of Wheaties growing
soggy in front of him.

As if they'd waited for him to complete this exact
thought process, the parents now come alive, both
speaking in unison.

"Didn't you tell that man never to come back?" the
mother asks, while the father looks at him and shouts,
"Yes! Now who the hell are you? What have you come
here for?".

I am now truly standing in *The Sunken Town*,
Wieland realizes, speaking to characters of my own
invention. I have confounded the levels, crossed the
wires, in a way that might have disastrous

consequences for us all. He flashes back to his old dream of the walls crushed like wet paper and... somebody stomping through to carry them all away.

Wieland almost wishes it would happen now, if only to be delivered out of the town and back to the mountaintop without all the grief that, he senses, will otherwise intervene.

"Mom... dad," he manages to whisper. "It's me. It's..." He knows the pain the name will cause, but he forces himself to utter it anyway. "It's Jakob."

The name silences the room.

"Jakob's right here," the mother says, nodding at the doll. The father nods too, but neither looks entirely convinced. "Our family is complete," she swears. "You're the only interloper. Which is why you must leave now."

"Yes, right now," the father says, rising to his full height and summoning his sermon voice.

Wieland wonders what he's really doing here, why he felt compelled to make this scene. Am I praying they'll protect me from the couple from another town? That they'll tell me it isn't too late to go on being Jakob, that I haven't thrown that away for good?

He shudders and says, "Look at me. I know I'm changed on the outside, but inside I'm the same. Can't we all stop pretending?"

In the grueling silence that follows, he looks at the doll-Jakob and intuits what has to be done. He swallows, moving his eyes over the father's wiry frame, aware that he's about to cross a line that can never be uncrossed.

Then, before either of the parents can stop him, he lunges across the table at the doll-Jakob and wraps his hands around its neck, squeezing through the soft cotton flesh to get at the wooden bones below. He grabs and twists as much as he possibly can in the one or two seconds of shock before the father is likewise upon him, trying to wring his neck just as he's trying to wring the doll's. He presses the doll's face into the ground and hammers the wooden armature with his palms, feeling the front of its throat splinter as cotton and thread wisp out, and he flashes back to the father destroying his show at the Town Museum and he thinks, Now we're even.

Or, at the very least, we will be soon. As soon as I force the end. He flashes back to himself as the Lone Lecher, standing on the lawn in anticipation of the Apocalypse. Now, he thinks. Now, now!

He squeezes harder as the father's hands close around his own throat and his consciousness wavers. It wavers so hard that, looking down at the mess of stuffing issuing from his replacement, he finds he can't remember which materials are supposed to issue from dolls, and which from people. Blood, pus, wire, thread... some go with one, he thinks, and some with the other. But which is which?

He clamps down harder still, forcing these questions out of his head as the doll's head comes off in his hands and he hears a death rattle shoot out of his own mouth.

Just before he blacks out, he thinks, The violence of this instant represents the final rupture of the collective illusion. When I wake up, if I'm still alive, I will be reunited with my family in the only true reality there's ever been, on the far side of the Apocalypse, where all the imposters and lost futures are gone, and the giant key in my desk upstairs unlocks the gates of the real New Jerusalem, never again to deny us entry.

On his way there, Wieland falls into a room beneath the kitchen, a culmination of all the basements he's lived and worked in so far.

He sees his life's work arrayed on all the walls and laid out on a series of benches. The Future Museum, it's called, the paradise for whose glory all true basement boys labor in obscurity. He senses, as he walks along the cramped aisles, leading himself on a victory lap, that the Age of Revelation is not yet over. It is always, he thinks, more ongoing than one wishes to believe. More suffering is always still to come. He sees *The Sunken Town* and *The Adoration of the Sunken Town*, and the cabin in Ragtown, and he sees his decapitated double and a model of the Tyson Meat Truck with eleven carcasses and one empty hook in back, gleaming with envy for the others, and he sees a dumpster stuffed to overflowing with Bellmers, and he sees Tobin and Greta and the Boys' Boys and the couple from another town, all stuffed and posed in whatever positions best express their significance in the Wagnerian epic of his life.

Though he knows he won't be able to stay down here just yet—that would be death, the end of all effort—he also knows for sure that it exists, and that nothing can ever nullify or cloud this knowledge. All you have to do now, he tells himself, once you leave this place, is devote the rest of your life to bringing it into the conscious world. Bring the town within the town into the town, he thinks, pleased with himself for the simplicity of this final formulation. "The first time I sent you up the mountain"—he can see that he's inhabiting the Demiurge now, talking to himself from on high—"you withered into a lewd and drunken old man. If I send you up there again, what are you going to do?"

Straining to move his lips as the pain in his neck begins to return, he mouths the words, "Devote my life to building the Future Museum and stuffing the surrounding woods with its overflow."

The Father's
Final Sermon

When Wieland comes to, he's sitting at the kitchen table before a bowl of Wheaties and a Training Mug of coffee, and his father is addressing him as Jakob. He can't tell how old he is, but he can tell that the doll he remembers having destroyed is nowhere to be found, and that its destruction has ruptured the very last of whatever coherence had allowed the family to go on functioning. The old, homey atmosphere of the kitchen is rushing out of the house, as if its seal popped when the doll's head came off.

"Jakob," his father says, "I have received news from the Demiurge. While you were sleeping, the long, long dry spell that I have unfortunately been fated to endure broke. I too nodded off, right here at the table, and was at last visited by an angel. And do you know what that angel told me?" He stops as his voice breaks and his eyes grow moist. Then he sniffles and continues, "That angel told me to make of you a sacrifice. There is an altar on top of the mountain that overlooks this town, the mountain in whose shadow this town was built, and the angel told me that you are to be sacrificed there. In the instant of your sacrifice, if I am brave and unwavering in my loyalty to the message I have received, the location of the New Jerusalem will at last be revealed. The far side of the mountain will at last become passable, and these long, painful years of exile, through which your mother has traveled steadfastly by my side, will be at an end. And fear not, for, though you will not survive in your current form, I will make another of you as soon as we arrive, so that you too might enjoy the fruits of my lifelong labor. I can hear the hinges on the gates of paradise creaking, Jakob, and, though I wish the secret to opening them were a more felicitous one, what must be done must be done. Like Kierkegaard's Knight of Faith—a vision of Jewish fealty expressed, as has occurred once or twice throughout Western history, by a Gentile seer too fervent to be contained by his own Christly dogma—who knew that God's call could never be doubted, even or especially at its most seemingly perverse, I have found the courage deep in my heart to do what the Demiurge has ordered. Now, please eat the rice pudding your mother is about to serve while I go into the garage to sharpen my axe."

Jakob—Wieland has consented to use this name for himself during these last few moments in the old house, decadent though he knows the indulgence to be—watches his mother, her face vacant as a sleepwalker's, prepare the bowl of rice pudding with three slivered almonds, a sprinkle of cinnamon, and a dash of whole milk, just the way she always used to. She puts it in front of him with a small spoon still warm from the dishwasher, and stands back, waiting for him to ingest the potion that will put him to sleep. This time, however, he's determined to witness the journey. He has no desire to be sacrificed by his father, but he can tell that remaining in town means ending up in the Tyson Meat Truck, speeding on a hook toward the Lincoln Tunnel. At least this way, he tells himself, spooning the rice pudding out of the bowl and onto the floor beside him, I'll get a ride up the mountain. Perhaps, once we're all up there, my father will reconsider. Massaging the spilled pudding into the floor with his toes, he pictures Tobin lumbering into the clearing at the critical moment and, in his graceless way, offering to haul a pig onto the altar in the condemned son's place.

Comforted by this remote possibility, Jakob finishes emptying his rice pudding onto the floor and hands the bowl to his mother with a glimmer of hope.

Back Up the
Mountain

Jakob's father is still grinding the blade of a yellow-handled Ace Hardware axe in the garage with the doors wide open when Jakob stumbles out into the driveway with his mother, who has his old black veil rolled up in her arms. He stands by her side and feels himself regressing to the age of twelve, The age I was when all of this began, he thinks. And, in a sense just beyond the limits of his understanding, the age at which he was born. He pictures himself as a twelve-year-old emerging from the darkness beyond the edge of the flat earth, summoned into the light for a definite but unknown reason, while Wieland watches from another part of that darkness, committing everything that's about to happen to memory.

Shivering, he looks up at his mother and tries to

send a signal to reestablish their bond before his father returns with the axe, but she just stands there, fingering the veil, staring into space, broken. He pictures the sculpture he'll one day make of her—the sculpture whose existence in the Future Museum he can already perceive—and he sees the cracks in her resolve made literal, the smooth porcelain of her face splintering as he taps it gently with a ball-peen hammer.

This image segues into that of his father looming up, full-sized, before them, axe in hand, as he says, "Okay, veil on. I'm starting the car."

Jakob slumps in the backseat with the veil over his eyes, just as he used to on those long-ago trips to Trader Joe's, and he feels the town melt and sink into memory as the station wagon drifts, hearse-like, through the sweltering summer streets. The bridge, the diner, the strip with Wing Hunt, Giant Chinese, and Mama's Pizza, the Town Museum, and even Chez Pierre, wherever it might be, melt into a thick black pool, over which the fabric of the veil forms a skin, like the skin atop a bowl of chocolate pudding. The hard surface of *The Sunken Town*: everything below, he thinks, as the car starts to lurch upward, is now classed as Raw Material, ready and willing to be used in any and every way I can dream up. It's all there for me, and for me alone. It has no form other than that which I give it.

As the car strains up the mountain, winding forward

and backward, hugging the potholed road around hairpin turns, no part of Jakob's mind is stuck on the possibility that he's about to die. It's not that I believe my father's hand will be stilled by any last-minute pang of conscience—after years of schooling, he knows his *Genesis: 22* as well as anyone possibly could—but, he thinks, the Future Museum is too real to die with me today, so either I'm immortal, or something will intervene.

Both parents gasp as the car lurches around a curve that must, though Jakob can't see, have revealed an especially sheer drop. A wave of loose gravel cascades off the edge and the front tires lose purchase; Jakob sucks in a mouthful of veil to keep from screaming.

After several more such curves and a number of slower, though equally steep intervals, the road begins to even out. The long approach to the summit, Jakob thinks, slowly letting the wet, bunched-up fabric out of his mouth, is almost over. By the time he's spit it all out and managed to sit upright again, the car has rolled to a gravelly stop and the engine has been shut off. The wet fabric slaps against his face like a curtain in an open window after a rainstorm.

"Okay," his father says, opening his door, which triggers the beeping sound that means the keys are still in the ignition. "This is as close as the vision can take us. The rest we'll have to cross on foot, feeling our way along like pilgrims in a new continent. Jakob, please remove your veil and leave it in the car."

Jakob does as he's told, kissing the fabric goodbye as he places it, like a cast-off skin, on the exact part of the backseat cushion where he'd been sitting. Then he takes his mother's still-numbed hand and walks with her a few paces behind his father, into the woods.

They march in silence, his father's eyes half-closed as he strains to match his innate sense of the altar's location to the actual topography that now surrounds them. As they march, they pass groves of Wieland's totems, and some soldiers posed on their way to or from the Battle for the Soul of the New Jerusalem, which Jakob knows must be raging in its eternal stalemate somewhere nearby. He sinks back into a memory of that walk, himself and Wieland side by side, preparing to part ways forever, though he didn't quite know that yet, and, in a deeper sense, it isn't quite true. He lets the two timelines swim atop one another, fluid and elegant as eels.

This image segues into the family's emergence at the edge of the clearing where his mother's cemetery lies in fading splendor. The neon of the graves has long since burned out, and many of the plots are choked with weeds and wildflowers, but the essential arrangement is unchanged. Jakob wonders when she stopped tending it; perhaps, he thinks, after I buried Wieland, or Wieland buried me. He looks at her as she surveys the work, and feels a wave of empathetic sadness break over his head as he realizes how little he truly knows her. What she really thinks, what she wanted all these years, even what work she did on the password-protected laptop all those afternoons, to buy us the fish and chicken we ate... I never once thought to ask, he thinks, gripping her hand though he knows she won't grip his in return.

His father is ecstatic. He waves his axe in the air and says, "I knew it! This exact image appeared to me as we were trekking through those woods back there, and now here it is! Nothing the Demiurge reveals in ideation remains excluded from the external world. My long, long years of fearing that the universe had succumbed to entropy and chaos are behind us now. All is as it should be forevermore."

Then, catching his breath, he grows solemn. "Here, in the exact center of these graves, is the altar." He looks to Jakob's mother and says, "Help me clear it off while our son prepares his soul for sacrifice."

On the Altar

Mother and father, one of them morose, the other ecstatic, clear leaves and dead flowers from the center of the clearing, while Jakob wanders the periphery, staring across at the cabin he once inhabited and still believes that he one day will again. The sun is high and boiling overhead and, though he hasn't consulted a calendar in what feels like months, he's certain that today is the summer solstice, the hot, wet heart of the year.

When the altar is ready, the father picks up his axe from the leaf pile where he'd stashed it, and says, "Alright, son, time to make your contribution to the family. The gates of the New Jerusalem creak open thanks to your courage in this instant. Know that your soul will journey on with us, to be installed into a new body as soon as we reach our new house, in the town we've been seeking all this time. Once the body you currently occupy has been buried, the path will open up, and then your mother and I will walk or drive along it, across the Desert left by the receding waters of the Red Sea, and then the long, exhausting centuries in Egypt will be behind us at last."

He begins to cry as Jakob traipses toward the altar. Though he still can't see himself dying, Jakob can feel the awareness dawning on him that perhaps his only survival will be as a disembodied soul, installed into a replica of himself in the next town his parents move to, where, inevitably, the cycle will repeat. He swallows the rising fear of this prospect while, at the same time, a far deeper, more insidious fear bulges in his belly: the fear that this has already repeated countless times. That I am, in the end, no more than *a* Jakob, a doll-boy built to inhabit a certain town and to die at its mountainous apex on the summer solstice before my parents move on yet again.

His vision begins to swim and his skin breaks into a sweat rash as he reaches the cleared spot and feels his knees give out under the pressure of his father's hand on his shoulder.

Before he manages to think anything else, he finds himself lying on his back on the ground, staring up at the blinding blue sky fringed by pines, his father's yellow axe traveling toward the top of what will soon be its downward arc. Somehow, he thinks, the babel of thought and conversation that has filled my life so far has proven to be non-infinite. The voices that spoke so freely have now said their piece. The seemingly endless economy of past and future has somehow—

"Stop!" screams a voice from the distance. It's so sharp and pure that it barely sounds human.

"Stop, stop, you can't kill him," it continues, softening just enough to resemble his mother's, but louder and clearer than he's ever heard it before. He swivels his head to look up at his mother staying his father's hand, pulling the axe back down to waist level, her gaze steely and clear, like she's just woken up from the sleep she's been in as long as he's known her.

"Look, there's something I have to tell you. I've been silent all these years, trailing in your wake, teaching your son whatever you told me to teach him, and do you want to know why? I did it because some small part of me believed you. I believed you really were a prophet, that you really would one day lead us through a doorway, out of the ruins of America and into paradise. After what happened to both of us in the Art World? I had to believe that. It was that or nothing at all, and believing nothing was unlivable. That should be clear by now. But this is too far. I will not stand here and watch this happen. I thought I had it in me to see it through, I really did, but, standing here before you now with our son on the ground like an animal, I swear I do not. Even if it costs us paradise, let him up right now."

His father shudders, somewhere between laughter and rage. Then, gathering himself just enough to speak, he says, "No, my love. This is precisely what Kierkegaard warned about. The temptation to relent at the final moment, to doubt the Divine Word and settle for Infinite Resignation. A life of security and compromise. No. Only a false prophet could do such a thing. A true prophet would..."

"I built all this," his mother interjects. "Everything here, all these graves, you didn't just dream them up. It was me. I snuck up at night and built them all. And not out of some holy compulsion. No, I built them as an art installation. A postmodern sculptural representation of Derrida's theory of Hauntology. The ache of Lost Futures, of collapsed potential. I built them, I confess to you here and now, with Jakob as my witness, as my entrée back into the Art World. During all the nights I spent up here working, I prayed for your death, or for some benevolent white van to appear on our doorstep and take you away, and then, not one second after that van pulled up the street, I would take our son, by then fully educated in the history of Gentile postmodernism, and buckle him into the station wagon and he and I would drive straight through the Lincoln Tunnel, where we'd..."

The crack of slicing skin and breaking bone reverberates through the silent cemetery, and, a moment later, a rain of blood spills over Jakob where he lies on the altar. Half of his mind prays that it'll turn out to be his own blood, the worst of dying already over, while the other half begins to cherish the knowledge that it isn't. Blood falls and falls, like rain, until the ground beneath him is so wet he's sinking into it.

Though he feels completely enervated, he manages to swim over to the nearest gravestone and grip it hard enough to climb to his feet, from which vantage he watches his father hack the rest of his mother's head off. Half of his mind is mute with horror, while the other half thinks, giddy with adrenaline, Here, at last, is the Primal Trauma that will infuse my work with the edge of madness all true Genius requires, the capstone on the origin story that, in time, every educated person on earth will know about me.

Epilogue to the

Father's

Sermons

Father and son stand beside the body in the center of the high woods as the sun begins to set and midsummer tips onto its far side, setting the long approach to winter in motion. Neither speaks as the shadows of the graves lengthen, shrouding the mother's head, which sits perfectly still, likewise not speaking. It wavers, in Jakob's perception, between the recently living remnants of the one person in the universe who ever loved him, and just another chunk of Raw Material, intriguingly fleshy but awaiting animation as patiently as the blades of grass around it.

Soon, he vows, I will find a way to grant you the life you deserve. Then he looks up at his father, his face obscured by twilight, and nods to signal that he's ready for the reckoning to begin.

Receiving this signal, his father says, "What's happened is most unfortunate, but a usurpation of the sanctity of the Demiurge's will cannot be tolerated, not even for a millisecond, and most especially not within the family, which is the last remaining bulwark against the rank duplicity of the outside world, of which the Art World is but one unholy manifestation. No suffering, no death, is too high a cost to preserve the sanctity of the family. Remember that, Jakob, when you have a family of your own. And remember also, long after you've come to believe that I'm no longer with you, that I will be with you then, too. Then more than ever. I am an eternal entity, a trans-dimensional being, a spirit embodied in this flesh only incidentally. I stand before you today in the midst of only one of my infinite lives, as the father of one of the infinite families that I will sire in the fullness of time, and yet the wisdom of that infinitude is concentrated within this frail mortal frame. It pains me nearly to bursting to contain so much wisdom, but it is here, and it stands before you now. It has spilled blood for you, Jakob. That your vision might be pure, the work of your hands true. That the living hell of the Art World might remain far from your soul, its ravenous teeth chomping only in the farthest distance, as a warning. Do what you know you must. Become great. Do not let the energies released by this sacrifice fade away. And know that, every time you look out at these woods," he gestures with the axe at a blackening wall of trees, "I'll be among them. I'll be out here always, whispering to you, watching you, waiting to see what you make of yourself. One day you'll see how much you have to thank me for, so let me tell you now that you're very welcome. Everything I did, I did for you, and also for myself, because, here at the very end of our shared story, there is nothing at all to prevent me from admitting that we are the same. You and I, Jakob, are two versions of the same man, two of the Demiurge's unending revisions of itself, and thus my immortality is yours as well. Use it wisely."

With this, he leans into the space between them, as if for a hug, but then seems to think better of it, or to lose his nerve. He shrinks back, dropping the axe onto the soft ground as he turns to leave. Jakob watches as he vanishes into the shadows of the foreground and, a moment later, palpable only acoustically now, into the shadows of the background. Jakob pictures the wall of trees opening to receive him as the paths and trails that he'll wander for the rest of eternity etch themselves onto what had been, until this instant, an unmapped black-green expanse of virgin forest.

The Mother's

Note

When the father's footsteps have gone silent, Jakob—calling himself by this name for the last time—bends down and picks up his mother's head, cradling it in his arms as he walks back toward the cabin. The air turns chilly as he passes the looming spiders, taking credit for them at last. The first and boldest manifestations of my authentic self's need for protection, he thinks, lifting the rotten latch and shouldering the front door open in its warped frame. The smell of marrow stew hits him as soon as he's made it over the threshold, and he feels the name Jakob slough off and drift through the greasy air, into the same enchantment that now pervades the woods. He remembers his old thoughts about the Wilderness and the simultaneous necessity and danger of going out into it. An artist has to be able to dwell in the Wilderness, he reminds himself, setting the head on the kitchen table and taking the bottle of clear liquor down from the shelf, but he also has to be able to come back home. That's the line—the only line—between art and madness. And don't you ever forget that.

Okay, I won't! he promises, at last certain that he knows what it means.

Taking a deep swig from the bottle, he stares at the head and rummages in the pockets of his raincoat until he pulls out a rolled-up slip of paper. Unrolling it, he discovers a chunk of black handwriting, which forces him to turn on the light. The bulb buzzes and burns a dim orange, just barely enabling him to read the following:

Dear Jakob,

Something bad is about to happen; a sort of Apocalypse. But don't ever let that make you doubt how much I love you. All these years, I tried the very best I could. I tried to teach you what I believed would enable you to find your way into a deeper regime of existence, beyond or below the scummy plane of everyday life. If life in America is going to remain viable for your generation and those that follow, it is going to have to occur on this plane. The surface is no longer capable of supporting human existence, if it ever was. But beneath this surface, I fervently believe, a deeper frontier is still open, awaiting the arrival of a courageous few. Please know that both your father and I, although we expressed it in different ways, never wanted anything more than for you to live and work on this sunken plane, which we firmly believe you are capable of reaching.

If you do reach it and find yourself able to serve as an intermediary between what you find there and the surface, there is no reason why you shouldn't turn that immense gift to your advantage. Make the best work you possibly can and sell it for as much as you can get. You deserve to live well, better than I did. The part of you that is your father's son is surely now turning against me, beginning to believe that my pen has been possessed by the devils of the Art World, but please just know that...

Wieland crumples the paper and stuffs it down the head's throat, as deep as he can without it coming out the bottom. Then he drains the bottle and shuffles off to the bedroom that he died in. As he crawls into the cold, stiff sheets and looks up at the vast panoply of maps and charts adorning the walls and ceiling, he stretches out and thinks, I've made it to the high place at last, out of the deep bowl of chaos and confusion below. Drifting into his first mature dream, he imagines a future scholar discovering the rolled-up note in his mother's skull, and earning tenure at some East Coast university after writing a 1000-page biography that argues for this single document as the key to the entire Wieland Enigma.

Wieland's

Dreams

This dream leads to a deeper one in which he reemerges as the Lone Lecher in the now-familiar Art World alley, just behind Chez Pierre, holding his shrouded bundle and waiting his turn to present himself at the window that will decide whether to grant him access to the next level, or kick him back to the one below. Success is a vertical climb, but altitude has the soupy, swimming quality that all dimensions in the dream have taken on. The frenzy to move upwards and the terror of moving downwards are ever-present, but it's grown impossible to say which direction is which. Which terminal leads to the bus station and the long, bumpy ride along country highways, out of the City forever, and which leads to the yacht off the coast of Cannes and the Lido at the Biennale in Venice? He leans against the soot-covered pillar that defines one edge of the alley and wraps his arms tighter around the bundle and resolves simply to hold on until whatever is going to happen next happens.

At the same time, like an adjoining exhibit hall in the multi-floor retrospective of his life, another dream is underway. In this dream, he's already a major figure, feted not only by the couple from another town but by thousands, even millions, of such couples, his face regularly adorning the covers of *Frieze* and *Artforum* and other publications so rarefied he's unable to dream up names for them. He gives lectures to packed university halls on the import of Bruno Schulz and Joseph Cornell, and yet, all the while, whatever's alive inside him dreams of a drafty cabin on a mountaintop surrounded by woods, conjuring a single still point in the increasingly entropic universe of his fame. He leans against the lectern at RISD, his hands shaking, and looks out across the sea of rapt faces and thinks, If there were anything at all I could do to trade places with the version of me that lives on that mountaintop, making his models and dioramas for no one in the unheated tranquility of his basement, I would do it a thousand times over, and a thousand times after that.

When he wakes up throughout the night in his bed in the cabin on the mountaintop, he is rocked sometimes by a sense of smothering desolation, and other times by a relief so profound he can think of no way to express it except by saying to the empty room,

"Thank you, whoever you are, for seeing to it that I ended up where I belong!"

Tobin's Pig

A pounding on the door wakes him again from these dreams, to which he knows he'll often return over the years and years to come. The pounding goes on until it's convinced him that it won't stop until he gets up to address it, so he hauls his feet off the creaky old bed, pulls his blue robe over his naked body, and shuffles to the door. Peering through the front window, he allows the spectacle of Tobin with his pig on a leash in one hand and his butcher knife in the other to sink in slowly, like an artwork that will yield its hidden meaning only to the most patient of witnesses.

He opens the door and, yawning, says, "That for me?"

Tobin gasps with laughter as he shouts, "Yes! Yes! Yes!" Jumping up and down with his butcher knife high over his head, he adds, "You said you'd come back and now here you are! Now we can be happy?!"

Still beaming, he drags the pig onto the grass at the bottom of the porch steps and sets to work stabbing and sawing and chopping into it at unpredictable, sideways angles, the blade running black with blood as the pig squeals and shrieks and scrabbles at the softening dirt. The relief on Tobin's face is orgasmic as all that's insane in him comes out through his hands, his left continually slipping on the leash, only to catch it again a moment later, as the next swing of his right hand finds home.

While the pig segues, one chop at a time, from an animal to a mass of Raw Material, Wieland ruminates on the fate of his Jewishness. He remembers Jakob keeping Kosher, following his father across the endless wastes of an American Egypt, as if every interstate were the Red Sea and salvation were only ever one town away, and he remembers his father's sermons on Nazism, on how all finished work is, in essence, a rebuke to the endless revision of matter that is the Demiurge's core tenet, and thus the heart of what it means to be a Visionary Jew.

That pig, he thinks, is going to be finished soon. Its body can be revised any number of ways, but the story of its life as a pig is now ending forever. He finds, for the first time, that his certainty that all objects are equally alive has wavered. He finds that he has put that childish thing behind him, though the prospect of living without it brings no comfort. He flashes forward a few hours to an image of himself sitting alone in the dimming kitchen, surrounded by freshly smoked pork with his mother's head at the center of the table, and though he can see the beauty of this tableau, he finds that he can no longer filter out the attendant clamminess of its reality.

Returning his attention to Tobin's hacking, his thoughts likewise return to the question of his Jewishness. What have I become? he wonders, as an empty pool in his memory fills with images of childhood in Bavaria, near the Austrian border, while the First World War was raging. He conjures a mother who named him Wilhelm and taught him always to finish his work, to render in definite form every idea he ever had, for fear of ending up a Wandering Jew, a relativist like Einstein, a living rebuke to the integrity of the universe itself. He conjures a father he never met but was told died in France defending the homeland, and, though it brings tears to his eyes, he feels his heart swell at the magnitude of that sacrifice.

As Tobin finishes hacking the pig's head off and begins dragging the piecemeal carcass out to the smoker, Wieland retches in the bushes beside the steps, then collapses on his hands and knees and weeps openly. He sobs and shakes and expels the last of his belief in the childhood he led in the town below, in the story of his mother and father and their series of new houses. From now on, he decides, wiping his eyes, that story will live only in one of the alternate cabins up here, while the counterstory—he ages himself into his late twenties and places that man in Poland in 1944, then here, in this cabin, in the 60s, waiting for the children from the town below to feed themselves to his spiders—will live in another cabin, and I will live in a third, enacting a third story, that of a lonely old man on a mountaintop, preserved in an eternal present, and all will be equally real, all made tangible in wood and foam and wire, and my visitors, when they come up here in their tens of thousands, will be left to sort out the meaning of the larger constellation for themselves.

Wieland previews this constellation as he joins Tobin by the smoker, barely managing to nod when Tobin asks, "Ready for a ragbag from Ragtown?"

A while later, once the pork's been cooked, Tobin smiles almost benevolently and says, "Okay, little fink, look for me tomorrow with lots and lots of toys!"

When he's gone, Wieland takes a dozen heaping armfuls of meat into the kitchen and sits in the twilight with them piled on the table, forming a wall around his mother's head. He sits and stares, not eating, not drinking, until he's tired enough to go to sleep, desperate to drift back to his moated castle and the tigers he's collected over the years.

Thereafter

As they always do once he's settled into a new place, the days and weeks and months begin to speed by. To punctuate their lonely passing, Wieland summons the Blood Clot as often as his increasingly frail body will allow. Whenever the cabin grows eerily quiet, as it often does in the midmorning and late afternoon and just before he's about to try falling asleep, he searches his scarred surface for a decent font to summon her from. Then he runs the bath. Sometimes they make love, but more often they simply talk about whatever's on his mind and, when he remembers to ask, whatever's on hers. He tries, sincerely, to be a better listener, a man able to absorb life from the outside, not only to generate it from within. He and she used to talk about having a child, but, as time goes by, the conversation becomes increasingly theoretical. In a sense, though neither quite acknowledges this, they are, in Wieland, already raising the only child they'll ever have. They alternate according to their moods, or allow this child to be both at once, a son and a daughter, twins or a twinned soul in a single body. "If we can conceive *of* him or her," they often say, "how is that not the same as conceiving him or her?"

This logic soothes Wieland when he's so deep in his work that the Blood Clot's company, and that of their child, becomes all that tethers him to the human race, which, despite everything, he feels neither willing nor able to abandon just yet.

Still, part of him knows this is his last chance. There will be no shunting the burden into the future this time. Insofar as he's able to face the truth of this, his work proceeds at a frantic pace. He descends into the basement with a bottle of clear liquor and a pail of pork, and reemerges in a new season. Sometimes the Night Crusher—himself beginning to show the weight of time—emerges to assist him, and sometimes he's on his own, with nothing but his mother's skull on the workbench for company.

He roves from one cabin to another to another, and even begins to sculpt the moated castle with its den of luxury tigers, using the materials that Tobin brings from Ragtown to flesh out the figures that correspond to the several lost versions of his life, the adjacent Edens from which he was, like all mortals, expelled at birth. He fills the woods with connective tissue, tendrils that link the many cabins, breadcrumbs of deeper meaning for his future biographers to fight over.

Sometimes he listens for the footsteps of his father, and often he senses his presence lurking behind trees, or high up in their branches, or just underfoot, but he never sees him, and rarely, aside from Tobin and the occasional hunter, does he see anyone else.

And what of my public? he often wonders. What of the tens of thousands who will one day make their way up this mountain to see what I have rendered? For the time being, the Blood Clot graciously serves as his gallerist, replacing Greta, who disappeared, he likes to imagine, into the realm she glimpsed when she conjured Chez Pierre. When he has a new piece ready for display, he summons her in the sink—chewing through scar if need be—puts on the dress and heels he found in a chest in the bedroom, and carefully leaves himself behind to travel on as her, carrying the precious bundle down the mountain.

At the bottom, she installs it in the increasingly derelict Town Museum, which she now thinks of as the terrestrial analogue of the Future Museum that exists in its truest sense inside her, and in another, expanding sense, in the woods that surround the cabins.

Then, satisfied that the Wieland legend is growing, she orders a milkshake and a plate of fries at the diner. Afterwards, if her energy holds out, she walks the streets and alleys of the Sunken Town, feeling them sink ever deeper underfoot. Sometimes she passes the plaza that still contains Wing Hut, Giant Chinese, and Mama's Pizza, and looks there for the Tyson Meat Truck, wondering what she'd do if she ever found it idling, anxious to beat the traffic in the Lincoln Tunnel, but she never does. It's gone for good, she understands, as the day grows dark, which means that it's time to make her way across the Tick-singing Meadow, over the bridge, and, following the ghost of her mother, back up the mountain again.

Acknowledgements

Tremendous and heartfelt thanks to Miette Gillette for taking this project on and turning it into the beautiful book you're holding now. Huge thanks also to John Kazanjian, Avinash Rajendran, Matthew Spellberg, and Mike Natalie for their thoughtful feedback as this story took shape, and, as ever, to my wife Ingrid, my parents Lynn and Richard, and my brother Rob, for their unwavering love and support

About the Author

David Leo Rice is a writer and animator from Northampton, MA, currently living in NYC. He is the author of the novels *A Room in Dodge City, A Room in Dodge City: Vol. 2, Angel House,* and the story collection *Drifter*, one of the *Southwest Review's* "10 Must-Read Books of 2021."
He's online at www.raviddice.com and has taught animation and writing at Harvard, The New School, FIT, and Parsons School of Design.

About the Publisher

Whisk(e)y Tit is committed to restoring degradation and degeneracy to the literary arts. We work with authors who are unwilling to sacrifice intellectual rigor, unrelenting playfulness, and visual beauty in our literary pursuits, often leading to texts that would otherwise be abandoned in today's largely homogenized literary landscape. In a world governed by idiocy, our commitment to these principles is an act of civil service and civil disobedience alike.